Stratagem

CHRISTINA HAGMANN

www.ten16press.com - Waukesha, WI

To my husband and son, who know when to give me space.
To my family and friends, who know that I need space.
And to my students, past and present,
who know no concept of space. I love you all.

Chapter 1

I sat in the dark interior of the car, nervously spinning my earring and watching the shadows move behind the curtain in the lamplit house. Mr. Gray was saying goodbye to his poker buddies, all of whom had wives to get home to, making it an early night for him. It was 8:00 pm, and the streetlights cast an ethereal glow in the night. Conveniently but not surprisingly, the streetlight by Mr. Gray's house was burnt out.

Most families in this upscale neighborhood, one of many affluent suburbs of Washington, D.C., had retired in front of their televisions for the evening. I looked in the window of the house across the street. The drapes were open, revealing two kids, about six and seven years old, chasing each other around a kitchen table. They were laughing and playing as their mother sat at the table with a book. They didn't even know how good they had it, and they probably never would.

When I realized I was spinning my earring, a bad tell I had acquired, I pinched the diamond in the fleshy part of my thumb. It bit me, drawing blood. I watched a man, Mr. Gray's neighbor, exit the house. Now a single shadow moved across the living room.

I glanced out the rearview window at the black van that was parked a block away. The windows were tinted, so I couldn't make out who was in the driver's seat. It was usually the same guy, but I'd never seen him up close, and I didn't want to. I wondered how much they had briefed him about me. I wondered what he saw when he looked at me. I wondered if he knew what I was.

I flipped down my visor and examined myself in the mirror, something I often did, not out of vanity but out of reassurance. My green eyes were bright in the light of the visor mirror; they sometimes surprised me by how green they were, and I wondered if they were really my eyes.

Like the moon over a pond, the glow of the street lamp reflected off my black hair and illuminated my dark complexion. I quickly shut the visor, extinguishing the light and returning my attention to the house. Mr. Gray would be bringing the garbage out soon as per his usual schedule. I grabbed the petition, the one that had been supplied to me, off the passenger seat. I was sure the petition was for some real cause, just real enough for Mr. Gray to open the door for me. "They" were very good with details, but it wasn't a cause that mattered to me.

I reached for the door handle, feeling around for it in the darkness, and then pulled back, remembering I would need a pen. My purse was large and full of candy wrappers. I didn't have much else. After digging around and finding a pen, I paused. My cell phone sat in my purse. I picked it up and turned it off. I didn't know when I would see my phone again because this job was different and there was no emergency exit. If anything, that was what gave me some comfort during the last year, that they had planned a way out for me if I needed it.

Finally, I tucked the phone in my jacket pocket. I knew I would be in trouble for keeping it, but at this point, it didn't matter. The clean-up crew would report it missing, but I would already be in place. If they wanted it, they'd come for it.

My palms were sweating. I wiped them down the front of my sweater.

A quick tap on the driver's side window jolted me out of the whole cell phone conundrum. I jumped, my heart beating hard in my chest, and glanced up to see a young man, blond, his face filling up the window. He looked about seventeen, the same age as me. He was tall and lanky and kind of cute. His broad smile covered his face, but it didn't reach his eyes. I grabbed for the window button, but because the engine was turned off, I couldn't roll down the window.

Thoughts ticked across my brain. I couldn't ignore him, but at this point in the game, I shouldn't be talking to anyone besides Mr. Gray. I thought back to my cell phone in my pocket and had the strange sensation that something was wrong with this assignment. The boy lifted his hand in a still wave.

I grabbed the door handle. My palm was warm and clammy. I didn't know what to say to him, in part because I wasn't used to talking to boys, but also because this was the least ideal time to chat up some guy. Sweat began to dampen my brow. I opened the door a crack. "Yes?" I asked. Before I could get the whole word out of my mouth, he wrenched open the door.

Taken by surprise, I lost my grip. To my left, I saw movement coming from behind the vehicle. Instead of leaning out to see what was happening, I crawled back into the car, shimmying over the middle console, trying to get away from him. He snatched at my leg and grabbed me around the ankle.

I kicked wildly at his hands, moving back towards the passenger door, and that was when the second boy appeared, moving in from around the back of the car. He had short, brown hair and wasn't as tall, but he had a muscular build. As the blond pulled on my ankle, the brown-haired boy grabbed at my other leg. It was eerie how quiet the night was. All I could hear was my own heavy breathing and grunting as I tried to get away.

When they got me out far enough, the blond-haired boy tried taking hold of my waist. I grasped for anything that could anchor me in the car, but he was too quick and too strong. When he seized my waist, he was able to wrench my entire body from the vehicle.

I was unsteady as he pushed me into the arms of the dark-haired boy, and the dark-haired boy's large arms wrapped me in a bear hug and pulled me backward, away from the vehicle and out onto the road. I tried dragging my feet to slow us down, but my toes barely touched the pavement. I hunched over, trying to get my feet firmly on the ground, but he wouldn't let me gain control.

Struggling, kicking, my heart was racing. My mind went to the men in the van. They would come for me. An engine revved close by, and I turned my head, hoping to see the van, but instead, a rusty Pontiac squealed up next to my car. "No!" I tried to yell, but I had very little breath stored up in my lungs. I used all my strength to pull my arms apart, but it was useless with the boy's arms squeezing me tightly. I was sure that the men in the van had to be on their way. That was their sole purpose. To look out for me.

"They're coming," the blond yelled out. The boy holding me pulled me around to the back of the car. Everything seemed to be taking so long, but only a matter of seconds had passed. There was a click, and the trunk popped open. "Quick, put her in." The blond boy held a gun up. I squinted towards the rusty vehicle and the dark interior of the trunk.

"No!" I kicked, struggling for words, and jerked my head back, trying to hit the dark-haired boy who was holding me, but he was bigger than me, and my head only thumped harmlessly against his chest. My kicks were useless. I couldn't connect with anything. I tried to twist around, but he had a firm grip and was not letting go.

"The cuffs!" the blond boy yelled. The driver of the car, who I couldn't see, tossed something out the open window, but it missed its mark and clattered to the ground. Gunshots rang through the air. I flinched and stopped struggling, not sure who was firing. The dark-haired boy stopped and looked back long enough for me to see the men from the van running at us and firing their weapons.

"Help!" I screamed. It occurred to me that if they were willing to open fire, then maybe the target, Mr. Gray, no longer mattered to them. Maybe the assignment was void and they would have to go with Plan B, which was riskier and had a higher mortality rate. That was what I was told going into this, warning what would happen if I failed or refused to follow through. More importantly, they didn't need me for Plan B.

I kicked again, but the boy holding me was too strong. The blond held the trunk open as the dark-haired boy lifted my legs in. He fumbled with me as I used my legs to push off the edges of the trunk, or whatever I could get my feet on. Instead of losing his grip on me, he pushed himself forward and folded himself over me. With his weight heavy against my back, he forced me down and hopped in the trunk with me. More gunshots fired. Bullets pinged off the side of the car. The trunk closed, wrapping everything in darkness.

I tried to get away, moving towards the back of the trunk. My senses heightened. Our breathing was heavy and loud in the dark trunk. It smelled of gas. There were muted shouts and more gunshots as the vehicle pulled away. The force of the forward motion and the fact I was off balance caused me to roll back to the boy who was holding me. I tried to wiggle away again, but his grip was firm and his arm locked securely over my arm and around my stomach.

A bullet loudly ricocheted off the side of the vehicle, and I froze, listening to the muffled voices inside the car. Suddenly, the boy shifted, and his head moved down over me and closer to my ear. "Sorry for being so rough." His voice was gentle in my ear, and a prickly sensation shot down my side. I held my breath, wondering what the Agency would do now that I hadn't completed the assignment. What would they do now that I had gone and gotten caught?

"Are you okay?" his voice broke through. I didn't say a word. I didn't know what these boys wanted or what they knew about me.

Low, faint voices came from the inside of the vehicle. It was cold in the trunk, and there was no way of telling how much time had passed. The boy's rhythmic breathing warmed my neck. His body, solid and heavy, pressed up against me. What would a bunch of teenage boys want with me? Dark motives crossed my mind, and my panicked brain circled and circled around thoughts that I kept trying to push out. I was on the verge of a freak-out, and I couldn't afford that. After what I had been through, I should be able to handle a bunch of teenage boys.

I had come a long way from a year ago. Back then, I was living in my home in Oak Park, Illinois, with my father—the librarian—and my sisters, Ginger and Georgia. I was worrying about the girls at school accepting me and regretting what I had done to make them accept me when a group of men broke into my bedroom one night and took me. They knew what I was, and I knew it was my fault, even though my dad had warned me. And my poor father, a regular guy who had already lost his wife six years earlier, was forced to give me up without hope of ever seeing me again.

I closed my eyes tightly, but the blackness in the trunk was darker than that of my mind. I thought about the cell phone in my pocket, but with the boy's arms wrapped around me, there was no way to get to it. If I waited for the right time, it might be my only chance to escape. My only way to get back to the Agency.

These thoughts jumbled in my mind like clothes in a dryer.

Though I had no idea how much time had passed, we were moving out of the city. The vehicle had slowed at certain points in the trip and made brief stops, probably at traffic lights. When we finally slowed to a complete stop, I strained to hear what was going. "Shh," the dark-haired boy whispered in my ear. There were voices outside. I sucked in my breath, prepared to let out a piercing scream, but suddenly a large hand clamped down on my mouth. The hand was warm and smooth but damp with sweat. It gently drove my chin down and my neck and my head into my chest. The pressure was uncomfortable, claustrophobic. I felt like I was suffocating. Like I would never be allowed to breathe again. My body prickled.

"You don't want these people to know you're here," he whispered. "They will not be kind to you." I had no idea what he was talking about. But if I couldn't yell out, there was one other thing I could do. That thing was my specialty. I grabbed his hand on my mouth and concentrated on his voice, closing my eyes. My head began to buzz. "Stop." He pulled his hand away like he had touched a burning ember. "What are you doing, Meda?" I hesitated for a moment, startled he knew my name. My skin was ablaze with pins and needles, and the backs of my eyelids burned. "Shit," the boy whispered, squirming away from the heat of my body. I began to fill up the trunk. The car moved again.

Chapter 2

I lay waiting, breathing heavily. These guys seemed like a bunch of future frat boys who were looking for a dark thrill, but frat boys wouldn't know my name. No one knew my name. So maybe they were a part of some other group I didn't know about, rogue members of the Agency? If so, why was the getaway car a rusty Pontiac? I knew it wasn't in my best interest to underestimate anyone, but it was the only thing that kept me calm and in control.

Then I began to wonder what the boy in the trunk with me was thinking. He had moved away from me, sensing some change in me, and was now pressed up against the front of the trunk. He knew my name, so maybe he knew what I was. He would be ready when they stopped, and he would be the first one out. The first one they would see. I tried to think quickly about my element of surprise, how I could fool them, but the vehicle finally pulled to a slow stop before I could come up with a great plan.

"So, is it okay we didn't cuff her?" I heard a voice ask from outside.

"Well, we'll see when we get there, but I think Brody can take care of himself just fine." Brody. The name of the boy in the trunk with me. I mentally recorded the information.

"Guys," Brody said, his voice loud from the interior of the trunk. "Guys, she did it. Be prepared." Damn it. They knew about me. I still could surprise them though; everyone was always shocked by what I could do.

I moved towards the boy, trying to get closer to the door. He tried to grab me, but I was now as strong as him. We fumbled in the darkness for a minute, and I felt my elbow connect with his face. "Shit," he said quietly. His words were muffled, so I could tell he was grabbing at his face. He let out a groan. Suddenly, the trunk popped open. It was still dark, but there was a glimmer of dawn on the horizon, and I tried to use that to my advantage.

I jumped up quickly, brushing Brody's arms away. "It's me!" I yelled, trying to move quickly out of the trunk so that they wouldn't have a chance to take in all of the details. I shot out, and as my feet hit the ground, I stumbled, my body stiff from being confined, and caught myself with my hands to the ground. "She's in there!" I yelled, standing and pointing at the trunk. I was ready to run.

"Holy shit!" one of the boys yelled. I was hoping they would be looking at the trunk, but as I looked at them, the tall blond pulled his gun up and aimed it at me. The two boys stared at me, the blond and the driver who had a shaggy fringe of dark hair. The driver looked at the trunk, and I turned to see what he was looking at.

Brody was sitting up in the trunk, holding his nose where I hit him. "Damn, that stings." He pulled his hand away and wiped blood on his blue jeans. More blood dripped down the front of his leather bomber jacket.

I glanced down at my own clothing, a sweater and leggings now stretched to the size of a man. It was a dead giveaway that even though I looked like Brody in every way, I was an imposter in the skin of their friend.

"Nice try, Mimic," the blond boy said. "Dan, grab her."

Dan must be the driver who I hadn't seen. He had a chiseled, clefted chin and muscular physique. His build was like the blond's, kind of lanky. In fact, they had many similar facial features. Dan stepped towards me, eyes open wide. "Man, I wouldn't have believed it if I hadn't seen it with my own eyes, Aaron. Dude, she looks exactly like Brody." I knew I was done. I couldn't compete with a gun. There were other mimics who could, but I wasn't trained to.

"My dad wouldn't lie," the blond, who I now knew was Aaron, said, pulling out a set of cuffs. I remembered that they had dropped cuffs earlier. I should have known then that they were aware of what they were dealing with. For being an expert at observation, I hadn't noticed the obvious with these boys, but most likely, I just didn't want to acknowledge the obvious.

The real Brody pulled himself out of the trunk. Aaron handed the cuffs to him, and he walked towards me, standing face-to-face with me. He stared at me, his eyes traveling all over my face. I knew he was trying to look for differences. They all did. But I was able to take anyone's form down to every minute detail. I saw the mole above Brody's lip, and I knew he would see the same mole on mine. I was an exact replica.

"This is insane, Aaron. For real," Dan said, breaking the silence.

"Put the cuffs on her," Aaron motioned at Brody. "That should stop her." Brody grabbed my hands. I didn't struggle as he gently clicked the cuffs in place. They burned as they settled down onto my wrists. I couldn't help myself as I cried out in pain. I studied the cuffs. They were silver. Yes, these boys had done their homework. I felt pins and needles, and my knees turned weak. I was going to pass out.

"Grab her. She's going to fall." Brody stepped forward, and everything went dark.

Chapter 3

When I awoke, I was tied tightly to a chair with rope around my waist and my ankles. My wrists burned from the silver handcuffs that remained on them. The boys also remembered to tighten the handcuffs once the silver forced me to shift back to my own form. I kept my eyes closed and my head limp, pretending to be asleep.

In my mind, I quickly went over the information that I had gathered about my captors. The boy that was in the trunk with me was named Brody. I also collected the names of the blond, Aaron, and the driver, Dan. The shift had been a bad idea, but if they hadn't known, I could have caught them off guard. Aaron seemed like the leader. He was the one who had told Dan about my ability to shift. They also knew that I couldn't shift when in contact with silver.

I remembered Aaron saying something about his dad not lying. I wondered what he meant by that. So, his father knew about mimics? Maybe his father knew about the Agency. But what did these boys want with me? Did they know about my mission?

"So, what is she? What do we call her?" Dan asked.

"Well, there are many names. Skinwalker. Mimic. All Native American lore."

"That shit is real? Does that mean werewolves and vampires are real too?" I heard a sigh. "Dude, Aaron, I didn't believe until I saw it with my own eyes." I squinted my eye open so I could see them. None of them were looking my way.

"Like I said, my dad wouldn't lie. Neither would Smith, well, at least not about this," Aaron said. I could see his eyebrows were creased. "I wonder how many like her are out there?" He had no wonder in his voice. It was angry. Accusatory.

Then Brody spoke. "I wonder how many out there are being used like her." I opened my eyes to see his brows drawn together in a frown. His words took me by surprise.

"Brody, you have to stop thinking of her as a victim." Aaron was shaking his head at Brody. "She's not a victim. She chose this. And she's a monster." I clenched my jaw, fighting back anger. His words proved that he didn't know much about me.

"Aaron, you have to stop thinking of her as the bad guy. There are bigger fish to fry here. You don't know what her story is. You don't know what they're holding against her."

"Ah, guys," Dan interrupted. "I think she's awake." Suddenly, all three boys stared at me. Dan stepped forward. "Welcome," he said, smiling. Aaron shoved Dan away.

I scanned the room. There was a gas lamp and a fire in the fireplace, probably no electricity. The room had high ceilings with exposed beams. There was a kitchen with the bare minimum furnishings and a small, round kitchen table with three chairs tucked underneath. I was currently tied to the fourth chair. There was also a living room area, and situated around the fireplace were two ratty loveseats and an overstuffed recliner with a floral pattern on it. The windows were covered in plastic, probably to keep what little warmth there was inside.

My teeth began chattering. My sweater hung down off one shoulder after being stretched out when I shifted into Brody's form, and my leggings were hardly enough to keep me warm on a cold fall day. My hair hung limply around my face, and I tried to toss it back.

As Aaron whispered something to Dan, Brody approached and bent down to look me in the eyes. "Are you okay? Do you need something to drink? To eat?" I tried to clench my jaw, be strong, but I couldn't stop the chattering of my teeth. Brody watched me until Aaron pulled him back by the elbow.

"What are you doing?" Aaron whispered fiercely, but it wasn't quiet enough for me not to hear.

"I'm making sure she's comfortable," Brody answered matter-of-factly.

"That's not our job." Aaron motioned between the both of them. Dan watched the back and forth. The boys seemed to forget about me, so I repositioned myself in the chair.

"Aaron, she's a person. I'm not going to let her sit here starving and freezing."

"Not until she tells us something." Aaron turned to me. His eyes were cold, and his mouth was set in a line. He straightened up and then asked a question I wasn't expecting. "What did you want with Mr. Gray?"

I turned away, not wanting to give anything away. These boys did their homework. Even at the Agency, my mission was a secret, but these boys knew my mission had to do with Mr. Gray. Well, I *was* sitting outside his house.

I ignored his question and studied the flames in the fireplace. They must have learned about the mission from Aaron's father, the same person who told them about mimics. But what would make them want to come and kidnap me? Revenge? Ransom? What were their plans for me? If it was some kind of revenge, then they could have killed me right away. They wanted answers for some reason. But

I knew that if I gave them answers, I would be dead, either by their hands or by the Agency.

Aaron leaned close so I couldn't ignore him. "I said, what did you want with Mr. Gray?" I clenched my jaw again, trying to make my teeth stop chattering, trying to look braver than I was feeling, but my body started shivering instead. I was sure they could sense my fear.

Aaron turned to Dan and Brody. He punctuated his words with anger. "We're not giving her anything until she starts to talk." He grabbed the ax that rested by the door. My breath caught, and I froze, bringing my shoulders up. I wasn't able to do anything to protect myself. Though the boys didn't seem violent, I knew that I couldn't underestimate what they were capable of, especially Aaron, who seemed to hold a particular hatred towards me.

Aaron noticed that I was watching. "Oh, don't worry about this." He let out a humorless laugh. "This is for firewood. I have something else in mind for you." With that, he turned towards the door, taking the ax with him, his shoes heavily thumping across the wood floor. As he left, he slammed the door behind him. Dan acknowledged Brody, concern in his eyes.

Brody went into the room that was off the living area. He came back with a fleece blanket. Dan started, "But Aaron said—" Brody walked by Dan and tucked the blanket around my shoulders and legs. I felt the heavy warmth of his hands through the blanket. I tried to sink back in my seat to get away, but his hands didn't linger a moment longer than necessary.

He turned back to Dan. "Watch her. I need to go talk to him." And with that, Brody was out the door, and I was left alone with Dan. He plopped down on the kitchen table, his feet dangling inches from the floor. I watched him as he watched me. Dan had blue eyes and a t-shirt that said Gearhead Garage, and he had to be about 6'3".

He flicked his hair out of his eyes. He began to swing his feet, and I could see that he was the type of person who got bored easily, and that probably got him into a lot of trouble.

When Aaron walked out the door, I had gotten a glimpse outside. The cabin wasn't as remote as I expected because through the trees, I could see another home. We couldn't have been too far out of the city. Besides, we weren't in the vehicle that long. I felt queasy, remembering the last time I was in the woods with my father. I was ashamed. I pushed that thought out of my mind.

Finally, Dan broke the silence. "I hate the smell of this place." When I didn't respond, he continued. "See, that's the thing about Brody. He has this sense of right like no other. The dude reminds me of Clark Kent. He's a good balance for my cousin, who loses his temper easily."

I knew then that Dan was their weak spot. He wasn't as focused as the other two. It made sense that he was cousins with Aaron, seeing as they resembled each other. He seemed like a good-time guy, not a businessman. Not as angry as Aaron. My mind flicked through tactics to use on him. At the Agency, I studied for situations in which I had to think on my feet, read body language, and react. I was trained in observation, but it wasn't my actual strength. My strength was shifting and doing what I was told.

"Dan," I said quietly. "You have to let me go." I tried to muster tears. Acting wasn't my strength either, but I thought I sounded convincing.

Dan jumped off the table, surprised I spoke to him and even more surprised that I called him by his name. "We can't." He moved closer, studying me. He clenched his fists open and closed. He was nervous but trying not to show it. "Why were you after Mr. Gray?"

"I can't tell you, Dan. People are in danger. You have to let me go. Please." My eyes welled with tears. As Dan moved closer, his eyebrows raised in sympathy and his mouth twisted with concern.

"Don't do that." Dan put one hand up to his forehead. "Don't cry. You're safe for right now." I squinted my eyes, causing the tears to spill over the edges. "You're fine," Dan repeated.

I let out a gentle sob, my body rocking. I found that real tears were hidden behind the fake tears, and soon, I really was crying. I was scared. I had never been cut out for this business. I was a normal girl who grew up in a normal house, besides the fact that I was a mimic, which I didn't even learn until I was ten. I was just a teenager. I consciously tried to push away my self-pity. It would do me no good in this situation.

My real fear was not these guys. These guys seemed normal, whatever their motives were. Though Aaron was intense. I was afraid that he would snap. There was some raw emotion, something about me that gnawed at him until he couldn't stop from swatting at it.

What I was really worried about was the Agency and what they would do to me when they got me back, or worse yet, what they would do to me as a result of my failure in the Gray Mission. It would be easier if they took me back. They would put me back in my little room, tucked away from the world. They would initiate Plan B, whatever that was. But if they didn't get me back and they knew that I was still out here, there was no doubt in my mind that they would do a clean sweep. A kill order. I knew too much to be left alive, even though in the scheme of things, I didn't know all that much.

My tears were wearing out. The early tears left cold streaks on my face. I turned, trying to wipe them off on my shoulder, but I couldn't quite reach.

Dan moved closer. "No, really. Don't." He turned away, his eyes scanning the room for something, maybe a tissue, and when he couldn't find what he was looking for, he reached out his hand to wipe the tears away. I turned so that he couldn't touch me, but as I turned, I faced the door just in time to see Aaron enter with Brody behind him. They both froze, staring at us. Brody's mouth hung open like he was confused, but Aaron's face turned red as he stared at Dan, who was too stupid to put his outstretched arm down.

Aaron took a step forward. He spit his words at Dan. "What do you think you're doing?"

Dan put his hand behind his back, embarrassed. "Nothing." He smiled crookedly, a smile that probably worked on most people, especially women.

Aaron moved right in front of him. "Why are you talking to her? I told you that wasn't your job."

Dan shrugged and cast his eyes downward. I wouldn't be surprised if he kicked at an imaginary pebble. "I was trying to get information, and she's easy to talk to."

"That's because she's tied up, you moron." Aaron turned to Brody. "I told you she was dangerous." He turned back to Dan. "Do not talk to her. She is going to try to manipulate you to get what she wants. That's what they do. That is what they are trained to do." I was surprised to hear Aaron say that. And though that was what I was supposed to do, I wasn't very good at it, but I knew that there were other mimics who were.

Dan's ears turned red. "Aaron, don't talk to me like I'm a child. I'm here, aren't I?" He straightened up, now standing about an inch taller than Aaron.

"You aren't ready for this, Dan." Again, I was surprised, but this time I was surprised that Aaron would talk about Dan that way in front of me and paint him as the weak link. Maybe Aaron wasn't as smart as he seemed.

"He wasn't doing anything wrong," I whispered. I couldn't help it. I knew it would get me in trouble, and I knew my speaking up could make me appear vulnerable, but I hated seeing someone picked on.

All three of the guys turned to me, stunned I had spoken. Only Aaron came at me. He was across the room in seconds. He grabbed the armrests on my chair and yanked the chair forward, the wooden legs slamming on the floor with a thump. I flinched.

He spoke with a quiet intensity that set off an alarm in my head. "Why, if Mr. Gray is so important, wasn't there more security detail?" His hot breath hit my face.

I kept eye contact with him, not wanting to show any signs of weakness. I was startled by his question. He was traveling in the wrong direction if he thought that Gray was the important one, if he thought that they would plant a large security detail around such a secret assignment. My eyes were still damp with the tears I conjured for Dan. I wanted to wipe them away so I didn't look fragile or exposed.

Aaron reached out and grabbed my neck. I tried to recoil as he squeezed, but there was nowhere to go. He leaned in close to my face. Behind him, Brody and Dan turned away, unable to watch this sudden brutality. He spit as he talked, and his squeeze was unyielding. I tried to shake his hand off, but I couldn't. I tried to keep my cool, to keep steady, but my brain was reacting to my body's distress at not getting enough oxygen.

I gasped, unable to suck in all the air I needed, again, trying to shake him off, but his hand was immovable. Finally, with what little breath I had stored, I spoke quickly. "Mr. Gray was not important."

Aaron let go as soon as I spoke, but I could still feel a phantom hand on my neck, squeezing. I took large gasps of air. As he reached in his pocket, I looked past him to see Dan watching me and Brody trying not to make eye contact with me.

Then Aaron pulled out a small electronic device and the keys to the handcuffs. He pushed the device into my face. On the screen, which was smaller than a phone, was an image of a file folder that Aaron clicked open. I couldn't read the words because Aaron shoved it so close to my face. "This is Gregory Gray's file. He is a security officer at a small firm. He is single. Middle-aged. Healthy. What did you want with him? He is unremarkable and inconsequential. Why would the Agency send a mimic in?"

"It was a short position," I answered. I breathed slowly, keeping my heart rate low. I would only tell enough to keep them satisfied for the moment. Only enough to keep his hands off me until I came up with another plan.

Aaron's face deepened a shade of red. "My intel is legit. People lost lives for my intel, so quit lying to me and tell me the truth. Who is Mr. Gray? What was the end game, you little freak?"

His words stung. I decided I really disliked Aaron. Of course, the choking didn't help, and the name-calling didn't either, but also, I wasn't fond of the way he had treated Dan, which was curious because I didn't even know Dan. Aaron was an asshole.

I set my jaw to keep my cool and lifted my chin at him, holding my head high. My neck burned. I would not give him any more information and tightened my mouth shut. I had a moment of weakness before, but now that I knew who this guy was, what kind of guy he was, I wouldn't give him the satisfaction.

Aaron raised his eyebrows at my defiance. He stepped closer, but then Brody spoke up. "Aaron, I think we need to take a little break."

"Oh, I'm just getting started." He glared at me. Brody reached over and touched Aaron's shoulder. That broke Aaron's gaze. He motioned at Aaron and shook his head. It was the kind of nonverbal communication that seemed to reference a previous conversation, possibly the talk that they had outside. Brody considered me. "I'll watch her. You guys go lie down." I glared back. I was relieved that Brody stepped in, but I didn't want to show that.

Dan began to speak. "But what about—" Brody shook his head.

Aaron slid the device and keys back into his pocket. "Come on," he said to Dan. Dan seemed to have forgotten how Aaron had talked to him only moments ago, and he followed Aaron into the bedroom. I followed them with my eyes, and as they opened the door, I could see shapes in the room that looked like bunk beds. When they shut the door, Brody was still staring down at me.

He crossed his arms. "That was a pretty neat trick you did, shifting into me." I didn't respond. He motioned towards the bedroom door, and then back at me. "But you shouldn't mess with Aaron. And leave Dan alone too. Dan might be a nice guy, but he can handle himself. Don't push him." Brody took a few steps away and then turned back. "You should try to get some rest as well. We're in for a long day." It looked like there was one more thing that he wanted to add, but he didn't. He turned away and walked over to a ratty loveseat and plopped down with his back turned to me. He didn't look back.

I waited to see if he would say more, but he didn't. I didn't trust him. He seemed too nice. There had to be something behind that, some kind of act. Good cop, bad cop. But Dan didn't fit it. He seemed to be along for the ride. Brody and Aaron were the two I had to watch out for, and Aaron was a live wire. And though he worried me, there were bigger things I should be afraid of, like the Agency.

After a couple of minutes, I quietly tried to lift my legs from the chair, but they were tied down tightly with each foot sternly anchored around a chair leg. My waist and arms up to my elbows were taped around the chair back, and so were my shoulders. My wrists were still cuffed together, and the silver burned a deep red ring into my flesh. I had gotten a glimpse of the red before Brody covered my hands with the blanket. I tried to rub my wrists together under the blanket to ease the itch when I hit something in my inner pocket. I had completely forgotten about it. My phone.

Chapter 4

Brody was turned away from me, his head resting on the back of the loveseat. I was surprised he wasn't watching me. He seemed a little too trusting. I could only hope.

I didn't have much time. Under the blanket, I pushed the flap of my jacket back and gently pulled out the cell phone while trying not to move the blanket too much. When I had it in my hands, I tucked it between my legs, trying to remember the buttons, feeling them and counting them to find the number that I needed. My life depended on it.

"Why you?" Brody spoke softly, but suddenly. I jumped, and the phone almost slipped out of my hands and would have clattered to the rough hardwood floor, but I clamped my legs together to catch it as I held my breath.

"Why you? Why you, when there are others?" He was quiet.

I didn't want him to come over and find the phone, but I couldn't answer his question because I wasn't sure what he was asking me. "What do you mean 'others'?"

"Others. There are others like you, right?" His head still rested on the couch.

I thought about his question. I didn't even know how many mimics there were. I only knew of my mother, but I hadn't seen her in years. There was one. My guard, John, told me about her. He was the only person at the Agency who ever talked to me, even though he wasn't supposed to. He also delivered books to me to keep me occupied in my one-room cell. I don't know how he knew that I loved to read, unless someone told him I was the daughter of a librarian. He told me about a mimic who was younger than me, and from what he told me, she sounded ruthless. She arrived there as an orphan and was trained to be an assassin, a product of the Agency. Unlike me, she was loyal. She wasn't a prisoner. I wouldn't share this information with Brody though. I didn't want him to think of me as unique or valuable. That seemed dangerous.

"There are enough," I lied, trying to make myself sound unimportant.

"Why you?"

I looked down, my thoughts flitting to my mother and then back. "I'm good," I finally answered. "I'm good at what I do." I wasn't sure how accurate that statement was, but I got the job done.

"Well, you got caught, so you can't be that good."

And then, what came out next I knew I shouldn't have said after it left my lips. "I have everything to lose," I answered quickly, then bit the corner of my mouth. I silently cursed myself. But I wanted Brody to know that he was right, what he said to Aaron. That this wasn't a choice that I made for myself. I was forced. I didn't know why it was important. I guess I thought that it would help him get over what I was about to do to these boys.

Brody turned and eyed me from the loveseat. "Don't you think others have things to lose? Don't you think that they are holding things over their heads?" He leaned forward as though to get up, and I held my breath, not daring to move a muscle. Then Brody turned back and stared into the fire. "So, you're good at pretending to be other people?"

"I've always had to pretend." I pushed the first button on my phone, holding my breath in hopes that it didn't make a sound. When it didn't, I exhaled gently. I must have silenced it before I put it in my pocket. I closed my eyes, trying to picture the numbers. When I got to the final digit, I hesitated. I wasn't sure what the Agency would do in a situation like this. Maybe they would reward my loyalty. They could still use me for the job, but if they found out what I told these boys, and they thought the boys knew too much, Brody, Aaron, and Dan would be dead right along with me. There was no way that these three could outwit the Agency. They were teenagers.

I held my breath and pushed the button. Brody turned, his eyes boring into me. I had the sudden sensation that he knew exactly what I did. My face flushed. "You should rest," he said, turning away. My heart pounded in my ears. I slipped the phone back into my pocket and sat and stared at the fire. There was no telling when they would arrive. I should have been prepared, sharp, but instead I was exhausted. My eyes were heavy, and my head kept drooping.

I dozed here and there but awoke abruptly when Brody opened the door. He held it open and let the cool fall air enter. I could smell the grass on the breeze. When we arrived, it was dawn, but now the afternoon sun was fading into the night. I wondered if I pressed the right button on the phone. I somewhat hoped I didn't. If the Agency came and I was lucky, I would go back to my preexisting state. If the Agency came and decided to erase every trace of this mission gone wrong, then the struggle would be over. Either way, I seemed doomed to be held captive or be dead. My fate would be decided for me. The more I thought about it, the more I realized that I probably hadn't done the right thing by notifying them, but truthfully, it had been a long time since I knew what the right thing really was. I was so used to following orders.

The bedroom door opened, and Aaron came out. He didn't so much as look at me but made his way to Brody's side. Brody looked back at him. He raised his eyebrows, and Brody nodded. More nonverbal cues that I couldn't decipher. The two interacted with an ease of a close friendship, like they had known each other for a long time.

I broke the silence. "Who are you guys? Who do you work for?"

"You wouldn't know us," Brody answered, still searching for something outside.

"What do you care?" Aaron asked, studying me.

"I don't know if you know who you're dealing with." I frowned. It came out sounding like a threat.

Aaron laughed. "Honey, you don't even know who you're dealing with. In the grand scheme of things, you're only a pawn. You have no real power, though you think you do." Aaron walked into the kitchen and grabbed an apple. He pulled a knife out of the drawer and slowly quartered the apple. He was wrong. I knew I had no power.

"They'll kill you if you know things," I said. What was supposed to be a warning, again, came out sounding like a threat. I was trying to get it across to them the danger that they were in.

Aaron looked up, away from the apple. Before Brody could react, Aaron took three long strides so he was standing in front of me, then crouched down. "Are you stupid?" Aaron yelled at me, spit hitting my face. He was an inch away, and his cheeks were flushed, and his ears were red. I tried to stay calm, but I couldn't take my eyes off the knife clenched in his fist. Aaron was unstable. There was no telling what he would do to get the information he wanted. "You don't think I know that? Do you really think they will ever let you go? Or your family?"

"Aaron," Brody called out. He grabbed Aaron's elbow and pulled

25

him back. "You're not mad at her. She's not responsible for this." Brody was once again defending me. Who the heck was this guy, and what game was he playing? I willed myself to believe Brody couldn't be that nice. It would make what happened next easier.

Aaron shook Brody off. "Yes, she is. She's a coward. If she refused…"

"Then her family would be dead." Brody said those last words gently, but the fire had not gone out in Aaron.

Aaron threw down the knife with such force the tip of the blade dug into the wood floor and held. "Instead mine is." He pushed by Brody and walked out the open front door. I could hear his large boots stomping down the porch steps.

Brody bent down and pried the knife out of the board. He examined it, then looked at me, his brow creased as though waiting for me to speak. I couldn't. Aaron's family was dead. I had no idea if whatever happened resulted in a general hate for mimics or if it was something I, specifically, had done, but I didn't kill. That was one thing I didn't do on my missions. I was beginning to understand why Aaron hated me so much, but there wasn't anything I could do about it.

Brody walked to the table and put the knife down. He pulled a chair in front of me and pulled me closer so our knees were touching. He slowly drew the blanket from me. He was calm. I was not. "So, what was Mr. Gray supposed to do? You have to tell me, Meda. Aaron won't wait forever. We can't make our next move until you tell me the truth."

I didn't answer. I couldn't.

"Please. Haven't I been kind to you? Haven't I tried to give you all the fairness I can? Treat me with some respect. Tell me."

I wanted to help. I fell hard for his good cop act. I wanted to share everything with Brody. He had been kind. In fact, I had not received this much kindness from anyone in a long time, but I couldn't tell. I couldn't put my family at risk, not to mention Brody. And soon he would know about my betrayal anyway, so none of it mattered. And then I would find out if he was just playing good cop.

The door opened, slamming hard into the wall behind it. Aaron rushed in, eyes wide and breathing heavy. In the breeze, the whir of an engine made its way into the small cabin. "They're here," Aaron whispered. "She did it."

Brody's eyes bore into me as he opened the side of my jacket and plucked out my cell phone. He knew exactly where it was. He had known it was there the entire time. "I felt it on you when we were in the trunk."

I was confused. Why didn't he take it?

"Meda, I knew exactly when you signaled them. My computer notified me of the indicator." He shook his head, sighing.

"You tricked me?" So much for the good guy. I spoke quickly, words pouring out with no fear of their reaction. "I'm sorry, Brody. I had to. If I don't get back to them, they'll kill my family. I have to follow orders. If I don't do my job, my two little sisters are dead. So is my father."

"Yeah, I get that. But instead we're dead," Brody answered. His voice was flat. Dan had made his way into the room with a gun in his hand and dressed in a warm flannel jacket. Aaron shoved one of the ratty loveseats aside to reveal a door leading to a basement or cellar.

"Maybe not," I said in tears. I hated the way Brody looked at me. I hated disappointing people, even if they were complete strangers, but the boys weren't listening to me anymore. Brody pulled a duffel bag from behind one of the loveseats. It had been blocked from my view. They had a plan the entire time. They weren't waiting for me to tell them about Mr. Gray, though I was sure they still wanted answers. They wanted me to send out the signal. But why?

Brody pulled out what looked like a cell phone. Dan spoke up. "Tell me again. Why are we waiting for them to show up?"

Aaron spoke up after heaving the cellar door open. "We had to consider that they had some kind of tracking device on her or that she would alert them in some way. We can't afford to have them follow us after this point." He regarded Brody. "Ready?"

Brody moved over to me and began to roughly tear the tape from my legs and chest. He spoke quickly. "I need you to follow me. You are now expendable to them. They probably think you've turned."

"No." I shook my head. "I sent the signal. They'll know I'm still working for them."

"Not after what happens next. Come on." His orders were direct, emotionless. He kept my hands cuffed in the silver locks and turned back to Aaron. "Ready." I followed as Brody pulled me down the steps into the dark basement, wondering where they were leading me.

At first, I couldn't see anything. Then, when my eyes began to adjust, I noticed boxes with red numbers on them. Mechanical devices with wires attached to them. "Don't even try anything," Aaron said and handed Brody jeans and a sweatshirt that he pulled off one of the shelves.

"Yeah, one false move and pfow." Dan made a gesture with his hands. I had no idea what they were talking about.

Brody, holding the clothes, turned to me. "I need you to change." I held out my wrists. He hesitated for a moment, and Aaron watched, tense. Brody tucked the clothes under his arm and began unlocking the cuffs. "Don't try anything. We have to assume they could be tracking you using anything, articles of clothing, jewelry. Lose everything." He removed the cuffs and handed me the clothes.

I stared at the clothing in my hands, not sure how to begin. I was embarrassed to get undressed in front of the boys. Aaron turned his gun on me. "Do it or you're staying behind. Believe me. It would be safer for us."

"Turn around," I said. The boys, realizing they were watching me, averted their eyes, but remained close enough to me that I had no chance to escape. I began stripping down.

As I was undressing, I glimpsed around the room. When I pulled the sweatshirt over my head, I suddenly realized what I was looking at. I couldn't help myself. "Are those…" I asked quietly.

"Explosives," Dan said, his back still turned. "We're going to blow these guys sky high."

"That isn't the plan," Brody said sharply, almost angrily.

"Done," I said quietly, putting my arms out. They turned around, and Brody settled the cuffs back on my wrists. I winced in pain.

Aaron stepped close to me. "Lose the earrings," he said. Brody reached up to take the earrings out, but I twisted my head away in time to see Dan disappear through a passage into the dark.

"Not the earrings," I said firmly.

"Everything," Aaron said, stepping towards me. "I'm not sure when you began to feel it was okay to make demands on us, but you are following our orders now."

"These things never leave me. I promise. They don't have a tracker in them. They never had a chance to put a tracker in them." I wouldn't let them take the only thing I had left that was mine, mine before the Agency came and took me.

"You say that like we can trust you after you just signaled for them to come get us. I said lose them," Aaron said. He turned to Brody. "We don't have time for this."

There was a quiet thump upstairs. Aaron glanced up to the ceiling. "That would be the smoke bombs."

Brody reached up for the earrings, but I turned my head again. "Please," I said urgently. "They're the only thing I have left from my mother." Brody studied my face. I was sure he didn't believe me. I wouldn't have believed me.

Upstairs, the room exploded in gunfire. I instinctively ducked while the incessant chatter of machine guns continued. Had I been up there, I wouldn't have survived. My stomach buzzed. The Agency must have decided on Plan B, the plan they didn't need me for. "Come on!" Aaron yelled.

Someone upstairs yelled to cease fire, and the gunfire stopped, but heavy footsteps pounded across the floor above us.

The three of us made our way through the dim maze. The basement seemed to be larger than the upstairs. There was a doorway on the far side of the room, and Aaron led the way over the threshold followed by me and then Brody. We were inside some kind of dark tunnel. My shoulders ricocheted off the narrow walls as I was pushed and prodded down the hallway.

A light came from behind, and I saw Brody had the cell phone he pulled from the bag. He glanced at the screen but kept pushing forward. "We've got ten seconds!" he called out.

The tunnel ended in a large cavern that had high ceilings carved from stone. I blinked wildly, but before I could take in everything in the vast room, Brody pushed me to the right where a van was parked. Dan was already behind the steering wheel, revving the engine.

Brody guided me towards the back and shoved me in. "Time!" he yelled. There was a muffled thud as he climbed in after me. Dan reached up into the visor and punched a code on what looked like a larger version of a garage door keypad. The stone wall rumbled as it rolled up in front of us. A cloud of smoke streamed through the door we had just run through, but we didn't wait around to see what happened. As soon as the door lifted high enough for the van to get through, Dan stomped on the gas and the van rocketed out of the cave.

"Woo-hoo!" Dan yelled. I couldn't believe it. He seemed to be having a good time. The van moved uphill and then down. Brody had one arm over me, holding me to the bed of the van so I wouldn't be jostled too much, or maybe he was afraid I would try to get away. Dan punched a code back in so the garage door would shut. A series of rumbling "thunks" came from behind us. I jumped a little, craning to see the reaction on Brody's face.

"Secondary explosives," he said quietly. Brody put his mouth close to my ear. "Meda, we're good guys. I need you to remember that, but something bad happened to Aaron. He's angry, and I can't control him." He paused, and then continued, "You will have to tell us the plan for Mr. Gray. There is no getting around that."

I bit my lip. Was this good cop again, even after I had dialed the kill orders?

I was confused. There were no more orders to follow. No more contingency plans. It wasn't my own life that concerned me so much, but I didn't know if my family was in danger or dead. If the Agency knew or even thought I turned on them, there would be no hope for my sisters and father. There would be no reason to keep them around, especially since my father knew about mimics.

So, there I was, inexplicably tied to the three boys in the van, whether they trusted me or tried to kill me, and I knew that if the Agency couldn't get their hands on me, they would stop at nothing to kill all of us.

Chapter 5

Aaron had insisted I wear a blindfold. Brody objected but submitted to Aaron. It wasn't worth the fight. I could hear Dan humming along to 80s rock music that played on the radio. Occasionally, Brody would ask how I was doing, but any other discussion among the guys was whispered so that I couldn't make out what they were saying. I ignored Brody, determined not to fall for the good guy routine.

We switched vehicles twice along the way. Both times, Brody gently led me by cuffed hands to the next vehicle, bending my head down so I wouldn't hit it on the doorway.

We pulled off for bathroom breaks. Brody would uncuff me and let me know his back was turned. It was only then that I removed the blindfold, but there was nothing to identify our location. The roads were overgrown and badly paved. We were always traveling on some kind of backroad system. Brody would stand guard, and when I was done, I would put the blindfold back on and call for him.

We ate fast food in the vehicle. Brody would hand me the food, and I would eat whatever he gave me, no questions asked. Aaron didn't try to talk to me at all. They didn't ask me about Mr. Gray, which was unexpected, but they must have had other plans to get the information out of me. That was why Brody warned me in advance that I would need to talk.

By the time the vehicle stopped and Brody said, "We're here," I couldn't tell how long we had been on the road. I was disoriented from the blindfold and the starting and stopping. I didn't even know if it was day or night. They unloaded me out of the vehicle, and we began walking.

I walked on unstable, unlevel ground. The feeling of damp grass soaked through my shoes. I could smell the trees and the cool fresh air. I heard someone grappling with a lock, and Brody took me by the elbow and guided me down several steps. I heard metal scrape on metal, and my arm brushed against a wall as we moved forward. Wherever we were, it had a tinny smell. Like the inside of a soup can.

When we stopped, Brody began removing the blindfold. He pulled it away, and I got my first look at the room they led me to, the solid door we had come through, and the cramped, dark kitchenette we currently stood in.

"Welcome home!" Dan called out, not to anyone in particular. No one laughed, and Dan seemed nervous, like he was trying to break the tension. He went to the fridge and grabbed some water bottles for everyone, including one for me. It was clear he was struggling to see me as a prisoner, and I knew I had to take advantage of that.

"Thank you," I whispered.

Dan's mouth dropped open, and he sputtered a "You're welcome," as any polite young man would. Aaron glared at him angrily.

Brody began removing the cuffs from my raw, oozing wrists. I glanced at Aaron to gauge his reaction, but he just rolled his eyes and breathed a heavy sigh before disappearing through an even thicker door on the other side of the room. He was not happy with how "human" his companions were treating me. Dan followed Aaron through the door, leaving me alone with Brody. And while Brody was a lot smarter than Dan, he was also kinder than Aaron, but I couldn't let that cloud my judgment.

The walls were made of large cement blocks, and everything was gray. I rubbed my raw, blistered wrists. My skin had that kind of reaction to silver. I winced and turned them over, inspecting the damage. Then I glanced around the room once more, my eyes settling on a map on the wall. It appeared to be a map of a national forest. There were no cities on it. "What is this place?" I chanced a whisper to Brody, not wanting Aaron or even Dan to hear my question.

Brody studied me for a moment as though weighing the risks of giving me an answer. "It's our little fallout shelter, for when we need to get off the grid. Aaron's dad built it, and no, he wasn't a doomsday freak. He knew what was going on." He set the cuffs on the table, offering no more details. "There's a place for you to shower and clean up." He pointed towards a curtained room, which I thought could have been a pantry.

My face flushed red with the thought of my possible aroma, something I shouldn't have cared about, but I couldn't help myself. Brody led me to the curtain off the kitchen. Behind it was a room sparsely embellished with a stainless-steel toilet and a shower stall. There was a small sink and a tiny mirror above the sink. Brody disappeared for a moment and came back with a travel bottle of shampoo, toothpaste, toothbrush, a comb, and a razor. Under the toiletries were neatly folded towels and a pair of scrubs. "Sorry, this is all we can give you right now."

I took the items, and as Brody turned to leave, I whispered, "Thank you, Brody."

He turned and opened his mouth, then paused. His face went blank again. "I'll be right outside." Brody pulled the curtain shut, and I was left alone. I looked around the room. There were no windows and nowhere to go, so I began to undress. Goosebumps appeared on my arms. It was chilly in the underground bunker.

It took a few minutes for the water to warm, but I didn't mind the wait. I stood and let the steaming water pelt my face and sink slowly through my pores. I took my time soaping up, not knowing when I might get another chance like this. As I washed, I replayed the events that brought me here. It all happened so quickly, and I tried to imagine if I had done something different, anything different, if there could have been a better outcome.

I thought of the Agency and how they would view my actions. If they thought I was colluding with my captors, my dad and sisters were at risk. They were always being watched. The Agency kept close tabs on them at all times because they knew what motivated me, my family. So, they also knew if I were to ever get out, that would be my first stop. My gut told me that my family would be safe for now, but I wondered if the Agency knew about these boys. Who were they working for? What exactly did they want?

These boys had intel and had carefully planned their firework show at the cabin with the thought of taking out some members of the Agency. It was an extremely clever move which made me think they weren't operating alone. My guess was it had something to do with Aaron's dad.

Then my thoughts, like rocks skipping across a lake, landed on Brody. I couldn't shake my suspicions about how kind he was when he didn't have any reason to be. It's not that I didn't believe there were nice people in the world. The problem was I wasn't used to being treated that way by anyone, especially after they knew what I was. People were uncomfortable around different. It's always been that way, historically speaking. It had to be part of the plan. Aaron was meant to scare me while Brody was meant to gain my trust to get information. It had to be. And I couldn't fall for it.

Because I didn't want to leave the warmth of the shower, I closed my eyes and imagined what Brody would be like outside of the craziness we were in, as a normal teenager. There was no harm in imagining it, I told myself. I thought of where he would have fit in at my high school, before I was pulled from my normal life. He was probably just as nice to everyone he met and treated everyone with respect, which meant everyone would love him. Undoubtedly, he would have been the most popular guy in high school. He was kind and extremely attractive in that underwear model-esque kind of way. My face flushed. I had no idea if his body was model-esque, but he was strong and cute. He was smart and loyal to his friends. My heartbeat sped up. I was being stupid. I needed to be serious.

But then, as I scrubbed my arms, remembering how Brody had held me both in the trunk and in the back of the van, I shook my head, trying to shake loose the stupid thoughts. I was glad no one could read my mind. I was being a silly teenager, and I needed to stop. I was their prisoner. They were going to use me to find out the plan and for whatever else they had in mind which I still didn't know about, yet I couldn't help the guilt that burned inside when I saw how disappointed Brody was when I triggered the attack at the cabin. And I couldn't help the feeling that I was feeling right now. But I could hide it. I had to.

I knew sometimes prisoners or kidnap victims did that with their captors, began feeling like they belonged with them or felt sympathy for them. Stockholm syndrome, I think it was called. And though I didn't think this Brody was an act, I knew I wasn't meant for happy endings, so it was important to push my feelings away, down where no one would see them, not even me. And with that last thought, I felt my disappointment hit the surface and sink down, deep.

I stepped out of the shower and toweled off. I tried to squeeze the water out of my hair, but droplets still soaked into the blue scrubs. I examined my face in the mirror to make sure I was still myself. When I confirmed my own reflection, I opened the curtain and walked right into the middle of an argument that was taking place in the kitchen.

Brody and Aaron stood nose-to-nose, but as soon as I stepped out, they stopped talking and stared at me. Aaron's face was red, and I could feel the anger radiating off him as he glared at me. Dan stood off by the refrigerator, watching Brody and Aaron.

Aaron's stare was startling, and I backed up. Even though I didn't mean to, I found myself moving in the direction of the door that led outside.

"Where do you think you're going?" Aaron asked, his eyebrows creasing in a feral manner. I froze. I looked behind me and saw the door, then turned back to Aaron.

I put my hands up in surrender. "I didn't mean…" I started, but Brody cut me off.

"Aaron, lay off," he said, his voice low but firm.

Aaron moved towards me, swiftly. I tried to stand my ground, but there was an intense anger and energy to him. He was moving like he wasn't going to stop. I recoiled, closing my eyes, but then opened them immediately. He stood right in front of me, looking down at me.

I moved back a step, but he was still too close. He leaned down, and I felt his hot breath on my face. He reached out and flicked a clump of my wet hair off my shoulder. I flinched in surprise. Then his eyes grew wide, and I knew what he was seeing. I tried to put my hands up, but it was too late.

"Brody, she still has those earrings." I twisted them, gripping them tightly. I backed up, feeling weak, and I knew in that moment

I was weak. I needed to stand my ground. I decided then and there that I would not let him take them. I would not let him bully me.

Aaron stepped towards me with his hand out, palm up. "Give them to me."

"No," I said, finding my voice. I backed up as far as I could go. My shoulder blades pressed against the cold metal door that led outside. I protectively shielded the earrings from him.

"Give me the earrings." Aaron stayed back, waiting for me to hand them over.

I knew I was being stupid. He was my kidnapper. He had total control, but I couldn't give up the one thing I held onto through all of this. Everything I had done was for my family. What more could this boy do to me? "I won't," I said, lifting my chin up at him.

"Meda," Brody called softly but sternly. Aaron stepped towards me, leaving no space between us.

I was backed into a corner. I remembered before, the feeling of his hand squeezing tightly around my neck, and found that I couldn't physically control myself anymore; it was fight or flight. Without thinking, I swung a tight right hook that connected with Aaron's cheekbone.

Aaron stumbled back, shocked. Dan covered his mouth with his hand. I braced myself for the repercussion. Before Brody could move to stop him, Aaron rushed me. He shoved me so hard against the door that it banged open. I lost my footing and collapsed in the hallway, but I could hear him breathing, heavy gasping breaths, and I knew he wasn't done.

I scrambled to my feet and turned to run towards the exit. From behind, two hands shoved me hard against the outside door, which luckily, had not been bolted shut. I stumbled on three steps directly outside the door and lurched up them, but I wasn't fast enough.

Rough hands grabbed the back of my scrubs and pushed me down into the patchy grass at the top of the steps. The wind was knocked out of me as I hit the ground, but I caught myself with my hands before my face connected with the grass. The air was still, and I saw tiny ants scrabbling in the dirt in front of me.

Aaron reached down and grabbed the back of my arm, pulling it back and turning me so I faced him. I didn't want to look at him. I saw the oddly peaceful blue sky, and then, behind Aaron, I saw Brody trying to get up the steps to us, but Dan was holding him back. "Let go, Dan! Stop it, Aaron! Stop!" Brody yelled, fighting against his friend. But Dan was bigger, a muscular gearhead. They seemed too far away, even though they were only a couple of feet.

My ears were ringing, and everything felt hollow. Aaron picked me up again by the collar of the scrubs, and I heard it tear at the neckline. He shoved me down in the grass again, knocking the air out of my lungs. I tried to focus my eyes on him, but everything was blurry. Leaves crunched beneath my back. I tasted blood in my mouth. I must have bit my tongue.

Aaron screamed at me. "Why were you after Mr. Gray?" He leaned down and grabbed me by the collar again. I tried to squirm away, scuttle through the grass and weeds, but he twisted his hand tight so the scrubs were like a noose around my neck. I reached up, trying to pry his hand loose to give me some relief, but there was none.

"What were you going to do?" he yelled in my face. I closed my eyes tight, trying to fight the tears, trying to will him away, or will myself away. I couldn't breathe, and everything was fuzzy. That was why I didn't see his hand coming at me, but I felt it. It landed hard, stinging the left side of my face and breaking loose the dam of tears.

"Aaron, stop!" When I opened my eyes, I could see again, but it was like looking in a tunnel. I could see Brody wrestling with

Dan, trying to get to Aaron. Then Aaron shook me, my head jerking violently back and forth, my brain throbbing.

"Why Mr. Gray?" he yelled. He shook again.

I couldn't hold it in anymore. My body was screaming with pain. I was gasping, trying to speak, but words wouldn't come out, and finally, my voice cracked, causing Aaron to pause, fist in the air as though he was going to strike me again.

I sobbed, ashamed at myself, and sputtered, "My primary target wasn't Mr. Gray." I spit out the words at him. Blood went with, droplets spotting my borrowed scrubs. I was angry at the tears streaming down my face. I gasped, but it sounded like a sob. "Mr. Gray was just a pass-through." Aaron was inches from my face, breathing heavily. It was nauseating.

"Then who was the primary? Who were you trying to get to?" He twisted his fist, pulling my collar tighter. I grabbed at his hands, hitting them, but without any real force, trying to knock them free. I could see over Aaron. Brody stopped struggling against Dan.

Aaron let his grip loose just enough for me to get a big breath of air. It felt good to be able to take a full breath, but I could see Aaron's fist balled up, ready to strike again. The fight seeped out of me. "The President," I whispered, my lips bubbling with blood. "My primary target was the President of the United States."

Chapter 6

Aaron held me like that for a while, hands froze in a ferocious grip. He was encompassing, all I could see, and I wasn't sure if the violence was over, but when he spoke, the rage in his voice had subsided to a dull hatred. "You were going to kill the President?"

I struggled to speak. "I don't kill anyone," I said, trying to defend myself, but I had to admit, even to me it sounded weak.

Aaron lifted me close to him. I flinched as his hot breath hit my face. "What do you think happens to people once you become them?" I stared at him. "Do you think they just let them hop back into their lives, with no recollection of the events you lived through? Don't you think that would be suspicious?"

"I don't know what happens. That's not my job." I knew it sounded stupid when I said it, like I was making excuses.

"Not your job? Not your job? You have no clue what your job is. You have no idea what is going on." I held my breath in fear that Aaron would hit me again. I could feel his anger rising. "You better pick a side, freak. Because right now, you are completely expendable—to us and them." He continued to hold me close, glaring at me. I still wasn't sure if he was done with me or not. I tried to look strong, show that he hadn't affected me, but I didn't know what he was seeing.

Then, Aaron let me go, my shoulders dropping the last few

inches back to the ground with a dull thump. He angrily kicked a lump of dirt and grass, causing me to flinch, but he didn't kick them at me. He turned and walked toward Dan and Brody. He pushed by them roughly, and they both got out of his way.

Dan followed right behind Aaron, looking back at me only once, while Brody made his way toward me. He slowly came to my side and opened his mouth as if to speak, but no words came out. He bent down and reached his arm out as an offering.

"No," I said, shaking my head. I didn't want him touching me. I didn't want anyone touching me. I stayed there on the ground. My hand found the corner of my mouth. It was wet. I pulled my hand away and saw red. Fresh tears streamed down my face, and I felt Brody just standing there, staring at me. I wanted him to go away, but I knew he wouldn't. He couldn't. I was their prisoner.

He reached down, moving to wipe the blood off my face, but I turned my head and wiped my mouth on the upper sleeve of the scrubs, then self-assessed to make sure everything was still where it needed to be after the beating I'd taken. I reached up and rubbed the back of my neck. It throbbed. I probably had whiplash from Aaron shaking me. I took a deep breath, and I felt the pain in my ribs and gasped.

"Are you okay?" Brody asked.

I'd nearly forgotten he was there. I looked up at him. "I'm not on their side." My words came out as a whisper, more to myself than anyone else. "I'm not on anyone's side."

He reached down and offered his arm to me again. I stared at it. "Meda, there is a way you can make things right. If you cooperate, we might be able to change things. To fix things."

I turned my eyes to him. I felt defeated. "There are some things that can never be fixed."

"But you can try." His eyes flickered with determination. I don't think this guy ever took no for an answer.

"I'm not a killer. I've never killed anyone." I took a breath and continued. "If I didn't do it, someone else would. They could have gotten anyone to be Mr. Gray. They could have gotten anyone for this job. I'm not their number one." I spit blood out of my mouth and into the grass, wiping my hands on my legs.

"But why you? If they had other choices, why did they choose you?" Brody asked.

"I don't know," I answered. I stared at his hand and finally reached for it. He hoisted me up, and I grimaced in pain. I allowed myself to put my weight on him as he walked me back to the underground bunker.

The first time we came through, I was blindfolded and hadn't seen the large bolted door. Brody hoisted me through the door and into a small hallway that ended in another door. There was a key swipe and a punch code, and then we were back in the kitchenette. That was as far as Brody took me. He pulled out a chair at the table. Aaron and Dan were nowhere to be found. I suspected they were behind the second large metal door at the back of the kitchenette. That door was also equipped with a code panel.

"Tell me about the job," Brody said, sliding the chair gently under me. "Why Mr. Gray?"

I sighed. Brody was the only one who treated me like a human, and they were right. I was expendable. The gunfire at the cabin had proven that. I decided that whatever happened, it didn't matter anymore how much I revealed to Brody. He and I were both dead already. Well, I had a chance if the Agency decided I was valuable enough to keep, but they had no reason to keep him alive.

I slumped down in my chair. "Mr. Gray's security firm was

chosen to help do security for the President's visit. Gray was the obvious choice because he had no family. No one would know, and he wouldn't need to be eliminated, leaving an unnecessary trail." I turned to Brody. "It was the easiest in. The least suspicious. You have to know if I don't do this, someone else will."

"I know," Brody said. He was facing me, leaning over the table. "That's why we need to stop it. So, what does that mean, Gray was the obvious choice?"

I rubbed my wrists, still red from the cuffs. "I was to infiltrate Gray's security team through Gray, set up back doors in the security, and then, eventually, take over for the President."

Brody persisted. "But what would happen to the President?"

I looked up at him, throwing my hands in the air. "They don't tell me those kinds of things." I knew it sounded stupid when I said it. This was exactly what Aaron was talking about. I was responsible because I didn't ask questions, not that they would tell me.

"So, you know it probably means they plan on getting rid of the President, right?" I didn't answer Brody. He continued. "Why don't they just assassinate the President using the security back doors that you create?" He said it almost like he was talking to himself.

"All I know is that I had a series of appearances to make on an issue, which they didn't disclose to me ahead of time. They were going to brief me when I was in place. They don't trust anyone enough to tell the plans to in advance. Plus, this one is a game changer. That was why the security team was so small. They didn't want to raise suspicion at the Agency. The Agency is big and far-reaching, meaning that, though the chances are small, there are opportunities for double agents to sneak in."

I paused. I wanted him to realize how big this was, if he didn't already understand. "Anyway, then I had some papers to sign, and that was it. I do know it was supposed to be my longest placement ever. I myself wondered how sustainable it would be." Brody's eyebrows creased in confusion, so I continued. "I mean, it's easy to impersonate someone for a small period of time. But the longer you are in position, the more likely you are to get caught. And the President is so public…" My voice trailed off. I hadn't spent a lot of time thinking about the assignment because I had expected the Agency just to take care of everything, like they always did, and leave nothing to chance.

"Well, we have to stop it," Brody said, clenching his fist and dropping it on the table.

"You stopped Plan A. That's pretty impressive." I wasn't sure why I was complimenting him for kidnapping me and beating me.

"No, we have to stop the whole thing." His mouth was set in a firm line. I glanced at the door Aaron and Dan had gone through, waiting for them to come back out at any moment, but they didn't.

I turned back to Brody, confused. "How are you going to stop it? This is big. The Agency is big. You're just a bunch of…boys." By this point, I knew that they were more than just "boys" based off what I saw at the cabin, but I needed to get it across to Brody how serious this all was.

Brody looked at me and shook his head. "You still don't get it, Meda. We didn't stumble upon you. We helped set this entire thing up. We have a plan. Here, let me show you something."

He stood, pushing his chair out, and grabbed my arm and pulled me out of the chair. I was about to shrug him away, but my neck was still aching from the throttling that Aaron gave me. I let my body go limp with exhaustion.

Brody pulled me over to the large metal door at the back of the room. He punched in a code, and the door slid open. When I caught a glimpse of the room on the other side, I was surprised by the amount of electronic equipment that was there, not just computers, but other devices that I couldn't identify. Dan was also on the other side of the door, sitting with his feet up on the desk and blowing spit bubbles. When we walked in, he quickly dropped his feet, almost tipping out of his chair.

"Uh, what's up?" he asked, looking between Brody and me. When Brody didn't answer, Dan stood and continued. "Um, it's probably not good that she's in here." He spoke to Brody like I wasn't even there.

"She's with us," Brody said. "There's no turning back, and there's no getting rid of her. This is for better or worse."

"I know," Dan said. "It's just that…Aaron…and we can't trust her."

"Aaron better straighten up. He knew what he was signing up for," Brody said, "and the only way to build trust is both ways." Brody nodded at me, then a smaller door opened in the back of the room. We all turned to look in the direction of the bathroom. The toilet was still running when Aaron walked out the door. He looked up and saw me, then froze. His face did not reveal his feelings. Brody spoke quickly. "Aaron, you need to show Meda the files."

"Brody," I interrupted. "Maybe this isn't the right time." I reached up and touched the tender part of my face. My skin hurt, and I could feel where the bruise was forming. I didn't want to be anywhere near Aaron.

"This is the only time, Meda," Brody finished. "We aren't staying here long, and you need to be caught up to speed if you are going to be any help to us. You're on our team now, right?" Aaron clenched his jaw. I didn't say anything. Brody seemed to be putting a lot of trust in me for no reason. I didn't know if I could believe that he would trust me, and I knew Aaron wouldn't. I didn't understand it, but I'd go along with it. I would be on their team until it wasn't convenient to be on their team anymore.

Aaron still hadn't moved, so Brody stepped past him to the file cabinet that stood in the corner and started paging through the files. Dan sat back down, quietly looking between Aaron and Brody. He sensed their emotions bubbling like water in a boiling pot. I just hoped it stayed at a nice simmer.

I looked at Aaron, who glared back at me, cracking his knuckles. He stared for a moment longer and then barked out a dry, humorless laugh. I tried to hide my flinch, but I was sure he saw it. He was like a predator looking for a weakness in his prey. Then he walked by, knocking me a few feet over, and exited the room. I stumbled and caught myself against a desk. Letting out the breath that I didn't even realize I was holding in, I gathered myself and stood up straight.

"Well, that went better than expected," Dan said. I gave him a look that I was sure translated to "are you serious?" He shrugged.

Brody came back with some file folders in his hands. He motioned for me to sit down at a nearby desk that had some electronic equipment and what looked like a torn apart computer on it. "Dan, could you get us some water?" he asked, pulling out the chair for me.

Dan looked between the two of us, unsure if he should leave or not. "Are you sure it's okay?" he asked. "I mean, she doesn't have cuffs on or anything." He gestured at my still raw wrists.

"She won't change. Right, Meda?" Brody asked me. I nodded slowly. Dan looked back once and left the room. He seemed happy to go, and as soon as he was gone, Brody spread the folders out across the empty portion of the desk.

He pulled out a chair from a small table filled with wires and batteries. It made a loud scraping noise on the concrete floor, and he pulled it up so that the arm of his chair was touching the arm of my chair. "There are some things you need to know. And they have to do with you. And Aaron. Well, more specifically, Aaron's father."

I held my breath. This wasn't going to be good.

Chapter 7

Brody opened the folders. They were filled with documents and pictures. "You will probably recognize the people in these file folders. Aaron's dad got the intel before..." He paused for a moment as he shuffled the papers around before finding the one that he wanted. He held it to his chest so that I couldn't see it. "Aaron's dad was tracking the Agency, you in particular, Meda." I was surprised to hear that. I was careful, and the Agency moved me around all the time. It was hard to believe that anyone could have tracked me. The Agency was nearly invisible, or had been.

"Do you remember this man?" Brody put down the picture he was holding and slid it in front of me. It was a picture of an older man with shocking white hair and a serious look on his face. I immediately recognized him because the circumstances around that job had been so different from the normal. I remembered it clearly. It had been two months ago, and the Agency had sent me out in a car to an undisclosed location, which was really some road in the suburbs of D.C., on the north side, I thought. Two men in suits escorted the man into the car. The man seemed out of it, like he was doped up or something.

One of the men in suits placed the white-haired man's hand in mine, and as I stared into his eyes and started taking his shape, I saw something unexpected. It wasn't a look of horror, but a look of recognition. Usually people freaked when they saw me change, and rightly so. This man seemed like he knew what it meant. But that was the last I saw of him. The men in suits took the white-haired man away.

Then, they gave me a script to follow with some phone numbers. I was to place the calls from the back of the car and follow the scripts to the letter. I didn't even understand what the conversations were about. They didn't make sense to me.

After that, I had to go to a public place and make a scene. Once again, I was told exactly what to say, but it was incoherent ranting. I assumed it was to discredit the man so that people wouldn't listen to him. That would be one of many reasons to make a man look crazy.

I made a scene at a local restaurant. It wasn't directed at anyone in particular. I walked in and started yelling exactly what they had told me to. Men dressed in police uniforms came and took me away. Of course, they weren't real police. They were Agency men, bringing me back to my little room at their compound when the assignment was done.

I was quiet. I didn't think it was safe to admit that I knew the man in the photo, but Brody could see it in my eyes.

"That was Aaron's father." He said it so quietly that I barely heard him. My stomach lurched. Aaron's anger made more sense to me now. Once again, I fought tears that burned behind my eyelids as I squeezed my eyes shut. What I had done made me responsible for Aaron's father, but I had no choice. I had to protect my family. I didn't know if the guy was a good guy or a bad guy. I hadn't thought if he had family. I couldn't think about those kinds of things.

I put my hand on my forehead, feeling sick. "After they used you, they assassinated his family and killed him as well. They made it look like a murder-suicide." Brody pulled the picture back towards himself and studied the photo of Aaron's father. It was curled up at the edges, as though it had been looked at many times before. I didn't know what to say. They killed his entire family? How would I know that they would do that? I thought of my sisters, and then I started to wonder if Aaron had any siblings, any younger siblings. I felt my stomach lurch and swallowed hard, trying to push the bile and my feelings down.

Brody continued. "Reg Monroe was a smart man. He was an aide to the Vice President of the United States. That was how he caught wind of the Agency and their far-reaching hands. That was how he uncovered the truth about mimics." Brody paused, but he wouldn't look at me.

"I was at the house that night." His voice quavered. "I often spent the night at the Monroe's, especially when my dad was on a bender." Brody looked up at me. He seemed surprised that those words had come out, as though it wasn't something he normally talked about. When I didn't react, he looked back down again.

"Aaron and I snuck out of the house that night to meet some friends at the football field. It happened when we were gone. When we returned, we first found Aaron's sister, Angela. She must have been trying to get away, maybe to come to us for help. They shot her in the head." His words hit me like a slap in the face, violent and unexpected. I felt like I couldn't breathe, and I noticed Brody's eyes beginning to glisten. He tried to blink the tears away. "There were still men in the house," he continued. "They shot at us, but we got away. We couldn't help anyone. We left Angela lying there." Brody didn't seem like he was talking to me anymore. He was speaking to the photo. "Aaron tried to stay. He thought he could save them. I had to drag him out of the house." Just then, Brody fought off a jerky breath, the kind of breath that comes with tears, but he remained composed as he continued talking. I held my breath, but tears had broken through and I couldn't stop them.

"Aaron called his uncle, Dan's dad, who met us outside of town at a gas station. He gave us cash, a duffel bag, and a tape made by Aaron's father and told us we needed to get out of D.C. He sent us to Chicago to meet with one of Aaron's father's associates. He also sent Dan with us, afraid that Dan wouldn't be safe."

I was quiet. Tears streamed down my face. The dam had broken, and there was no fixing it. The edges of my vision got a bit fuzzy.

"We made it out safe. Dan's family went missing soon after, but it turns out that they went on the run as well. Dan's dad had prepped to hide with instructions from Reg. This," Brody glanced around the metal tomb that we were hiding in, "was where Aaron's family was supposed to hide. But they never made it."

I looked at the picture in front of Brody. I understood. "I didn't know, Brody. I had no clue. You must believe me. Every assignment, I just did what I was told. They didn't tell me anything. They threatened my life and the life of my family. I didn't know…I mean…his entire family…" I shook my head, trying to shake off this new information. I now understood why Aaron hated me, and hate was a weak word for the situation. Because of what I did, Aaron's family's death was swept under the rug. Aaron's father was painted as a murderous crazy man. "I can't change this," I sobbed. "I can't fix things." I wiped my eyes with both hands. The guilt was crushing me. I suddenly wished that Aaron had done more than beat me up. Then I wouldn't have to live with the guilt.

"I know, Meda." Brody let out a deep breath. He didn't reach out to touch me or comfort me, and I was glad for that. He held onto the picture. To the memory of Aaron's father.

I spoke again, this time in choppy breaths. "It's just that, the only thing I could see in front of me were the guns pointed at my own family. That was what was immediate. That was why I did it all. I guess I never let myself think of anyone else." I ran my hand back through my hair and fidgeted in my seat. I couldn't sit still. "I'm so stupid," I whispered to myself. I couldn't even think of Aaron or what to say or do the next time I saw him. I could never make things okay. Reaching up to my ears, I removed the backs of my earrings, bundled the diamonds in my fist, and held them out to Brody. "Take them. I don't want them." It was selfish of me to want anything from my old life after what I had taken away from Aaron.

Brody studied me but didn't take the earrings. He got up and went to the shelving that contained old keyboards, monitors, cords, and various other electronic devices. He grabbed a box, sat back down across from me, and opened it. Holding the box out, he motioned to me. I gently placed the earrings in the box. He spoke quietly. "If these do have some kind of tracking device in them, they won't be able to catch the signal through here once we head to the city."

"It isn't important anymore, Brody. They are stupid earrings. Throw them away. Smash them for all I care."

Brody studied me again for what seemed like the millionth time. The sadness had drained from his voice. "Sometimes, it's the little things that we hold onto that help us remember who we are and why we keep fighting. If they were important to you before, they still are now." He closed the box and leaned forward, his hands resting on top of it. "So, there is a plan in place, but nothing that you need to know about right now. We're still working on it, and we have some help." I nodded. "Can I ask you a question?" he asked. When I didn't respond, he continued. "What was it like? How you lived?"

At first, I was horrified and confused by what he was asking.

What was it like becoming people? Pretending people were crazy? Setting them up for who-knows-what?

Brody must have seen the look on my face because he rephrased his question. "I meant, where did you live? Were you kept in a prison?"

I thought back to my room. I started out quietly. "I was kept on lockdown at all times. There was a computer with limited internet access. It was also where I was allowed to watch videos of my dad and sisters. They gave me books. I read over a hundred in the time I was there."

And then, I couldn't help it. My thoughts turned to my dad and the library. "My dad is a librarian," I started. "He taught me that reading books is a lot like reading people. You can't just look at isolated incidences. You have to see the whole picture, the whole plot, the character's past decisions. You also can't get hung up on what you think you know, because what you think you know keeps changing. If you get hung up on what you think you know, you will never be able to guess the end, but when you get there, you will realize that you knew it the entire time." Brody didn't say anything. I wasn't sure if what I said sounded like rambling mumbo jumbo or if he was thinking about my words. Maybe I'd said too much, but there was no turning back.

Though it pained me to even ask the question, I mustered up the courage. "Can I...can I see more of the files?" I didn't want to see them. I had never wanted to know anything about any of the jobs. But now I needed to know the truth.

Brody's face remained unchanged. "Are you sure, Meda? I don't think that would be the best idea for you right now." He held them protectively.

"I understand if you can't let me." I turned away, towards the wall. "I completely get it. I don't deserve it, but I need to know, and if not now, when?" He considered me for a moment, then slid the folder over to my side of the table. He quietly got up.

I heard him walk away then turned my attention to the folder. I searched the picture of Aaron's father, looking for something, I'm not sure what. Maybe some way to redeem myself.

Then I paged through the photos of the other targets. They only had a few, and a few weren't even my assignments. I paged through the files over and over again, replaying the assignments, Reg's and some of the others, trying to determine how many people I had affected. "Affected" was a gentle word. Killed? Ruined?

I stared endlessly at these people. Besides Reg, they were all nameless, only I knew that wasn't true. They all had names, and families, and friends. I felt my head dip and fought to pull it back up and keep my eyes open. I was exhausted. My energy flickered like the last embers in a burnt-out fire.

"You need rest," Brody said from beside me. I hadn't even heard him approach.

"I'm fine," I said, rubbing my eyes, aware that Brody was tired as well but seemed to be better at hiding it.

"No, you need rest." He stood up and pulled me out of the chair. My body was twitchy. I had aches and pains, and my legs were rubbery. Aaron really did a number on me, but I couldn't blame him.

My legs almost dropped out beneath me. Brody caught me and swept me up in his arms. "Let me down," I said weakly, embarrassed that I was being carried like a child. He ignored me and carried me to a curtain which was located next to the small door that led to the bathroom. My eyes drooped. Brody brushed the curtain aside to reveal cots. I was able to lift my eyelids enough to see that no one occupied them. My words slurred. "These are your beds?"

Brody tenderly placed me on a cot. I curled my legs up close to my body. Brody walked over to a shelf and grabbed a nubby navy-blue blanket. He covered me and tucked me in around my shoulders. I was drowsy, but not too drowsy to still be curious. "Why are you so nice to me?" I said, my rough voice cracking in the quiet of the small room. "After all I've done to you and your friends. Why?" I couldn't keep my eyes open. It was like I had been drugged.

Brody's hands froze mid-tuck. His lips closed tightly like he was searching for an answer. He reached down and brushed some hair off my face, and I was too tired to flinch back in surprise. "Most of the time, when people do bad things, it's not because they're bad, but because they're put in a bad circumstance." I searched his eyes, sensing a double meaning. He seemed like he wasn't just talking about me. I was suddenly a little less sleepy than I had been moments ago. "I don't think you're a bad person, Meda."

"What about those Agency men that you blew up back at the cabin? You understand that some of the people at the Agency are not there by choice."

"Our intention wasn't to hurt anyone. It was to throw them off. There was an alarm upstairs warning them to get out. The purpose was to fake your death. We left some artifacts behind so that they might think we were still there."

"What do you mean, artifacts?" I was confused.

"Human artifacts that we collected from a cemetery." Brody winced as he said it.

"That's...creative," I replied. Brody pulled his hand back and turned to walk out of the room. He looked back at me, his eyes softening with sympathy. "Thank you, Brody," I said, almost inaudibly.

When he got outside the room, I saw the shadow of someone approaching. Brody pulled the curtain closed, but not completely, and I could see Aaron step up to Brody in the open sliver of curtain. "She needs sleep," Brody whispered.

"Did you cuff her?" Aaron asked. "Because I'm pretty sure you didn't." Aaron held up the cuffs, which glinted in the cold glow of the digital lights on the electronics.

"I'm not putting those on her." Brody pushed by Aaron and disappeared out of the open curtain. I could only see Aaron.

"Brody, don't be stupid. Don't let being the good guy cloud your judgment. We can't leave her wandering around here with the ability to turn into any one of us."

"She's with us, Aaron. She told me everything," Brody defended me. I still didn't understand why.

"How can you be sure? She's an actress. She told you that herself. That's her job." Aaron was waving his hands around, the cuffs clinking together.

Brody stepped back in my vision and was inches away from Aaron's face. "She's a prisoner. She was before, and now she is again. Anyway, I'm sure she can't even move after you beat the shit out of her. I need you to drop it."

Aaron swallowed. "I lost control. But she is a monster. You have to see that," he said.

"The only monster I see is you, pounding the shit out of a girl less than half your size. All I can tell you is that it better not happen again. I will not stand by next time." Brody turned his back and walked away from Aaron.

"Don't forget what she's done," Aaron called after Brody.

I could still see Aaron in the doorway. He turned, his eyes burning through the darkness. He quietly whispered the words, and I knew they weren't meant for Brody. "Don't forget Angela." I closed my eyes into slits. It was dark in the room, and I was sure that Aaron couldn't see me in the dark, but the way he stood in the doorway, staring into the room, gave me goosebumps.

Chapter 8

When I awoke, my senses were struck by the smell of musty linens and a low hum that filled the bunker. The remaining beds in the room were still empty and made with plain gray blankets that looked old enough to be hand-me-downs. It didn't appear as though anyone else had come in. I let out a huge sigh. It would have been awkward waking up to this strange room and have it full of sleeping boys.

I sat up, unsure of what to do. I didn't want to leave the room for fear that I'd run into Aaron or Dan, or Brody for that matter. But more specifically, I was afraid of the way Aaron had looked at me. I tried to imagine how I would feel if I was in Aaron's position. I could see it clearly. Forgiveness was not an option.

I was lost in my own thoughts when Dan rushed through the curtain and into the room. I flinched awkwardly. Because I was sitting up, I couldn't even pretend I was still sleeping. Dan, his floppy hair a mess and his eyes rimmed red, looked at me and said, "Oh good, you're awake." He plopped down on one of the empty cots, immediately throwing his arm over his forehead and talking to me like I was not a prisoner. "I have to crash in an actual bed for a little while. Don't mind me." He was breathing heavily in moments.

"By all means," I said quietly. I decided to leave the room because

I felt even creepier watching Dan sleep. I tried not to rustle the covers too much as my feet padded on the cold concrete.

I tiptoed out of the room, even though there was no chance that I would be able to wake Dan. I stopped at the curtain that separated this "bedroom" from the other designated areas of the bunker and looked back. This room was just as plain as the others. Some kind of concrete, block walls, and no decorations. The entire room was gray and dreary.

I quickly ran my hands down the front of the wrinkled scrubs, trying to rub them smooth, which was silly, trying to make myself presentable for my captors. Then, I forced myself to reach my hand out and slowly pull the curtain aside. I scanned the room first. Brody and Aaron were nowhere in sight. They could have been in the kitchenette area, or some other area that I hadn't yet been introduced to, and that was fine with me.

I slowly walked over to the table where the files remained exactly where they were when I left them last night, if it was even morning. It was difficult to tell in the windowless underground bunker. Time had become a peripheral vision over the last couple days. I was aware of it passing, but the details were fuzzy. I slid into the chair that I sat in last night.

Shuffling through the pictures again, I looked for one in particular. Aaron's father stared back at me with his darkened, thoughtful eyes, eyes that had seemed confused and muddled the last time I saw them. There was a paperclip attached to the top right corner of the photo that I hadn't noticed last night. I removed it and flipped to two pictures that were attached. One was a picture of a beautiful middle-aged woman. I slowly slid the final picture out from behind the photo of Aaron's mom. I touched the hair of the smiling teenager. She had Aaron's eyes and the same blond hair. Angela.

I stared at the picture, trying to push the feelings away. This was once a real girl, not just a photo. She had a kind smile, and her eyes sparkled. I imagined her and Aaron sitting on the couch, joking around with each other. The real Aaron, what he was like before all of this. Because the Aaron I knew wasn't the Aaron that was. He was the Aaron that was created. Much like I was created by the circumstances I was put in that were beyond my control. Only Aaron wasn't allowed the opportunity to save his sister, like I was.

I clenched my fists and closed my eyes. I could picture Aaron finding his own sister, facedown in his bedroom, body limp, and nothing he could do to help her. For his entire life he was probably told to look after his sister, and this one time when she went looking for him and he wasn't there, the unimaginable happened. He probably felt that he should have died with his family, much like I sometimes felt that my death would make everything better in my own family.

Taking a breath, I looked at the photo one final time. This poor young girl's life had been cut down so early, and everyone who knew Aaron's family was tricked into believing that Aaron's dad had killed his wife and his own daughter when, in truth, he was only trying to protect them. He was trying to make sure that they lived in a world without lies and unnecessary death. And it was all my fault. Tears escaped my eyes, and I wiped the back of my wrist across my face.

The large door opened with a soft, whining squeak, and Aaron strode through with Brody stepping closely behind. I quickly shuffled the pictures around and tried to wipe the tears from my face. I jerked up from the table as though they caught me doing something I shouldn't be doing.

Aaron walked by me, moving towards the bedroom. He paused at my side. I could feel him breathing down on me as he looked down at the table. I followed his eyes. The photos weren't on top of the pile, which I was glad for. I tried to make myself smaller, hoping he wouldn't notice me even though he was standing right next to me. Without looking at him, I could see his head turn back to Brody. Only seconds later, he let out a sharp breath and knocked into me as he walked by, causing me to stumble back and catch myself on the table. A few papers fluttered to the floor, and I reached down to pick them up.

Brody crouched down to help me, but I shook my head. I gathered the papers up and turned in the direction of Aaron. "Aaron," I called out softly, unable to stop myself from speaking.

Aaron slowly turned around, anger and pain fresh on his face. The words must have been on the tip of his tongue. "You know what pisses me off the most?" He paused and shook his head. "You walk around here like you haven't done a goddamn thing wrong." He took a step towards me and pointed a finger at me. "You killed my father. You framed him. You made him look crazy." Spit flew from his mouth. He was breathing heavily, and his words were sharp, stinging.

"I...I'm so sorry, Aaron." I paused, putting the files down on the table. My words sounded so small compared to what I had done. "I had no idea." I clasped my hands together, willing him to forgive me. I moved closer to him. "You have to believe me."

Aaron stared at me, and I could see his lip beginning to tremble. There was something more he wanted to say. I held my breath. Then, Aaron shook his head. He turned, a dismissal, and disappeared behind the curtain into the room with the cots. I stood, staring at the curtain. I knew that there was nothing I could say that would make up for what I had done, but now that I knew the truth, I wouldn't stop trying.

A hand landed on my shoulder. I'd forgotten that Brody was in the room, and immediately, my attention turned to him rather than Aaron. All of my senses focused on the spot where he touched me. "Come on," Brody nodded at me.

"But I can't...I can't ever make it right," I said, crossing my arms into myself, more exhausted than anything.

"Let's have some coffee," he said, his hand still on my shoulder, leading me back through the metal door and into the kitchenette. He pulled out a chair for me, and I slid into it. He went over to the coffee machine and poured two cups, adding some powdered creamer to it.

We sat there at the small metal table with warm steaming mugs in front of us. I sipped on mine, my mind still on Aaron but trying to push it away and focus on what my next move should be. Brody's voice interrupted my thoughts. "So, there is something you can do to help make up for...it." I looked up from my coffee, startled at the sound of his voice breaking through the quiet. "You can work with us to take down the people responsible for all of this." He spun his coffee cup around.

I roughly swallowed and licked my lips. "Brody, I'll do whatever is in my power, but you have to understand that I don't have much power." Even with a night's sleep, I was exhausted. And defeated.

Brody nodded slowly and took a sip of his coffee, then continued. "Okay, well first things first. We need collateral. We need something that legitimizes us because, as you are aware, we're just a bunch of teenagers." I raised my eyebrows at him. I shouldn't have been surprised that he spoke the exact words that I had been thinking from the moment they took me. He wasn't only kind and strong, but smart as well.

I leaned forward, bringing the warm drink to my lips and considering what he said. Putting the cup back down, I pulled my legs up and crossed them on the chair. "What were you thinking?"

Brody placed both hands down on the table. "Well, we have to make a video."

I studied the serious look on his face, unsure of what to make of it. "What do you mean?" I asked, folding my hands together.

"We have to make a video showing that mimics are real. A video that could be revealed should anything happen to us. A video that we would give to Dan's family to release, in case they notice that we aren't acting in a way that we normally would." He must have seen the look on my face because then he added, "Don't worry. We won't have video of the real you. You'll just turn into other people. It will be completely anonymous. Then, we'll meet with some of Reg's contacts, some of the men that helped us get this far, and they will tell us our next step. We already gave them the intel on your original mission." I couldn't help my eyebrows creasing as I took in this new bit of information, but I didn't have the energy to process it. Brody took a sip of his coffee. I shifted nervously in my seat, and the chair made a soft scraping noise on the floor.

Brody leaned in and spoke softly. "Meda, I don't want you to worry about Aaron right now."

I ran my hand through my hair and sighed. "How can I not? After all that I did to him? How can you not be thinking about that?"

"Eventually he will realize the big picture, like I have. You didn't do this to him. They did it to him. You were just the tool that they used. But until he realizes that, I'll be in charge of making sure that he's calm. And he will get there. He's a smart guy." Brody turned and looked at the kitchenette door.

I nodded. I took a sip of my coffee then put the mug down. "So, when do you want to do this video?" I couldn't believe I was saying those words. Everything in me told me I had to hide what I was.

"Well, we have the equipment right now. Are you able to…" Brody paused, searching for the right words, but I knew what he was trying to say.

"Once I've shifted into someone, I am able to shift into them whenever I want. It's stored." I tapped my temple. Brody considered what I said, then smiled, a real genuine smile that seemed to show he was impressed. I wasn't used to that reaction. The usual reaction was horror and fear.

"So, do you know how many you have stored up in that head of yours?" He leaned closer, a boyish excitement gleaming in his eyes.

"I have quite a few, but it depends on what you want." I shrugged my shoulders, feeling a little cocky.

He paused in thought, then continued, "Well, a video is not going to prove everything. They could say that it was edited. But it's a start." Brody put his hands on the table and pushed himself up. "So, let's do this. Let's bring back the dead."

Chapter 9

Brody led me out the heavy metal door of the bunker and into a wooded forest. I filled my lungs with fresh air, and I could finally see that it was daytime. Growing up, I had only been in the country a few times. It was a luxury for us to get away from the city. The green earthy smell reminded me of my dad. My sisters. I pushed those thoughts away. They were dangerous.

Brody wanted to film outside to get better lighting, not the incandescent lighting of the bunker. I watched as his muscles strained with the weight of the cases of equipment he carried. I sat by a tree, looking up into the branches as the sun broke through the cover and permeated my skin. I had always felt like I was solar-powered, like the sun gave me energy. Once I was taken into captivity, the only time I saw the sun was on rare day missions. I'd like to think that my draw to nature had to do with my native background that I, in fact, was completely clueless about, but it was a tiny thread that connected me to my mother.

It was one of those fall days that was just warm enough to go jacketless, but not too hot. I heard the latches click on the camera case, and as I watched Brody begin to assemble a tripod, I twisted my hands together, my nerves getting the best of me. I wasn't sure how Brody was going to react to me shifting, and even though he had experienced it, seeing it was completely different. Brody was the last person I wanted to think of me as a monster.

He came over and dropped his body heavily in the grass beside me as he paged through the files that he brought outside with him. He showed me a few and seemed to consider my thoughts. As we talked, I rubbed my wrists, aware that there were no cuffs binding me out here in the daylight, in the wide open. For a second, I imagined what would happen if I made a run for it, but I blocked that thought out. There was nowhere to go, and I was weak and tired and wouldn't be able to travel far.

We decided on a few well-known men and women, mostly political figures. We didn't even discuss the idea of using Aaron's dad, and I didn't bring it up. Though it would prove Reg's innocence, Reg needed something bigger than this to make things right. I assumed that Aaron already had a plan in place of what they would do to right that wrong, and I was positive that they wouldn't make me privy to that info just yet.

Brody handed me a script of what to say. "So, are we ready?" he asked. "What do you need? Anything?" He smiled as he got up and moved towards the camera. He seemed excited, which didn't make me any less nervous.

"Um, if you have any candy or anything with sugar, juice or fruit snacks…I get really wiped out after…" I didn't finish. It was awkward to say it aloud.

Brody opened a messenger bag that he had hauled out with him. It had a couple of juice boxes along with some gummy worms and fruit snacks. I raised an eyebrow at him, wondering how he knew. He responded with a wink that made me blush. I brought my hand up to my mouth to hide my smile. It felt silly, but I felt close to Brody since he was the only one, in a long time, who seemed to care about me. Then, I felt like an idiot. He was only being nice to get what he needed. I wiped the smile from my face and moved over to the chair Brody set up.

Brody propped a sheet up between two trees as the backdrop, so there were no clues to lead anyone to our location. The camera would shoot from my head down to my feet, a full body shot to show the whole transformation. Brody situated himself behind the camera. Then, he peered over at me. "Are you ready?" he asked. I nodded slowly, and he counted down on his fingers, with a three, two, one, and I was on.

It all happened very quickly. I started as a young woman. I think she was some lobbyist I had mimicked. I started out very wooden and choppy, reading from the script. I usually had days to study the people, and it had been a while since I had shifted into this particular woman, so it was difficult to get the words out right.

The script signaled my next shift, which I did effortlessly. Shifting was the easy part. It was pretending to be the person, with their tics and nuances, which made it difficult. Not every mimic could successfully do what I could do, but it didn't come easily. It took a lot to study nonverbal body language and tone, even the way they stood when relaxed. When I was given an assignment, I was consumed by it all, which was why, as I shifted from one person to the next, I began to think about all of these people, the ones I had mimicked, who had probably died after I had taken their form. They died because of me. The female lobbyist, the male congressman, they were gone because of me, and I had never even thought of them. With each shift, I sank deeper into despair, but I was sure not to show it. It was easier to control my emotions when I was in the form of someone else.

I took a deep breath. "I think I need a break." And that was when I finally looked at Brody. His eyebrows were raised, and for a moment, he made eye contact with me. I couldn't gauge his reaction. He seemed surprised, not scared. People were usually scared, especially when I was shifting into them, or they were indifferent because they worked for the Agency and had seen it one too many times.

"That's a wrap!" Brody yelled as though he was talking to a crew rather than just me. I shifted back to my own form as he got up from behind the camera. His eyes flickered with confusion, and I didn't know why. I expected the worst, but as Brody approached me, his face lightened. He came and stood in front of me, taking a deep breath in. "Did anyone ever tell you how amazing that is?"

I smirked and shook my head. "Only the people who could see how it would benefit them. Only the people who could see how they could use me to get what they wanted. It's not amazing. It's evil." I didn't need to remind him that those people, the people from those files, were dead.

"I'm not talking about that. I'm talking about the ability to do what you can do. It's amazing. It's not something you should be ashamed of. They made it shameful."

I shook my head again, unwilling to see what made it amazing. My ability to shift was always supposed to be a deep dark secret. Something to hide because it made me different and dangerous. Only I knew the truth. I was powerless. I wasn't a danger to anyone. So maybe there was some truth to what Brody was saying, but it didn't change what I had done.

He handed me a juice box and grabbed one for himself, and as we sat there drinking our juice, it felt like Brody wasn't pretending. I wanted to believe it. Just being around him this way made me always want to see him smile.

He crumpled his juice box. "Well, Meda, I think it's cool. The way you can shift. It's so fluid and unreal, not creepy like in the movies." He moved closer to me. "And if people weren't abusing your unique gifts, it would be a blessing, not a curse." He reached out and squeezed my hand. I looked down at his hand gripping mine. My eyes slowly traveled back up, and I looked back into his eyes. "Oh," he said, looking at his hand over mine like he wasn't sure how it got there.

"Brody!" Dan called. Brody quickly dropped his hand and bent down to fold the tripod back up like nothing had happened. Dan walked up the steps, moving away from the bunker. He eyed us suspiciously. "Are you done? It's time to hit the road." Brody gave Dan a thumbs-up, and Dan turned to go back inside, only looking over his shoulder once.

I waited to see if Brody would tell me where we were going. He folded up the tripod and handed it to me, then grabbed the camera and stuffed it in a box with some other miscellaneous equipment. I followed him back to the bunker, disappointed he didn't say a word, but as Brody opened the door, he came face-to-face with Aaron.

"Where is she?" Aaron demanded. Then, when he saw me over Brody's shoulder, still at the top of the steps, he yelled, "What the hell, Brody?"

Brody looked back at me and then to Aaron. He knew why Aaron was angry. I did too. Aaron's voice was sharp. "What are you thinking letting her wander around without any cuffs? She could run at any moment." I stood still, not wanting to go near Aaron, but also not wanting him to think I planned on running.

"She's fine." Brody stayed between me and Aaron but motioned with his head for me to follow. I went as quickly as I could while trying not to bang the folded tripod legs on the doorframe.

"You're getting careless," Aaron said, directly in Brody's ear. "That's what she wants. She is fooling you, and you are falling for it. She's waiting for you to get comfortable, complacent, and then that's when she'll strike." I put the tripod on the kitchenette table and backed towards the bathroom door, trying to disappear.

Brody put the box on the table. He turned to Aaron. "We'll talk about this, but not here, Aaron."

"But…" Aaron started, his face turning red. He looked like he was ready to start punching again.

"I said, not here," Brody said calmly as his eyes flicked from Aaron to me. Aaron stared at him and then turned towards me. He glanced back at Brody, who raised his eyebrows as though he was making sure Aaron understood him. Aaron gave a curt nod and walked around Brody, heading towards the keypad door. Brody shut the outer door and made sure it was locked. Then, without looking at me, he turned and followed Aaron through the door.

I quickly slipped into the bathroom and tried to slow my breathing. I examined my face in the mirror to make sure it was mine. What was going on between Brody and Aaron? Was Brody playing a game with me? I thought he was sincere only moments ago, but then again, in my life, I've had a difficult time telling who was being truthful and who was pretending. I reminded myself I shouldn't trust anyone. Not even Brody.

Chapter 10

From the doorway of the bathroom, I watched as the boys gathered up various electronics and loaded them into the camper that was parked in the narrow tunnel located at the back of the bunker. Most of the items were unidentifiable; they seemed to be disassembled laptops and various odds and ends. There were also guns. I wanted to help, but I didn't want to ask what I could do to help and draw unwanted attention from Aaron, so I tried to stay out of the way as best as I could.

When they seemed to be finishing up, Brody came to get me and led me to the camper. This time he had me walk in front of him, though the cuffs were still MIA. When Brody directed me to sit on the sofa in the back of the camper, and still no cuffs appeared, I felt relieved. The camper was an older model. It smelled musty, but it looked clean. The sofa had rutty material that was hard on my skin, but the bright cheery yellow of the interior made up for that. We were like a ridiculously messed-up family going on a vacation.

Dan came in lugging a heavy green cooler. He opened it and pulled out a soda, popping the top and slamming it in one drink. I saw soda and various food items in the cooler. Aaron brought in duffel bags that were bulging at the zippers. They looked heavy, and Aaron's face strained to lift them.

Dan stumbled in a race against no one to the driver's seat. "I call driving!" He smiled with glee as Aaron followed and slid into the passenger seat, his long legs filling the space in front of him. Brody joined me on the sofa that was behind the driver's seat, which meant Aaron was able to watch us. He did look back at us once after Dan started the engine, but once the vehicle was in motion, Aaron opened up his laptop and began typing furiously. I was surprised they had WiFi in this old rig. They must have had a hot spot or something.

As we plodded along back roads, each bump jolted my aching body, and I had to brace myself. The old rig didn't travel well. It was a silent and painful first hour, but when Aaron shut his computer and leaned his head against the door for a nap, Brody turned and faced me, casually bringing one leg up on the sofa. I tried to pretend like I didn't notice as his leg brushed up against my side, but I didn't do a good job because I was staring down at the point where our bodies converged.

Brody didn't seem to notice. "Meda, if you don't mind my asking, how did they find you? I mean, how did they know about you?" I turned and looked at him sideways. "I mean, you clearly knew the danger of turning in front of someone. I'm assuming you were careful." He shrugged.

I pulled my legs up and crossed them, angling towards Brody. I also made myself smaller, something I had a habit of doing when I was in my own form. I didn't want to talk about it, but there was nowhere to hide, and I had Brody's full attention

"From the way you're looking at me, I can tell it's eating at you." He studied me. "You probably never had the chance to talk to anyone about it. It might relieve some of the guilt you have. We've got time. Want to share?" Brody raised his eyebrows. Aaron was asleep in the passenger seat, and Dan was watching the road and singing along to the music on the radio. It was hard not to trust Brody.

"It was such a stupid mistake," I started quietly, playing with the folds on the leg of my pants.

"It's okay. As kids, we're supposed to make mistakes."

"Yeah, but I couldn't afford this mistake. And I had been warned. I knew the consequences." Once I started, the words came out easily. "Generally, we don't change until we… you know…hit puberty," I said, cringing internally. "When the time came, my dad borrowed a friend's car; I'm guessing that he thought someone could be tracking his. We drove miles away, into the middle of the forest. I wasn't sure what we were doing. The trip lasted hours. I felt like we doubled back a couple of times."

"Your dad was a smart man." Brody smiled and rested his arm on the back of the sofa.

I nodded. "I think he knew they would always be watching. I just wish he would have told me enough so that I understood the gravity of the situation." I looked far away, to a different time. "That was the first time I changed. He made me shift into him. He coached me, obviously with tips he learned from my mother."

Brody tilted his head in confusion. "Oh," I doubled back. "My father was no mimic. It was my mother. But she was long gone by the time I was ready to change. Anyway, he made me look into his eyes and take his hands. It was strange, seeing his face reflected in his eyes. He then told me to never do it again. And to always assume people were watching."

I bit my lip and continued, the camper shaking my voice as it journeyed down the road. "I remember he had tears in his eyes. He said I looked exactly like my mother." I grabbed a piece of my dark, shiny hair and twirled it around my finger. "I looked nothing like my father. He was a redhead. My twin sisters have his complexion. Freckles and all. I have my mother's dark complexion."

73

I could tell Brody wanted to ask about my mother, but he was too polite to interrupt. "Then, when I became a teenager . . ." I paused and laughed. "God, I say that like I'm not anymore, but in a way, I don't feel like it. Anyway, I was rebellious. It was a big change for me, going from being homeschooled by my mother and then having her leave me. My dad dropped me into a public school, immersed in a sea of children with completely different backgrounds, some wonderfully creative and some terribly cruel. I had never witnessed such cruelty before as I did in that first year in public school.

"Anyway, we took another trip to the woods. He told me the truth, or his version of the truth, about how the government has been using mimics for centuries. How, as the story goes, it started when the settlers came and took over the land. The Native Americans long had the skill to shift, but only in a certain bloodline. They used their abilities to sabotage the settlers, but they couldn't hide it forever.

"Over the years, the government identified that bloodline. They signed treaties so the natives wouldn't share their secret. They gave them gifts in return. But they couldn't track all the bloodlines, and even some of the diluted ones, like mine, have the gift."

I paused. Brody's head tilted in interest. In fact, he looked more than interested, and it made me shift uncomfortably in my seat. I leaned back a bit. He nodded, wanting me to continue.

"I don't know where my father got his information. For all I know, he got some of it from my mother, but I'll never know for sure. I don't even know if it's true. It sounds like a made-up fantasy novel. Anyway, he went on to remind me not to trust anyone, not even my stepmom. I think he suspected she was a spy, but he went along with it for the safety of my sisters. He told me they took my mother, and before she left, she told him to remarry and to move on, though he never could stop thinking about her. I thought he was crazy. I thought he was making that up so I wouldn't be mad my mother left us." I shook my head, trying to shake out the painful thoughts. "But I didn't listen to my father."

Brody put his hand on my knee. I couldn't help but look at his hand, strong with vital blood coursing through his visible veins. "It's normal for teens not to listen to their parents, Meda. You shouldn't feel guilty about that." Brody's words didn't make me feel any better. I felt worse because, once again, he was being a little too kind. Just a little too understanding.

I started again. "I followed his directions until I turned sixteen. That was last year, on a stupid summer night. My friends wanted me to buy beer. They weren't really my friends. I mean, I was homeschooled by my mother until I was ten. Then my mother left. I didn't know how to fit in. So often I did whatever anyone asked me to do. Even if it wasn't the smartest or the best for me." I stopped and looked at Brody. "I guess not a lot has changed." I pursed my lips. Brody's face remained blank.

"I didn't tell them how I was going to get it. I wasn't that stupid. I knew enough not to share my secret with anyone. But I thought I could get away with it if I shifted into my friend's mom, and having already been in contact with her mom during a previous sleepover made it easy. I knew her mom was in for the night because we were at her house, and she was in her pajamas, so I thought I was safe.

"As it turned out, I wasn't. My stepmom was at the store. When I saw her, I was so nervous, but I knew she couldn't see through my skin. She couldn't know I wasn't my friend's mom. But I must have caught her attention, probably because I was so nervous. And then I saw her look to my hand. I was twisting my earrings, an annoying nervous tick I developed around the time my mother left. She looked to my hand, and I knew right then she knew who I was.

"My stepmother was the one who turned me in. She had been planted there by the Agency. I didn't even make it home before they grabbed me. They told me if I complied with them, my father and sisters would be safe. If I fought against them, they'd have to eliminate my father because he knew too much, only they didn't know how much my father knew, otherwise he wouldn't be alive right now. If he is alive…" I trailed off for a moment and then pushed the thought out of my mind.

"After that, they trained me to observe. That was my role. They tried to train me as an assassin, but that was one thing I refused. I couldn't kill or hurt anything. There was one mimic there that could. I never saw any of the others, but they talked about her a lot. They called her Isi. She was younger than me and cruel. Anyway, I was thankful they had her because it meant I wouldn't need that skill. I was their mimic who paid attention to details, and I was fine with that."

"And that's it. Fast forward to now." Brody tilted his head at me.

"Pretty much. They let me speak to my father from time to time, and he continues to play along with my stepmom in order to ensure my safety. I also get to see videos of my sisters. Other than that, I wasn't given much else besides a room in the compound and enough food. Even if I could get away from them, I have nothing to run to. They control every aspect of my life." I looked down, picking at my fingernails seeing as I didn't have any earrings to spin.

"You said you have nothing to run to," Brody interrupted my thoughts.

"Yeah?" I questioned.

He shrugged. "Now you have friends." He smiled.

I was confused. "What do you mean, friends?"

Brody stared at me. "Duh," he said.

I looked at Aaron, mouth-breathing with his head flopped to the side. "Yeah, a friend who would love to kill me," I said skeptically.

Brody looked at Aaron and then back at me. "He doesn't know you. He just has to see the real you."

"Yeah, *before* he kills me," I answered, rolling my eyes. I didn't think about it before I said it. I sometimes had a difficult time keeping my inside thoughts from spilling out. But Brody smiled. I shook my head. "I can't believe we're joking about this." Brody had reached out to me, and I appreciated that. He had all the capabilities of being dark and brooding, with his dark hair and dark eyes, but the crinkle in his eyes when he smiled gave him away.

There were people out there who always knew to do the right thing, reach out when someone was crying, listen when someone had a problem, laugh at a sarcastic comment. No matter how much I observed, I couldn't seem to pick up on those subtle nuances. I didn't know if it was because of what I was and because I never had a chance to become a real person, the person I was supposed to be, or maybe everyone felt the way I was feeling, but they kept those feelings to themselves. So even though everything inside me said to pull away, I did the opposite. I daringly reached over but then pulled back, unsure.

Brody studied me, his face suddenly growing serious. "Do you second-guess everything you do?"

I blushed, angry he could read my mind, and defiantly put my hand on his hand.

Brody looked down at my hand. I knew he could see through me. My discomfort. My nerves. He was probably thinking about how foolish I was. Maybe he was thinking I was stupid to think he would want to touch someone like me. Reaching out to someone was not in my nature, but when I went to pull my hand back, Brody held on tightly.

"You've heard enough about me. Tell me about you." My brain could barely focus on him as he held my hand. Even if this wasn't real, and if he was pretending to care, I could still use this to my advantage to get some information on him.

"Ah, there isn't much to tell," he started. "I was a high school athlete with a drunk dad. My mom left us when I was fourteen. She couldn't take care of my dad anymore, and I couldn't leave him." He stared at something off in the distance, maybe the trees racing by the window. "He taught me everything I know about sports." Smiling, he continued. "Anyway, he got worse, and I finally realized I couldn't change him. Aaron's family was the most stable thing in my life, and then one day, they were gone."

"I'm sorry," I said. I tried to focus on our conversation, but my mind kept zeroing in on his warm hand wrapped around mine. I wondered if he was feeling any of the feelings I was. How did anyone know what the other person was feeling? Was that possible?

"You have no need to be sorry. My dad was as sorry as they come, and he told me every single day, but I got over it. The only thing I regret in my life, the only thing I would change, would be what happened to Aaron's family. It was wrong. Reg wanted to fix things. To help the mimics. To stop the Agency. He wanted to right the wrongs, and for that, his family was assassinated." Brody's voice caught. I squeezed his hand. "It shouldn't have happened."

Brody said that Reg wanted to help the mimics. It made me curious, but this wasn't the right time. I needed to know the truth. "So how can you forgive me? How can you forgive me when Aaron's family was yours as well?"

Brody squeezed my hand tighter. "Because, it was my dad who taught me all about sports, but he also taught me that sometimes, good people are put in bad situations. Sometimes, good people can't help the things they do, but that doesn't mean they're still not good inside." He once again looked out the window at the landscape passing quickly by, and I could tell he was thinking about his dad.

My skin prickled and my eyes began watering, but I tried to fight it off. Brody had been through a lot, and I felt for him. I watched as he tried to pull himself together, then I felt guilty. I wished I could give him some privacy. I looked around the camper, and when I looked up to the front, Aaron was awake and watching us. Brody and me. His eyes narrowed when he saw we were holding hands.

Chapter 11

I quickly released Brody's hand and let my feet fall to the ground. Brody looked at me and then looked back over his shoulder to see that Aaron was awake. They made eye contact, and there seemed to some unspoken dialogue between the two. I stared at Aaron, waiting for him to say something or react, but he turned and looked out at the two-lane highway that stretched in front of us.

After hours in the vehicle, most of which were spent silently, Dan finally spoke up. "I gotta take a pee, and I need to shut my eyes," he announced as he pulled into a rest stop. It was clear he was too tired to drive but didn't trust anyone else to. When Dan got up and stretched, his eyes were bloodshot. Aaron couldn't stop yawning, and every time he let one loose, Dan would catch it and yell at Aaron for yawning again.

Aaron got up and crawled up into the bunk located over the driver's seat while Dan briefly left the camper and reentered just as quickly, returning to the driver's seat and reclining, probably to make sure no one else tried driving.

Brody stood up, grabbed a blanket from the cabinet towards the back, and handed it to me. Dusk had settled, and through the windshield, I could see darkness descend in the parking lot in the way station. It seemed it would be smarter to drive at night and rest during the day, but I wasn't in any position to make suggestions.

Brody interrupted the quiet as he sat back down next to me on the couch. He leaned close in a whisper, trying to make sure he wouldn't disturb the boys, though Dan was already snoring. "Meda, if you don't mind my asking, what really happened to your mother? Do you know?" I could see him by the light of the street lamp outside the camper.

I paused. It was something I didn't talk about, with my father, my sisters, with anyone, or with Aaron potentially listening in, but Brody had been so honest and kind that I felt like I needed to give him something.

I whispered, even quieter than Brody. "Well, I told you what my dad told me. That they took her. He didn't know about the Agency, but he knew the government used mimics, so that was what he assumed. I don't know what my mom told him. But what do I believe?" I asked Brody. Again, he remained silent. "Well, before he told me, for the longest time, I believed she left us. That she chose to leave us."

"What would make you think that?" Brody asked.

"I…I mean. I don't know. I know it couldn't be for lack of love. My father loved her so much, and she loved being a mother. She was the best mother a girl could have. But I remember her changing. I can't say exactly how. But I sensed it. A few weeks after the twins were born, she was gone. Maybe the responsibility of two babies along with me was too much for her."

He looked confused. "Do you really think that was it? Do you really think she just turned off the mother switch?"

"Mother switch," I huffed. "Nice."

"Sorry," Brody added. "I didn't mean…"

"No. It's okay. I mean, the thing was, my dad didn't talk about her past ever. A few times he had hinted at her rough life before they met, but he never went into detail. He tried to get it across to me that she was a free spirit, but free spirit to me means selfish. If the Agency did take her, it would make sense, but this last year I was with them, I never saw her, and no one spoke about her. I only heard of one other mimic, and even that was information I wasn't supposed to get. Who knows what really happened? I doubt I'll ever know."

Just then, I realized I'd given Brody a lot of information, and I tried to see his face through the now-darkened interior of the camper. He had pried it out of me. He asked me about my mother. I thought back to what I had said to him. Was there anything he could use? Then it dawned on me. Maybe he knew something about my mother. Maybe that was why he asked.

"Brody?" I asked.

"Yes?" he said. His voice sounded sleepy, but I couldn't be sure it wasn't an act.

"Why do you care about my mother?" I knew I sounded suspicious as soon as it came out.

"I . . ." He paused to yawn. "I wanted to know more about you." He reached over and squeezed my arm. "Why don't you get some rest. It's going to be a big day tomorrow."

I pulled my hand away from him and leaned over on the arm of the couch. I felt him settle in on the other end, then crossed my arms and rested my head on them. Thoughts of my dad and my stepmother and my mother and sisters swirled along the river that ran through my brain. While on one hand, Brody was right about feeling better by confessing to someone, I still wondered what he was digging for, and I thought about what I had left out of that confession as I drifted off.

I didn't know how long I slept when I awoke to a quiet clicking noise. I moved over to the window of the camper and pulled back the blinds. There was a soft glow of light in the darkness. I leaned closer to the window. Someone was out there, holding a cell phone. I felt my blood rush to my head. I could make out the shape. It was a woman. Then, the woman slowly looked up, and I stopped breathing. Outside the camper stood my mother.

Impossible, I thought, but even as that thought entered my head, we locked eyes, and I knew it was her. I continued to hold my breath. Then, my mother raised a finger to her lips, motioning for me to be quiet, and waved for me to come outside.

I pinched myself to make sure I wasn't dreaming, though since the boys had taken me, life itself seemed to take on a dreamlike quality. I cringed as my nails dug into my skin, then I looked out the window again. My mother was still there. She motioned to be quiet and waved again. Though I knew it was a bad idea, I made my way to the door and held my breath as I quietly slipped out into the night.

Chapter 12

I slowly pushed the door closed behind me, willing it not to make a creaking noise I would expect from an old camper. Luckily, there was no creak, just a quiet metal clink as the door shut. When I turned around, there was no one in the parking lot with me. It was empty.

I thought I was going crazy. I scanned the parking lot. There was a slight breeze, and I could hear cars on the main road. I walked around the back of the camper, avoiding the front just in case one of the boys awoke and glanced out the window. There was no one in the back. The other side of the camper faced a tree-lined forest. I didn't want to go to the forest side because I had an irrational fear that maybe what I had seen was a wild animal, like a bear. Well, considering where we were, it probably wasn't irrational.

My feet silently padded across the pavement as I made my way to the other side of the camper. I tensed, squinting into the darkness of the forest. There was no way I'd walk over there. I must have been seeing things, but as I turned to walk back around to the camper door, I stopped short of running into someone who had snuck up behind me.

I nearly screamed but clamped my hand over my own mouth and blinked a few times. It was my mom. She had the same dark hair, though it was chopped off in an edgy bob that highlighted her long, slender neck. Her features were dark except for her eyes, and even though I couldn't see them in the dark, I knew they were green like mine. I hadn't seen my mother for all those years, but she looked the same as she had in all of the photos.

"Mom?" I whispered. I couldn't move. She didn't either. We stood near the back of the camper, staring at each other. I wanted to ask her what she was doing here, where she had been all this time, a million different questions, but I couldn't speak.

"Meda, you've grown so much." She smiled, shaking her head and bringing a clenched fist to her mouth.

I was fighting back tears, but when she stepped forward to hug me, a few sprung loose. Her scent was spicy and unfamiliar. She smelled like the wilderness. Not like I remembered.

She pulled me back and whispered quickly, "We need to get you out of here." She kept one hand on my shoulder as she tried to guide me towards the forest.

"Where? What? How did you find me?" I tried to stop her. I needed to talk to her.

"Meda, there's no time. We need to go now. You don't belong with these boys. They'll get you killed." She kept pushing me along, but I resisted, and I wasn't sure why.

"But, where have you been? And what about Dad? And Ginger? And Georgia?" I blurted out, trying to get her to stop.

That made her pause. "What do you mean, what about Dad?" Her eyes flashed with anger, but only for a moment, and then she continued. "Your father will be fine. I already had him moved." I looked at my mother, confused. How could she have had him moved? How would she even get to him and then find me? What are the odds? Something tugged at my brain as she continued to usher me on. "You need to come with me now." She looked and sounded like my mother, but I was starting to have doubts.

Suddenly, the camper door clicked open and banged loudly against the outside of the vehicle. Because we were around the backside of the camper, whoever had exited was only seconds away from finding us. I looked at my mom, and her reassuring face was now a blank slate. She turned to walk away from me. "Wait," I called, taking a few steps toward her.

Brody came around the backside of the camper in a low crouch, and when he saw us, he trained his gun on my mom. "Don't move!" he called out. My mom turned and faced Brody. The corner of her mouth hitched up in a smirk.

"Mom?" I stepped hesitantly towards her but looked back at Brody.

"She's not your mother, Meda. Back away from her." He glanced at me but kept the gun on my mom.

I looked at the woman who stood before me and then back at Brody. "Mom?" I asked. My mom moved so my body blocked her from Brody's gun. I turned to Brody. "How do you know?" But when I turned back, I saw her draw her gun from the waistband of her black jeans. She stepped to the left and didn't hesitate before pulling off a shot.

I crouched down, putting my hands to my ears and closing my eyes. The sound of the gun was jarring in the night. Brody dove and rolled across the pavement, successfully dodging the shot, and was back on his feet with his own gun up.

My ears were ringing, and I was confused. When I looked back at my mom, or whoever she was, she now had her gun aimed at me. A shot rang out. My whole body clenched, awaiting the impact of the bullet and pain to follow, but no bullet hit me.

I looked back to the imposter, and a small bit of blood trickled down her arm. Her gun clattered to the ground as she grabbed her wounded shoulder. I followed her stare and saw Aaron, now standing at the front of the camper, gun in hand. He had hit his mark.

Then, my mother flickered, and I caught a glimmer of a different person. A younger girl. A girl with black, spiky hair and a thin, but muscular, rangy appearance. This had to be the other mimic. The mimic who the Agency used for kill jobs. It had to be Isi. Suddenly, she lunged at me. I was too slow because I had been watching her phase in and out, so she managed to grab at my arm, but she faltered. She was having a hard time keeping my mother's form. I wondered if the bullets the boys used had some kind of silver like the cuffs, and that was what was affecting her ability to shift.

When she lost her grip, I dove for the gun she dropped. She lunged with me, but I got my hands around it quickly. I watched people handle guns all the time, but I wasn't good with them because they scared me, but I couldn't let her see that. I picked it up and aimed it at her. Now all three of us stood, surrounding her. Brody to my left and Aaron to my right.

"You have nowhere to go," Brody said to her. "Just stay calm."

The girl looked at me, almost smiling. "Aw, Meda. You wouldn't shoot your own mother, would you?" She fake pouted at me.

"Who are you?" I asked. I was pretty sure I knew the answer, but I wanted to hear it from her. The girl looked at me and sighed. She began to shift before my eyes and turned into my stepmother. It was surprising to see her face again, and I began to understand why people were so easily fooled when I shifted into someone. You live your entire life learning to trust your eyes. "Stop it!" I yelled, shaking the gun at her. She flickered again, her face going smooth for a moment before returning to the form of my stepmother.

"Meda, honey. Don't you feel betrayed?" she asked with fake sympathy, closing her hands together.

"You're not her either," I spit at her. "I know who you are." I held the gun up but backed towards the camper. I didn't want her to lunge at me. I didn't want her to make me use the gun.

The girl who wore the face of my stepmother sighed and let out a huff of air like she was bored. "You're right. Good for you. You get a gold star." Her arms dropped to her sides. "Of course, I'm not your mother or your stepmother. I'm surprised you didn't guess that right away. I didn't think it would work, but they insisted you would fall for it. But, I mean, come on. You're one of us! How can you be so stupid?" She emphasized the last word.

"You're Isi," I said. She didn't answer, but her eyebrows raised slightly. She was surprised I knew her name. She moved slowly towards me as I continued to back up. Brody and Aaron kept their guns pointed at her.

"Neat trick. Where did you get my name?" I didn't answer. I knew enough not to show all my cards. "I know you. I know you're not going to pull the trigger. You never could."

A pebble rolled towards us, which made Isi look. Brody had been moving closer and closer. She laughed, looking at the boys who were now nearly at my sides. "Oh, you got me!" she cried in fake dismay. "I surrender!" She laughed, dropping to her knees and putting her hands behind her head. "I wouldn't do anything stupid if I were you. You guys are surrounded." She shrugged but kept her hands behind her head.

As if on cue, the sound of a helicopter caught on the breeze. All three of us looked up, trying to spot the bird, but Aaron wasn't going to let it get any closer. "Let's go!" he yelled. "Leave her." Brody moved to my side. He grabbed me by the arm and led me to the front of the camper. I didn't take my eyes off the girl. She continued to grin at me with her half smirk.

"Meda," she called to me as Brody dragged me away. "I do know your mom. She raised me like a daughter." She laughed.

I tried to pull Brody to a stop. "Wait," I said to Brody, confused. "Wait, did you hear what she said? We can't leave her. I have questions." Brody kept moving.

"We have to get out of here," Aaron said sharply. "They've tracked us. We need to ditch everything." He ran to the camper and knocked on the window. Dan immediately jumped out of the driver's side with a bag and a gun in his hand. He must have been at the window, ready to shoot or drive, whatever was needed. As soon as Dan's feet hit the pavement of the parking lot, they both started jogging towards the tree line, guns still ready.

"Come on," Brody said, pulling me along. I moved hesitantly as I looked back at Isi, who started to get to her feet and brush the gravel off her jeans. She smirked at me again. The engine of the helicopter grew louder, and I heard Isi yelling at someone, but I couldn't make out the words. I turned and began running.

We crashed through the forest, and I hoped we had a good enough head start. I was now running from the Agency. That was dangerous, not only for me but for my family. I knew I couldn't trust a word Isi had said, that the whole thing about my mother was to get me flustered, but it worked.

Branches slapped our faces as we ran in the night. I was disoriented and glad I wasn't the one leading the way. "Where are we going?" Dan yelled. I could see the glow of Aaron's cell phone as he tried to run and punch in numbers. He must have pocketed his gun. I could hear the chopper overhead now, and lights were beginning to sweep in the distance. There was no way we could outrun them. I began wondering what the Agency would do when they caught the boys. Kill them immediately? Torture them to find out where they got all their intel? I didn't want to even think about what they would do to punish me.

The chopper swept in our direction. "They must still be tracking us!" Aaron yelled. "She must have something on her." He motioned to me. I reached up to my earrings, but then remembered they were gone.

"We're not going to make it. Let's ditch her," Dan said. He pulled night vision goggles out of his back pocket and slid them on his face as he continued to run, and we followed his path. He sounded nervous; in fact, they all sounded nervous. If they were tracking me somehow, there would be no way we could get away from them.

"We're not leaving her," Brody said in a voice that meant it was not up for debate. "That's not part of the plan." I kept moving as a branch stabbed my arm and I gasped and stumbled. Brody still pulled me along, though he too was getting grabbed by the outstretched arms of the trees.

Aaron continued to watch his cell while weaving and ducking branches. When his screen lit up, making his face glow white, he called out, "Follow me!" Branches scraped my skin and caught on my shirt as the chopper swooped overhead. At one point, we almost ran right into the light sweeping the forest, but we managed to veer around it. I stumbled more than a few times and each time, Brody pulled me forward. I tried to imagine where a tracker would be on me. It couldn't be on my clothing. I didn't want to think about where it could be.

Aaron was still leading us, watching his phone and continuously changing paths and zigzagging between trees. We followed closely as he led us along a small stream and then up a hill. From the top, I heard traffic on the road below. Aaron moved to the edge of the hill, positive he was concealed by the dark. I looked back and couldn't see anyone. It was possible that we lost them. I hoped that meant there was no tracker.

"I contacted the safe house. They'll pull off onto the shoulder there." He pointed. He turned to Brody. "When we get there, we can take care of..." He motioned at me.

We all crouched down in the line of trees at the top of the hill. Dan faced the forest with his gun ready, waiting for movement. I hoped that we lost them. "How long will they be?" Dan asked, fidgeting but not taking his eyes off the forest where we had come from.

"They'll get here as fast as they can," Aaron said, annoyed. A stick crunched a short distance away. The boys turned and trained their guns into the woods. The trees were thick pine at the base, and we were crouched low, concealed under the cover of trees. There was no way they could see us, unless they heard us. The shadows began to make their way to us, figures with dark masks, like ski masks. Amidst the shadows was one figure without a mask. Isi.

Though we were completely still, I watched as her head turned, scanning the trees. Her mouth stretched out in a slow smile. I felt as though she was looking directly at me. Suddenly, she ran at us, faster than I anticipated her to be.

The four of us immediately turned, broke out of the tree line, and sprinted down the hill. Shots fired from behind. "Come on!" Aaron yelled, not at us, but at the people we were waiting for. And as we approached the road, with nowhere else to go, a pair of headlights veered off to the side.

We ran at the vehicle approaching us on the road. I hoped this was who we were waiting for, otherwise we could end up as road kill. As the vehicle got closer, they slammed on the brakes, screeching in the dark of the night and sliding a few inches forward.

Aaron ran to the car and slammed his hands on the hood. He looked in and must have recognized the man behind the wheel. He waved for everyone to get in. "Go! Go! Go!" he yelled. We all piled in as quickly as possible, Dan first and then Brody, dragging me with. Aaron hopped in the passenger seat. A bullet smashed through the passenger side window, and glass rained down on us.

"Go!" Aaron yelled. The man behind the wheel peeled out. More shots fired in quick succession as we all ducked low, bullets striking the body of the car. When the shots stopped and we were far enough away, I looked back out the window. On the side of the road was Isi. She must have run with us for a short way, trying to catch up. She stood motionless, dark, menacing eyebrows on a stark moonlit face. She raised her hand and flit her fingers in a little wave. I turned and watched the dark road ahead, still thinking about what she had said about my mother and still wondering how they had found us.

Chapter 13

As we turned down a long, dark dirt road, I could see a building in the distance. Even in the dark of night, I could make out the paint peeling off the sides of the rundown safe house. Various pieces of equipment, mostly what looked like car parts, were scattered around the rotted porch. It looked more like a drug den or crack house with all kinds of additional structures branching off the sides. I didn't feel safe at all.

There was movement, even this late. A cluster of shadows was walking off the porch and going around the back side of the house. Two men were sitting on the porch. I could only make out their shadows from the distance, but they looked like they were discreetly guarding the place. As we got closer and pulled to a stop, I noticed some of the men's clothes were drab in a way that was meant to be undercover, and it was clear they had military backgrounds from the way they carried themselves. Stiff-backed, with an air of efficiency about them. I had seen many like that back at the Agency. It was difficult to imagine them as real people. Then again, maybe the same could be said about me.

Dan and Brody got out of opposite sides of the vehicle, and Brody helped me out his side. He kept his hand on my arm to guide me up the driveway, which was shaded by trees. There weren't houses nearby, so the safe house was secluded, but it still made me nervous.

As we approached the house, all movement ceased, and the men stopped and watched us approach. I didn't like how their eyes stopped on me, much like the driver's eyes had. I was the enemy, and they knew it. I tried to make my face as blank as possible as not to antagonize anyone, but these men weren't like Brody, Aaron, and Dan. From what Brody told me, these men were part of a larger organization that specialized in calculating losses and seeking out potential threats, and I represented both categories for them. It seemed to me that I was getting out of the firm grasp of the Agency, only to fall into the hands of another giant. Only time would tell what this would mean for me, but I was anxious, and judging by the looks of the men, I didn't feel good about it. I couldn't help but think I'd traded one prison cell for another.

As we made our way up the porch and into the foyer, following the man who had picked us up, a different man approached. He was missing two of his bottom teeth. "So, this is her, huh?" He got close to my face and reached out, grabbing my cheek and pinching it. I turned my head, trying to get his hand off me, horrified.

"Hey," Brody said. He stepped between me and the guy. "What's your deal?" He put his hand out in front of the guy, ready to push him back if needed.

A man in a worn leather jacket stepped forward and pressed in front of the other guy. This man was older. He had a buzz cut, but there was enough hair to see that it would be stark white and full if he let it grow in. He had creases around his eyes, and his hands were leathery. "He's never seen one up close," the man in the jacket said, nodding dismissively to the other guy. "Name's Judge." He eyed my wrists as I tried to hide them, then regarded Brody, who set his mouth in a thin line.

Dan cut in. "Dude, we were attacked. Give us a break." He was flustered and raised his eyebrows in surprise at what came out of his mouth.

Judge studied Dan first and then surveyed the four of us, stopping to nod directly at Aaron. "I knew your father." Aaron stretched his mouth in a flat smile and nodded silently. Judge extended his hand to Aaron. "He was a good man." Aaron reached out and shook the man's hand.

Aaron pointed at each of us as he gave our names to Judge. The large man shook hands with Brody and Dan as well but did not extend his hand to me. "Follow me." He turned on his heel and led the way through the cramped, early 1940s home. As we weaved through the narrow hallways, it occurred to me that though these men had military backgrounds, they didn't keep their house very clean like I would imagine military men would. Maybe they were more like militia or trained civilians who were brought in. Or maybe they were too busy to be bothered.

We stopped at a doorway. When Judge opened the door, I could see it led down into the basement. I wasn't thinking when I grabbed Brody's arm. "No," I said softly. Judge turned around and eyed me, and then his eyes traveled to Aaron.

"What did she say?" he asked as he pulled a can of chewing tobacco from his back pocket and deposited a wad of it in his lower lip. He waited.

"It's fine," Aaron said, nodding. Judge looked at him again and turned to make his way down the steps. Aaron looked at me. "It's fine," he said, trying to reassure me. I was surprised to hear those words come from him, but it didn't make me feel any better.

Brody patted my hand that gripped his arm and then squeezed. He spoke to Judge. "So, this is where we can test for the tracker?"

"Tracker test and removal." Judge took the steps slowly as the four of us followed him down into the dark. I held tightly to Brody. Judge made it to the bottom of the steps and continued talking. "They're usually embedded under the skin in soft tissue. Fairly easy procedure, though it isn't for the squeamish." He looked at me briefly and noted my hand on Brody, then turned and walked across the room, flicking on lights and lamps.

"Brody, no," I whispered when the man was out of earshot. "You can't let these people touch me. They want me dead."

Brody thought for a second, then shook his head. I noticed he didn't disagree with me. He leaned in and whispered, "We'll figure something out. Let's see how it plays out." I stared at him, pleading with my eyes, but he turned away from me.

The basement looked like a torture chamber out of a horror movie. Trays were set up with various tools and cutting instruments. It crossed my mind that the room could, in fact, be a torture chamber, built to torture my kind. I tried not to think about that as we walked across the musty room.

"Put her here," Judge said, addressing the boys and not me. The chair was black with cracked leather and looked like something that belonged in a dentist's office. I looked at Brody. He nodded. I felt so weak, and I hated it. My life was completely in the hands of Brody and the men that were supposed to be helping them, men that I didn't trust.

I sat down and gripped the arms of the chair. Judge turned his back on me and grabbed a device that looked like a black light holder. It was long, and when he flicked the switch, it glowed red like there was a laser in it. Judge held it a foot away from my body and ran it down the length of me. It let out a quiet buzz when it passed by my thigh. I held my breath.

"Straighten your leg," Judge said. He held the device closer until he found the direct spot, the outer fleshy area of my thigh. "Jackpot," he said. "That should be easy to cut out. They usually don't plant it too far below the surface." I stared down at my leg in disbelief. Aaron studied my face, but my surprise must have been obvious. I had no clue how and when they would have inserted a tracking device in my leg.

"So, you've seen this before?" Aaron asked as though making casual conversation.

"Yep," Judge said, not explaining anything but tossing the device down on a nearby table that held more ominous tools.

"So, can you explain the procedure?" Brody asked, trying to alleviate some of my fears before I had a chance to voice them.

"It's real easy. I cut it open, use these babies," he picked out a very large set of tweezers, "and pull out the embedded tracker, and then we sew it up." He tossed the tweezers back down.

"Her up," Brody interrupted. "We sew her up." He watched Judge to see if he was going to correct himself, but Judge glowered back at Brody, standing his ground. I looked up at Brody from my spot in the chair, thankful he was with me.

"Look," Judge said, moving towards Brody. "I don't know what kind of thing you have going on—" He motioned between the two of us.

"If you think," Brody started, but Aaron held up his hand, stopping Brody.

"I'll do it." Aaron stepped forward. Brody did a double take, and my breath caught.

Judge paused, sucking on the chewing tobacco in his mouth before spitting a giant wad on the stained concrete floor. Then, the old man slapped Aaron on the shoulder. "You are so much like your father. Always willing to get your hands dirty." I looked down. If

Judge knew Aaron's father, I wondered what he knew about me.

Brody turned to Aaron. "Are you sure?" Aaron nodded. My eyes darted between them. Brody seemed to trust Aaron, but I still did not. Maybe this was a way for Aaron to hurt me the way I hurt him. Judge pulled Aaron in front of the tray and started going through the process with him.

Brody crouched down in front of me and whispered, "This is for the best. Aaron will take care of you, much more than that guy." He nodded in Judge's direction.

I started to shiver from the cold of the basement; the scrubs I was still wearing didn't do much to block out the chill. I watched Aaron as he nodded and listened to Judge's instructions. Brody awaited a response. I finally spoke. "I don't know, Brody," I said. "I am pretty sure Aaron is the last person in the world who would offer to help me out of the goodness of his heart."

"You don't know Aaron like I do." Brody squeezed my leg, and once more, I was very aware of his touch burning through the thin layer of clothing.

"Trust me when I say I will never get to know Aaron like you," I said. "Anyway, why would Aaron want to help me?" It was a valid question. Aaron could easily watch Judge take pleasure in digging the tracker out of my leg and not giving a damn about what it did to me. I was suspicious that there had to be another reason.

Brody looked at me like he couldn't believe I was asking the question. "Meda. Aaron is not a bad guy. I thought you would have picked up on that by now." Brody almost seemed annoyed I was still questioning Aaron's integrity as a human being. He continued, "You know you can trust me. And I trust Aaron." I studied his face, looking for a sign he was lying to me. The problem was, I didn't know if I could trust anyone, not even Brody, but he took my silence as an agreement. And as he reached up and grabbed my hand, I was still thankful he was here for me, which was more than I could say for anyone else in the world right now.

Once Judge was done talking to Aaron, Aaron dismissed him. Judge backed up, hands in the air, and muttered, "Suits me," and made himself busy in some corner of the basement.

I realized I would have to remove my pants, which was awkward, but in that moment, it wasn't the heaviest thing that weighed on my mind. The boys turned while I stepped out of my bottoms and awkwardly pulled the large top I was wearing down to cover my underwear. I looked to see if Judge had turned, and his back was towards me. I sat back down on the cracked chair, and it chilled my legs. I shivered. Aaron grabbed the cutting tool and moved over to my side. He looked nervous, which made me feel a little better, like he was taking this seriously rather than just hacking into me.

He scanned my leg again to make sure he had the correct spot, and when it beeped, he marked that spot with a Sharpie. Then, he crouched down as close as he could. "There's not even a mark there," he said as he studied my leg.

"Yeah," Judge yelled over his shoulder. "They're pretty good at covering their tracks." I could hear him spit again as Dan let out a nervous laugh.

"Covering their trackers, good one," Dan said, but there wasn't a lot of humor in his voice. He looked squeamish. I took in a deep breath and reached for Brody's hand. He gripped mine back.

I watched as the blade easily broke through my skin. It was razor sharp, and I didn't feel the sting until moments later. Once Aaron cut in, he was quick and efficient, which helped. I managed not to grimace too much, even though Dan kept making disgusting faces and saying, "Gross, doesn't that hurt?" That didn't help.

I almost cried out when Aaron got a grip on the tracker to tug it up from my flesh. There was a queasy sliding underneath my skin and a numb weightlessness when it was pulled free. It wasn't very big; in fact, it was about the size of a dime. When it was pulled free, Dan took it to Judge to dispose as Aaron prepared to stitch me up. "That wasn't too bad, was it?" he asked me. I was surprised he had even spoken to me.

"No, it was fine," I answered quietly. "Thank you." Aaron nodded. He skillfully put the stitches in my leg. Now the sharp pain turned into an ache of annoyance that hovered over that spot on my leg, and I grimaced as he finished up, hoping now that this was done, we could leave this place and never come back.

Aaron stepped back to admire his work, but immediately, Judge returned to his side after disposing of the tracker. "Aaron, can we talk?" Judge asked. Aaron looked at me one last time and nodded at Judge. The two walked over to the open doorway across the room. A smaller man with glasses emerged from the darkness of the room, pausing to talk to Judge. I quickly slipped my pants back on, and the man called, "Follow me," then led Brody, Dan, and I up the creaking stairs.

He stopped when we came to a bedroom with two bunk beds and a double bed. He motioned to the room covered with plywood walls and not much else. "You can stay here for tonight. Tomorrow you go to Opposition Headquarters in the city." I breathed a sigh of relief. I did not want to stay here any longer. In fact, I wasn't looking forward to spending the night here. Not one bit.

A pair of handcuffs materialized out of the man's pocket. "Judge says she has to wear these." He spoke to Brody and Dan, not to me. Brody went to protest, but I stepped forward, offering my wrists to the man. I nodded to Brody to show I was fine with it, especially if it meant they'd leave me alone. "We can't have her changing into everyone and their brother," the guy said, chuckling at his own joke. I was too exhausted to be offended by him.

The man disappeared through the doorway, and Dan let out a whopping sigh that sounded like he'd been holding his breath since we got here. "I call top," he said half-heartedly before hoisting himself up on the top bunk. He turned away, and his breathing grew heavy. Brody motioned for me to crawl in the bottom bunk, so I did. He pulled the blankets up over me and then grabbed blankets from the foot of the double bed and made up a spot next to me on the floor. I wanted to tell him it would make more sense if he slept on the bed with me, that he would get a better night's sleep, but I was tongue-tied. I thought about speaking the words, but in my head, they sounded like an invitation to something else, which embarrassed me. My cheeks flushed as the thought of his strong hands and full lips forced their way into my head, and I don't know when it happened, but I felt something for him, something I had never felt for anyone else. I cared about him, like a friend, but I was also embarrassed when my thoughts traveled elsewhere. I had zero experience with boys, and I felt foolish imagining something that wasn't even there, but how does a person ever know how someone else feels about them? I didn't know how Brody felt, besides that he was a kind young man trying to protect a young lady. I had no clue how Aaron felt at this particular moment. Dan seemed indifferent. Then I thought about my mother and what Isi had said. I started to wonder if I ever knew my mother and how she truly felt about me and my dad.

Aaron came in only shortly after, almost tripping over Brody as he entered. He collapsed onto the bed and was breathing heavily in an instant. I couldn't fall asleep as quickly. I thought about everyone who had been affected by the events of the last year, from my family, to Aaron and his family, to Brody and Dan, and even the men in the safe house. Though I knew I wasn't responsible for everything that happened, the guilt made it hard for me to shut off my mind and sleep, though eventually I did drift off.

The sleep was uncomfortable. My leg ached, and I had a hard time getting settled with my hands cuffed together. I could hear the boys' breathing, which was comforting because it felt as though they were the only people in the world right now who had my back, even if it was to their benefit. I realized there were plans for me. Plans Brody had potentially known about the entire time, so maybe he was just using me. My head was too mixed up to think about it.

Chapter 14

Though it seemed like I was awake the entire time, my eyes closing and then opening when I thought I heard someone moving outside the door, morning still came. Aaron got up quickly and got dressed in a fresh set of clothes that had been left in the room. I hoped he was also eager to get out of this place. He opened the door, and I could see men moving around, some with backpacks and gear, others like they were on their way to the shower.

Aaron looked back to see if anyone was awake and noticed me watching him, then slipped out the door. Brody woke up next, having heard the door open. He sat up and stretched. Then he realized I was watching him. He smiled at me. "How did you sleep?"

I looked around the room. It had paneling on the walls and ugly shag carpeting, but I couldn't complain. At least there was a bed. I tried to shrug, but my cuffed hands prevented me from doing anything, and as I lifted my hands and cringed, Brody could see the oozing red flesh that bled beneath the cuffs. "Meda," he said gently. He moved over to the bed and grabbed my wrists. I tried to pull them back, but he wouldn't let me. "Why didn't you say anything?" His eyebrows creased.

"It's not a big deal. I can handle it." I didn't want to make a big deal around the men who lived here. Something told me they would have very little sympathy for me. He turned my wrist around to see the extent of the damage, and I could see him really thinking about what the metal had done to my skin.

"Why . . . why does it do this?" He tried to hold the cuffs away from my wrists, but they were snug.

"It's basically an allergy. All mimics have this same allergy towards silver, from what I was told." I looked down at my wrists. The stinging was irritating but tolerable.

"I guess every superhero has to have a weakness," Brody said.

I nearly snorted. "Superhero?"

"Can't a guy sleep in?" Dan called out from his bed. Brody smiled at me. Dan sat up and looked down at us. Brody was kneeling by the bed and holding both my hands. "Really, Brody? You didn't even try to make a move last night? You had to wait until everyone was waking up?"

Brody's face turned red, and he stumbled over words to say. I looked away but peeked back at Brody. "Oh, don't play dumb with me." Dan got up, pulled his underwear out of his butt, and smiled at me. My face flushed, and I wondered when he had removed his clothes. His lanky body tripped over Brody and out the door.

We both stared at the doorway for a moment, and then Brody broke the silence. "I guess it's time to get up." He stood and stretched his arms. "Today we head to the city."

"Thank God," I said quietly.

"What?" Brody asked.

"I just mean, I can't wait to get out of here."

"You and me both," Brody said, helping me out of bed. We made our way into the kitchen. It was an old-fashioned kitchen, but it was an eat-in, so the breakfast table sat in the middle of the room as the counter space wrapped around two and a half walls. The curtains were a yellow that looked like they had once been white. At the breakfast table, Aaron sat with Judge.

Aaron motioned for us to sit down and reached over to Brody. Without saying a word, he handed him the keys to the handcuffs. Brody let my wrists go free as Dan scarfed down a large bowl of Fruity Pebbles.

"I'm so glad you have someone with good taste around here," Dan said between slurps. The cook who was working at the oven shot him a disapproving look.

Aaron had a file in front of him, and he and Judge seemed to be finishing up a conversation. He crossed his arms. "So, is that it?" Aaron asked, paging through the thin file.

"For now," Judge finished. He looked at the three boys, still avoiding direct eye contact with me. "I wish you kids the best of luck. You're going to need it." He saluted Aaron and left the table.

The cook slid oatmeal in front of Aaron, Brody, and I. "Nice hot meal is what you need. Not that your friend would listen to me." The cook nodded towards Dan, who smiled, flecks of rainbow cereal coloring his teeth. The cook walked away, shaking his head.

We all ate while Aaron went over the plan. Brody slid some juice my way, and I chugged it down. I was drained, and the sugar in the juice helped energize me. "The Opposition, which is the group that is helping us, has headquarters in the city, a hotel which provides cover for them. They are giving us a van to take to the hotel, and our contact is Smith." Aaron studied the folder as Brody nodded. I continued to eat. I wasn't a part of the conversation, but I couldn't help but feel hopeful because I was allowed to listen. "There is a reason we're going to the city. I've communicated with Smith already." I looked up, surprised. "They are providing us with resources and will help us plan a Good Faith Mission."

Confused, I looked at Brody, who glanced at me and then turned his attention back to Aaron. "What do you mean, Good Faith Mission?" Brody asked.

Instead of waiting for Aaron to answer, I spoke. "A Good Faith Mission is one in which they do something for you with the understanding that after that mission is done, you will follow through and do whatever they ask."

Aaron raised his eyebrows, surprised I could answer Brody's question. Brody spoke up. "So, what is this Good Faith Mission?" He placed his spoon down as he waited for Aaron's answer.

"Well," Aaron spoke slowly. "We are going to the city to meet with Smith because he has a plan to get Meda's dad and sisters out of the Agency's hands. We are going to get them back and help them disappear."

I stopped mid-bite. The words that came out of Aaron's mouth didn't make any sense. Why would the Opposition do that for me? Why would Aaron do that for me? I knew it meant I would have to do something in return, probably something big, but at that moment I didn't care. I brought my hands up to my face, my oozing, raw wrists exposed, and began to sob.

Dan looked embarrassed, and Aaron got up and threw his bowl in the sink. I couldn't tell what he was feeling. He didn't look mad. Brody reached over and squeezed my hand. I couldn't help myself. I wrapped my arms around him and embraced him, feeling his warmth as he wrapped his large arms around me. I pictured my dad and my sisters. I hoped they were still alright. I hoped it wasn't too late.

Then I heard someone take a deep breath. I looked up, and the man who had grabbed my cheek when we first arrived was standing by the cook, eating a piece of toast and sneering at us. I quickly released Brody, who was confused by my sudden withdrawal but smiled at me anyway. He turned and saw the cook and the man from before, the one with the missing teeth.

Brody pushed his chair back. "Come on, Meda," he said, emphasizing my name to show I was no "it." He grabbed our dishes and dumped them in the sink. The man continued to stare even as the cook turned back to the stove to make more food for the rest of the men.

Brody came back to me and addressed the man. "Do we have a problem?" he asked, stepping between me and the man. The man smiled and continued to chew. This guy was scary. He was beginning to bald, and I could see wisps of hair carefully combed over his bald spots, but he was well-muscled and looked strong.

Brody turned and led me back to the bedroom so we could make up the beds and get the hell out of there.

As we cleaned up, Brody disappeared to shower. Before he left, he asked if I'd be okay, and I assured him I would be fine. There was no way I was leaving that bedroom without Brody as my escort. I was determined to pee my pants if it came to that.

Only a few minutes went by when there was a knock on the door, and when it opened, I expected to see Dan or Aaron, or even Brody, having forgotten something. But it wasn't any of them. It was ol' toothless. He must have known Brody wasn't here to protect me.

"Oh, yes?" I asked, trying to play it cool and not show any fear. I remembered how roughly he had grabbed my cheek when we first arrived, and I looked out in the hallway to see if anyone else was out there, but we were alone. I quickly stood up from the bed. "Can I help you?" I stayed near the bed, not wanting to get close to him.

The man had stubble on his chin, and his body odor was sharp, pungent. He moved towards me. "Judge was right when he said I ain't seen one of you up close. Mind if I take a look?" I didn't know what to say so as not to offend the man. His energy was like a live wire. He was a little crazed in the eyes, but I wasn't sure if it was real or my imagination.

"Um, I'd rather not." He moved closer anyway. I noticed his belt was open as he stepped closer. I backed up, tripping over a small rug. The man continued to move forward slowly and animal-like.

"Well, ain't you got a little attitude on you. You're lucky we took you in. I think you owe a little appreciation for that." He moved faster than I could back up, and he soon took hold of my wrist, which was still raw from the cuffs. I grimaced and tried to shake him off. I didn't want to call out because I thought that might force him to do something worse than what he planned, whatever that was.

I could smell the stink of his breath. "I want to touch your skin. I was wondering how it felt, if it was like clay or loose and rubbery." He rubbed his thumb on the raw part of my wrist, and I couldn't help but speak.

"Please, that hurts," I said, again worried I would offend him, but my patience was wearing thin. He suddenly pulled me to him, uncomfortably close. He was bigger than me, and stronger. I could smell some kind of alcohol on him, but I couldn't dare risk shifting, not after they let me loose of the cuffs.

While still holding my wrist, he brought his face to my neck. I had the irrational fear he was going to bite me as he took a long inhalation. "Hmm, you smell like a woman." I closed my eyes and turned away, nearly gagging, and then suddenly, just like that, he let go.

When I opened my eyes, Aaron stood behind the man. He had a blade pressed down on the man's neck. "What in the hell do you think you're doing?" Aaron snarled in the man's ear. I'd seen Aaron look angry before, but for the first time, it wasn't directed at me.

The man tried to shake Aaron off. "Get your hands off me, boy."

Aaron swiftly turned the man around and pushed him down on my bed. He leaned forward and put the knife to the man's neck again.

"If you even look at her funny again, I will cut you." Aaron didn't even blink.

The man sneered but started to look unsure. "Kid, what is your problem? She's a mimic. An animal."

"You are my problem, but you won't be anymore if you go near her again." Aaron pushed the knife down, not enough to cut the man, but to let him feel the pressure. "Get it?" The man gave a quick nod, and Aaron stood up and stepped away, leaving the man room to get up but also blocking the man's view of me. The guy got up and spit on the floor before walking out of the room.

Just then, Brody walked in. He was rubbing his hair with a towel but froze when he saw Aaron standing there with a knife. Aaron quickly slid the knife into his pocket. "What's going on?" Brody asked, immediately moving to my side. I was sure he could hear my heart pounding in my chest.

"Nothing," Aaron quickly answered. He walked by Brody and out the room. Brody turned to me, but I didn't know what to say.

"What happened? Did Aaron do something?" Brody's eyes searched me, making sure I was okay.

I shook my head vehemently. "It was that guy. I...Aaron saved me." Brody looked confused, probably as confused as I was.

Then Dan came in the room. He was completely oblivious to our tension and walked between us, picking up his bag. "Time to go, ladies," he said, smiling at Brody. Then he stopped and looked at Brody's flushed face and then mine. "What?" he asked.

"Let's just go," I said. With the promise of seeing my dad and sisters again, I didn't care about anything else, even if it meant heading towards another unknown.

Chapter 15

Though they had provided fresh clothes for Aaron, Dan, and Brody, they didn't think to provide me with any. Brody managed to track down some unisex clothes. I slipped into an old Ozzy Osbourne t-shirt and some black sweatpants that were too big for me, but considering I had been running around in scrubs before, I felt this was a much better look.

The van we loaded into looked like a corporate van, white and windowless. Dan slid into the driver's seat. I got the sense he enjoyed driving. Aaron was in the passenger seat and immediately pulled out his cell and started clicking away. Once again, Brody slid into the back of the van with me, his dark hair still wet from the shower. He shook it, and a few water droplets flew off his close-cut hair. I could smell his shampoo from my spot across the van.

Once we rolled out of the driveway of the safe house, I felt relief. Even though I wouldn't call the boys my friends to their faces, they felt like it, and even Aaron didn't scowl at me as he looked back to make sure we were all ready to go.

I was back in a place where I at least felt safe, and we were on our way to my family. I tried to tell myself I shouldn't get my hopes up, but hope was all I had. I didn't even want to think about what the Opposition was going to ask me to do in exchange for my family, so I tried to enjoy the trip, if that was possible.

We were on our way to Chicago. It was the first time I knew where we were, well not exactly, but at least the area. Prior to this trip, no one thought it was important enough to let me know. I laughed at that thought. This was the first time in over a year I didn't feel like a prisoner. Brody looked at me and smiled. Aaron had his window down, and the breeze rustled my hair. I closed my eyes and felt my dark hair flutter on my cheeks. This was what freedom felt like, even if it was an illusion.

While Dan drove, he babbled on about the Opposition, using his free hand to emphasize important points. "There are three groups. First, there are people like us. The revenge-seekers. The normal folk who got their lives taken away, erased." I looked up at Aaron in the passenger seat, and I felt the pang of guilt. I reached up to spin my earring but forgot it wasn't there. I gripped my ear instead. Aaron looked back like he sensed my eyes on him. He made eye contact with me, gave me a tight smile, and turned to the road once more. I dropped my hands in my lap.

"Then there are the up-aboves," Dan continued. "Many of these guys used to be part of the Agency. They know all the insider trading tips. They have connections. They dress in nice clothes." He swiveled his neck around, indicating that he thought they were a bit uppity. "And finally, there are the military grunts. These are the 'for hire' men the Opposition gets to do their dirty work. They'll do anything for money, though some of them are in it for the right reasons. They hate mimics. The most important thing to remember is you can't trust any one of the groups."

I looked up, speaking loud enough to be sure Dan could hear me. "So, you're saying I can't trust you guys?"

Dan slammed his hand on the steering wheel and glanced at me in the rearview mirror. "That is exactly what I'm saying. And it would be in your best interest to remember that." He shook his head at me, and I couldn't help but smile. I looked across at Brody, who had his hand over his mouth, trying to cover his own smile. His legs were stretched across the van, and he nudged me with his foot. I hit him back, and he brought his hand down to show me his smile. He had perfectly straight teeth, like he used to have braces. I wanted to ask him, but I thought that would be weird. There was so much I didn't know about him. But I wanted to.

As we entered the heart of Chicago, I admired the tall buildings through the windshield. I felt lighter than I had in a long time. I felt different as well. Even before I was taken, I always had to hide what I was. I didn't have to with these guys. They knew my secret and had accepted it. Sort of.

Aaron pointed straight ahead. "We'll be staying in the top floor of that hotel."

It was one of the tallest buildings I had ever seen. I stared up at the top of the hotel. "Isn't that…dangerous? Like a trap?" I looked from Brody to Aaron with concern on my face. I was also a little afraid of heights, but I didn't want anyone to know.

"The entire floor is stacked with security," Aaron said. "No one else on the floor. It's a major penthouse suite, so it's easy to secure the floor from intruders. No one else should be going up that high." Yes. No one should be going that high, I silently agreed. Aaron continued. "They have retinal scanners, which makes the place a mimic-free zone. I mean, besides you, of course." I nodded and lifted one corner of my mouth in a half grin. He turned and watched as we approached the building. I continued to look at the back of his head, his blond hair mussed with the wind. In the time I'd known him, it was the most he had spoken to me without yelling at me or hitting me.

When we arrived at the hotel, Aaron said something to a man at the front desk. He called someone on the phone, and then another man appeared next to us. There was no need to check in. He led us through the lobby to a service door. It smelled like laundry and food, and then we were at an elevator. No one crossed our path which made me feel a little more secure.

The man produced a key card and swiped it on the panel. The elevator climbed the shaft, and I grew anxious and light-headed, watching each of the floors light up as we passed them. The elevator jumped to a stop, and the light indicated we were at the top floor.

The doors opened to the foyer of a large suite. I took a deep breath as the man pointed to the cameras that were trained on the elevators, explaining the security to us. "The cameras take pictures of anyone arriving on this floor; granted, they need the code to be able to open the elevator doors. The images taken are then sent to a computer that runs a retinal scan. So, if someone gets here and knows the code, the scan will identify them in our database. Which reminds me, we will need to scan her."

He motioned to me. "Mimics are a bit trickier as you know." The man nodded at me. "You guys can change the color of your eyes to match your likeness, and you also change the shape of your eyes, which is what our computer measures. We do have a way to identify mimics, though we wouldn't want to give away all our trade secrets just yet." He smiled and winked at me. This was much different from the last place, when the men wouldn't even look at me. I stood a little taller.

Though this was no vacation, when we entered the hotel room, Dan and I, with a sense of childish wonder, oohed and aahed at the luxury around us. Apparently, I wasn't the only one used to minimal living quarters. The suite seemed to go on forever. It was bigger than my home had been, with an open concept kitchen and living room and an entire wall of windows. The kitchen was shiny granite and stainless steel, and the sofas were a deep, rich shade of red. It even had an expensive smell, like cologne.

Dan sprinted over to the window and pressed his forehead against the glass, trying to look down. I joined him, afraid to look, but when he looked at me, smiled, and motioned for me to do the same, I stepped closer and looked down. It felt like I could fall, but Dan nudged me. "Cool, huh?" I laughed, and it came out louder than I meant it too. Dan looked startled, and I laughed again. It had been a while.

Then Brody joined us, and Aaron came along, lagging behind. "Woah," Brody called out, and Aaron couldn't resist. He stepped up to the window as well. Standing there, the four of us, with our foreheads pressed against the glass, I was reminded that we were all just teenagers, and there were still things out there that could surprise us and fill us with wonder. And just like that, I felt like I belonged. Like I was one of them. And I was surprised not only by the beauty of the view, but the beauty of these boys, and their youth and their goodness.

I glanced at Aaron and then at Brody. Sometimes I was amazed at how beautiful people could be. Even the most unexpected people have something beautiful about them. There are so many different variations of beauty, from eyes, to graceful hands, to a curve in the hip. There is so much beauty in the world, and not many people pay attention enough to see it.

"Ahem." Behind us, someone cleared his throat. We all turned at the same time. The man who stood before us looked like he was in his late twenties or early thirties. He wore a suit that had not one wrinkle or crease, and his skin was a dark mocha color. Aaron was the first one to straighten up and step forward with his hand out. "You must be Aaron," the man said, gripping Aaron's hand.

"You must be Smith," Aaron said in return. The rest of us approached the man as well. He shook hands with each of us, including me. Surprisingly, no one tried to put handcuffs on me. "Thank you for accommodating us," Aaron said graciously. I was surprised by what a gentleman he could be. I guess, considering the position his father had held, he was used to meeting people in formal situations.

"Aaron, I'd like to go over a few things with you." A looked bounced between Aaron and Brody, and Brody gave a curt nod. Smith nodded at Brody.

Smith continued. "You can join me in the debriefing room." Then he turned to the rest of us. "The fridge is fully stocked. Go ahead and make yourselves at home." He motioned to the living room. Brody made eye contact once again with Aaron, and Aaron nodded before he disappeared behind an oak door with Smith leading the way.

In seconds, Dan was at the stainless steel, double-door fridge, emptying its contents. "Yeah, cake!" he yelled. I looked around. There was a man sitting in the foyer who seemed to be keeping watch.

I stood by Brody. "When are we going to be debriefed?" I asked quietly, not wanting to sound ungrateful. "I mean, I can understand why they wouldn't want to tell me all the plans, but shouldn't you know? And Dan?" Brody shrugged, but I could tell that once I said it, it bothered him. I felt guilty. I hadn't meant to plant a seed of doubt in him, but this mission was important to me, and I wanted to know what they were planning. I also thought if anyone would look out for the best interests of my family, it would be Brody. Then I felt even more guilt. I needed to start trusting Aaron after what he did for me.

Dan interrupted, talking to us while chewing, "Would you two quit yapping and grab some sandwiches?" Brody and I stopped talking and followed Dan's orders. We grabbed our sandwiches and planted ourselves in front of the large screen television. Brody tried to get Dan to watch the news, but Dan kept switching it back to a movie that involved illegal street racing and women in scantily clad clothing. I could have guessed this would be the kind of thing Dan would enjoy.

After we finished eating, Dan dozed off on the couch. I dozed off too, my stomach stuffed. The couch moved as Brody got up. He was talking to the man who sat watch, but I was so comfortable I didn't care. I didn't need to be nosy anymore. I continued to fall asleep, but then felt as if someone was watching me, so I jumped awake. When I looked up, Brody was standing over me.

"What?" I asked, sitting up.

He reached his hand down and whispered, "Come with me."

I felt a little like I was dreaming as I got up and walked behind Brody. Brody looked at the man and pointed like he was asking permission, and the man nodded. Brody took me by the hand and led me down one of the hallways, and I stumbled drowsily behind him. When we got to the end of the hall, there was a door with a sign that said, "To Rooftop Balcony."

I looked at him questioningly. "We shouldn't go anywhere," I stuttered, suddenly nervous. What were we doing? I wasn't sure what Brody wanted from me. "We don't know who could be out there," I blurted. "What if we're seen?"

"It's fine, Meda. I checked." He smiled at me. "Come on. Live a little." Then he pulled me out the door. It didn't exit out to the roof, like I thought it was going to. It brought us to another door marked "Fire Exit."

"Where are we going?" I asked. Brody didn't answer, but he seemed to know the way. Now I knew what he had been talking to the man about. He pushed the door open and pulled me into the stairwell with him. It was all concrete and white, and there was no carpet, so it seemed like an area that wasn't meant for guests.

He turned, smiling. "Come on," he said, motioning up the steps. He took the first couple two at a time, dragging me behind him. His strides were longer, but I was quick. It was dark in the stairwell except for the security lights.

"What are we doing?" I asked.

"We're going all the way to the top," Brody responded.

"I thought we were on the top."

"Not quite." Our feet echoed in the stairwell, and I tried to hold back a smile. A fluttery feeling burst in my stomach. I was excited and scared all at the same time. It didn't feel right to feel this in our current circumstances, but I had been feeling like an entirely different person ever since we left the safe house.

We came to a landing at the end, and Brody went to push the door open that said, "Rooftop Balcony." I grabbed his arm. "Wait! Are you sure the alarm won't go off?" Brody smiled and walked out the door.

He pulled me in a rush out to the rooftop. The cold air outside hit me immediately. Then, the vastness of the night struck. I didn't realize that as we napped after our meal it had turned to night. Stars flickered above me. It was dizzying. "Beautiful," Brody said quietly.

"It is," I said, looking at the stars. I dropped my eyes to Brody and noticed he was looking at me. I was immediately embarrassed and struggled to say something, but my mouth didn't work.

Something glimmered in Brody's eyes as he moved towards me, cautiously. I didn't back away, though everything in my body tried to make me. Brody's words traveled quietly through the night. "It's a shame you were born a mimic." My stomach dropped, unsure of what he meant. Then he continued. "Because a face this beautiful should never be allowed to change." I laughed. It was so cheesy I couldn't look at him, but I also found a deep blush lurking up my neck. I always wondered why, in books, women seemed to fall for the cheesy lines. I knew now it didn't matter how cheesy the line, because when a man you care for compliments you, everything in the world brightens.

One hand slid delicately to my hip. "Meda, I want you to trust me," Brody said, his smile replaced with a look of earnestness.

I had a difficult time finding words when all my attention was focused on his hand at my hip. "Of course I trust you, Brody. Look at all you've done for me." Then, his other hand dropped to my other hip, and he slowly pulled me towards him.

"What I meant was, I won't let anything happen to you." His voice had a dreamy quality. His hands slid from my hips and met each other at my lower back. I had been hoping, wishing the entire time, that it wasn't all in my head. Willing myself not to trust him. I had no way of knowing until that very moment how he felt, but I couldn't return his embrace. I stood with my arms dumbly hanging at my sides.

"I know," I said, but I felt stupid. I was speechless. I was afraid to hold onto someone. Those people had a way of being used against me. Brody gently placed his hand on the side of my face. He brushed my cheek with his knuckles and brought his hand under my chin, and suddenly his warm mouth was on mine.

I closed my eyes and sighed. Now I had stars in my eyes. Starbursts of color flooded my senses, and I felt every inch of his lips. Then, I pulled back. He looked into my eyes and saw my concern.

"What is it? Tell me. You aren't alone anymore." He continued to hold me, not letting go.

"I don't know if I can do this." I shook my head. "I'm afraid." He studied me. "There is always something to lose. The more people I get to know, the more people I have to worry about."

"Stop. You don't have to worry about me." His brows drew together. "It's my turn to worry about you. You have people on your side. You're not alone," he whispered.

Though I fought it, tears welled up in my eyes. I shook my head, amazed. "How do you always know the right thing to say and do?" It was that very reason why I didn't trust him in the beginning. He seemed too perfect. Like a cardboard cutout of the perfect guy.

Brody laughed and shook his head. "It's funny to me you see it that way."

"I'm not the only one who does. Dan told me you're like Clark Kent." I tilted my head, studying him, waiting for his answer.

"Meda," he sighed. "I don't know what is right any more than you do, but I trust in myself. That is what you need to do. Instinct will get you far, but confidence in your choices will get you the rest of the way. And you are a good person. You should be confident that you will choose to do the right thing when the time comes for you to make such a decision."

I threw my arms around Brody's neck and kissed him deeply. He stumbled back a bit, and I could feel the smile creep up on his face, so I kissed him harder. His hands traced their way around my waist. This was what it felt like. This was why my dad held onto the memory of my mother. This was the feeling I'd been waiting for. The feeling that life was worth all the trouble.

I pulled back. "Well, I feel like that was the right choice." I smiled.

"I second that," Brody added as he ran his hand through my hair. "Sadly though, I think we're out of time." He tilted his head. "We'd better get back to the guys." He reached his hand out, and I grabbed it. He pulled me along, back to the door, back to the stairwell, and back to the room.

When we arrived, Aaron was sitting on the couch next to Dan. He only looked up briefly, but that brief look said it all. Aaron knew there was something different between Brody and I, and his look showed that he thought it meant nothing but trouble. He shook his head.

Brody and I sat down on the loveseat across from the two. "Where's Smith?" Brody asked.

"Gone. I'll go through the debriefing." Aaron opened up his computer and turned it to face us. "We will be initiating the switch at the zoo to get Meda's family back."

"Wait, what switch?" Brody asked.

Aaron looked to him. "Meda's going to have to shift." Then he looked at me. "Hopefully you remember what your stepmother looks like."

Chapter 16

When my father had first introduced me to the woman who would be my stepmother, I was surprised. Beth was the opposite of my mother. She was small and agreed with my dad on everything while my real mother and father got into epic fights that ended with a lot of kissing and probably other stuff I didn't want to think about. My mother's personality could fill the room while Beth faded into the background. I didn't know then, but that was why she was the perfect operative for the Agency.

Ginger and Georgia were still young when my dad brought home the auburn-haired, mousy-faced Beth. Like any woman auditioning to be a stepmother, she was kind to us, but there was always a coldness about her. I knew I could never get close to her because Dad told me not to share my secret with anyone, which meant I couldn't even let my guard down at home.

At first, I couldn't believe Dad had betrayed our family that way, even though it had been years since we had last seen my mother. But Dad still talked so lovingly about Mom and was so different around Beth, I soon realized Beth was not a replacement, she was a stand-in. If and when Mom returned, Beth would be dropped in an instant. Which made Beth tolerable but also made me feel a little bad for her, until I found out she betrayed our entire family and had been working for the Agency the entire time.

That was why I was speechless at first when Aaron told me I would be shifting into the woman who betrayed me, the woman who had taken the place of my mother, and who, even though she had been cold, had pretended to treat me like a daughter. Yet, I listened intently to Aaron's plans. I could see many ways in which it could go wrong but focused on the way it would go right. When it did go right, I would be reunited with my family.

The switch would take place at the zoo, where my father would be taking my sisters and stepmother. This was all orchestrated by Smith, who had someone in the Agency who could get to my family. A secret double agent. My father told my stepmother about the planned trip, and she, in turn, informed the Agency. It was a pretty great plan. It was clear the public place was necessary just in case people were watching. Even the Agency wouldn't risk a shootout at the zoo. At least that was what I hoped.

"How does that sound?" Aaron asked. I was surprised he wanted me to weigh in. Then again, I was the expert on my family.

I shrugged. "I mean, there are things that could go wrong, but the same can be said for every plan."

"We'll have a back-up team waiting as well." Aaron closed his computer and looked between me and Brody.

"So when does this happen?" I asked, reaching up to my naked ear to twist my invisible earring.

"Tomorrow," Aaron answered. My hands dropped. I wasn't sure if I was prepared to go undercover again. I was getting used to being myself. "Let's all try to get some sleep." Aaron clapped his hands together and stood. "We have a big day tomorrow."

The man, whose name I now knew as Bill, if that was his real name, showed us to our rooms. We each had our own room, and

I was sad to separate from Brody, who had been by my side for the last few days through this whole wild trip. It was hard to believe that only a week ago, I was at the Agency compound, locked in my room, prepping for my biggest assignment. Only a week ago, I had no idea there was a boy out there named Brody who would sweep in and change my world. A boy who made me feel like I could be myself but also made me nervous because I didn't know who I was. So while I was sad to see Brody standing by the door of his room as I made my way down the hall to mine, I was also relieved. I had enough to think about without worrying about spending the night with a boy I just made out with.

Bill showed me to my room and shut the door behind me, but not before Brody gave me a wave goodnight. I smiled and waved back as the door shut in my face. I turned and took a deep breath.

The room was bigger than my father's master bedroom at home. The bedding was fluffy, white, and crisp. A far cry from the places we had been so far. A cabin, a camper, a sketchy safe house later, and we had finally hit the jackpot. A table by the entryway held a vase full of fresh flowers. There was a gas fireplace with a smart TV mounted over it. I flicked the fire switch on and off a few times and smiled to myself.

I walked across the white carpet to the bed and tested its firmness. It was a king-size bed, and I couldn't wait to crawl in. But first, I walked over to the door by the bed and opened it. Behind the door was the most amazing bathroom I had ever seen. On the long stretch of countertop was some kind of gift basket. In that basket was a robe, slippers, a bath bomb, and other toiletries. That was when I turned and looked at the massive jetted tub, and I knew the perfect way to relax in order to prepare for the stepmother swap. I began to run the water, once again smiling to myself.

In the morning, after a night of soaking in the tub, indulging in trashy television, and sleeping heavily, I shuffled out to the vast kitchen area to get a cup of coffee that was already brewing in the pot. Apparently, Bill's station was a stool by the coffee machine, and when he turned with my cup, he raised his own cup at me. I nodded and raised mine in return. Of course, Aaron was already awake. Smith had returned. And Brody sat eating a banana in the living room.

"Hey, sleepyhead," he called out. I made my way over to his side.

After Aaron debriefed us, Brody led me to a room, different from the one in which Aaron met with Smith. This room could only be described as a wardrobe room. It was the size of a bedroom, but it was filled with clothing racks on wheels. There were six racks total, three on each side, parallel to each other.

"This is where we find your outfit of the day." Brody smiled. He handed me a picture he grabbed off the side table when we entered. "They already have a picture of what your stepmother is wearing for the day."

I took the photo from Brody's hand. Beth looked exactly the same. She never seemed to change, and her clothes were as boring as ever. The picture looked like it was taken without her knowledge by someone hiding a cell phone. She stood in front of Georgia, braiding her hair. Georgia looked like she was talking animatedly, but Beth had a bored, vacant look on her face. As I looked at the picture, I grew angry. My sisters deserved more than a fake mother who pretended to care about them.

Brody and I walked between the racks. There were regular clothes, glitzy dresses, police uniforms. I pulled out a white lab coat and held it in front of me, raising my eyebrows at Brody. He smiled, and I kept going. There was men's clothing and women's clothing, even some children's clothing. I tried to imagine why a child would need this wardrobe, hoping they didn't have children mimics working for them, but this suite also operated as a safe house, which meant the Opposition probably brought families here before they placed them in hiding.

I bit my lip and turned to Brody. He only had to look at me for a moment to realize there was something wrong. "What's going on, Meda?"

"I don't know why, but I'm kind of afraid to see her," I said, holding up the picture and studying it again. Brody looked down at it with me.

"She can't do anything to you." Brody focused on my face.

"It's not that. I'm not afraid of her. It's just… I'm afraid of what I will do when I see her."

Brody sighed, relieved. "You only have to see her long enough to change into her."

"I know, but Brody, this is a woman who pretended to care about me. She pretended to care about my father and my sisters, and the entire time, she worked for the Agency. It's not fair. It's not fair to my father or my sisters."

"Meda, you are strong enough to do this. Remember, Beth is just a woman doing her job. Try to take the emotion out of it."

"Easy for you to say." I let out a huff of air.

"It's the same thing I told Aaron," Brody said, more quietly. I was struck speechless, but only for a moment.

"Wait, you're comparing me to Beth? I had no choice. I mean I did, but at the expense of my own family. Beth had a choice. This is her job."

"All I'm saying is you'll never know why someone chooses to do what they do until you know them, and you don't know the real Beth. I mean, I'm pretty sure that's not even her name."

"Stop." I was getting mad. Brody was trying to make me feel bad for Beth, and that wasn't going to work. It was different than my situation. She was supposed to be part of my family. She gained our trust and then betrayed us. I held my tongue because I was afraid if I spoke this aloud, it would come out angrier than I wanted it to, and I was trying to remain calm. Brody, of course, could see right through me and tried to change the subject.

"I'm sure you'll be in control. It's perfectly okay for you to have these feelings. In fact, I like to see this side of you. The side that decides to fight back." Brody grinned prominently, displaying his dimples that were usually hidden. "Anyway, I'll be there with you."

His words stoked the flames of the fire that was building. I forced a smile back at him and shook my head. "Not the entire time."

"In spirit?" he said stupidly but laughed. "Just remember, the sooner you do the switch, the sooner you'll be with your family." Once again, he knew exactly what to say.

He walked over to a clothing rack and dug in, sifting through the colorful garments. "Here. This looks close to what she's wearing, and they're quite stunning. Very matronly," he joked while handing me some jeans and a top. I rolled my eyes and went into the bathroom to change.

I came out, the clothes a little baggy on my tiny frame. I spun around, and Brody cringed and mouthed, "Yikes." I shoved him and sighed. "Can we go over this one more time?"

Brody waved to a spot on the plush carpeted floor in the room. "Ma'am, do you need a hand getting down there?" He smiled. I rolled my eyes and plopped on the floor. Brody sat very close to me, crossing his legs.

He looked directly in my eyes as he spoke to be sure I was getting the full plan. "Okay, your father and your sisters are going to the zoo with your stepmother. That is where we'll do the swap."

"Got it," I nodded. "And we know this for sure."

"For sure. We even got notice that your stepmother made the call to the Agency to confirm the trip. The Agency will have people there, watching them from a distance, but hopefully, if it all goes right, they won't realize the difference after the swap, and by then it should be too late."

"Okay." I clasped my hands together. "Where do we swap?"

"We'll wait for her to use the restroom."

I turned my head, confused. "How do you know she'll use the restroom?"

Brody smiled. "Because your dad knows he can't leave until she does."

"Who talked to my dad?" I asked, suddenly very interested.

"The Opposition has a person in place. They found an untraceable way to communicate with your father. The mole sent a series of codes for your dad to decipher, and your dad was quick to pick them up. Once your dad set up the trip and Beth pushed it through the Agency, our double agent was able to get assigned the job." He picked up the picture he had set next to him. "Hence, the photograph. Anyway, your dad is a smart man, being able to follow the codes. So, Smith set most of this up, but Aaron filled in the blanks."

I raised my eyebrows. "Aaron?"

"Well, we needed to make sure we had someone who was looking out for your best interests, not just what would be easiest. Anyway, I told you, he's looking out for you. In a way, he's doing this for you, Meda." Brody paused.

"Well, and to get me to do whatever the Opposition wants of me when I'm done."

"No. Aaron went to bat for you. He told them there was no way you would do it unless you had your family back. They could have found a different way to coerce you, but Aaron's word means a lot to them because of his dad." He looked down.

"But why would he…" I trailed off as Brody looked back up. I shook my head, knowingly. "He didn't do it for me, Brody. He did it for you."

His face flushed, and he smiled. "I mean, he did owe me something for all his crap I put up with."

I moved forward and squeezed his hand. Brody gave me a squeeze back and then got up and walked over to the walk-in closet in the room.

"There is something else." He disappeared for a moment, and when he came back, he held a black box. I got up off the floor, and we met halfway. Brody held the box out in front of him, and I moved closer, curious about the contents. He gently slid the lid off the box and tilted it so I could see what was inside.

My mouth dropped open, and I was instantly confused. Brody started speaking. "I know what you're thinking." He shook his head sadly. "They aren't the same. The original ones were lost at the bunker. But I sent the man at the front desk to find a pair that were similar."

I regarded the earrings that looked like the exact earrings my mother had given me. Brody must have paid attention to what they looked like in order to find these duplicates.

"Wait, when did you do that?" I asked. He hadn't been out of my sight.

"Last night." Brody smiled.

I felt tears in my eyes. "Brody, they're perfect. They look exactly the same." I absently wiped the corner of my eye. "In fact, they're even more beautiful than the originals." I was embarrassed that I was getting emotional, but a boy had never given me jewelry before, and this jewelry meant something to me.

"They are going to help your dad identify you. I'm not sure he quite trusts anyone, which is wise." I took the earrings out of the box and began putting them on. Brody watched, his face hard to read.

"What is it?" I stepped closer to him.

"Nothing. I just—" he stammered. He reached out and brushed his hand down my face. "I just don't want to see you get hurt again." A dark cloud passed over his face. "I will do everything in my power to make sure no one can hurt you again."

I shook my head. "You can't do that. I don't want you to make promises you can't possibly keep. You are not responsible for the situation we are in, even though I know you feel some sort of guilt. You can't live your life that way. Things will eat at you." I thought of my own feelings, about how I felt responsible for my father's current situation. Then I thought about my mother and how she probably felt responsible for me. It was a vicious, never-ending cycle. And I knew that even if we got my family back, there would still be people who were hurt. We wouldn't be able to end it all.

There was a quick rap at the door before it swung open. Dan stood, looking between the two of us. "Everything okay in here?" I wiped the remaining tears from my eyes. Dan gave me a once-over and nodded, knowingly. He stepped forward and patted me on the shoulder. "It's okay, Meda. Your outfit is…nice." He didn't wait for a reply. "Let's go!" he yelled as he turned and walked out the door. Brody and I followed, Brody gripping my hand the entire way.

Chapter 17

We were back in the living area. Aaron was sitting with Smith, speaking in low tones. When they saw us walk in, they both got up from the couch and joined us near the foyer.

"Before we go," Aaron started talking, "let's go over a few things one more time." He was speaking quickly, and I saw the traces of perspiration on his forehead. Nerves were contagious, and soon I was breaking out in beads of sweat.

"Brody and I will be in one vehicle." Aaron pointed at Brody when he said it and then directed his words at me. "We'll be keeping your stepmother contained in the restroom while you take your position." He looked at Dan. "Dan will be the back-up getaway driver." Dan's face dropped, and he scowled at the floor. He knew the plan, but that didn't mean he couldn't be disappointed. The fact that he wasn't the actual getaway driver, just the back-up, was a blow to his ego.

Aaron gave Dan a nudge on the shoulder. "Sorry, bro. We can't afford the risk of anyone recognizing you, even if you are the most qualified driver." Dan smiled at Aaron, and I realized something I hadn't before. Aaron acted like a big brother to Dan. Sure, they were friends and cousins, but Aaron was protective of Dan, probably because Dan had a childlike quality that made him seem too trusting and too naïve to the world. You had to get to know him to know there was more beneath the surface.

Just then, the entryway door opened, and a man in a suit led an older woman into the suite. She was wearing a uniform and seemed to be a regular employee of the hotel. Smith brought the woman to me. "Jillian," he said to me, making sure I understood he was using a false name for me. "I want you to meet Cynthia. She is one of the newest members of our staff. Quite motivated. I'm sure she'll go far." I stepped forward to Cynthia and shook her hand, staring into her eyes. She seemed confused, not sure what this meeting meant for her but hoping it meant she was doing a good enough job that one day she would move up in the ranks.

As she left, Smith brought me, along with Brody, into the room behind the large oak door. It looked like Smith's office, with an executive-style desk in a cherry veneer finish. There were computer monitors and gizmos and gadgets on the shelves that covered one wall of the room. "I hope you don't mind, Meda. We are going to record your shift for our own purposes." Smith grabbed a video camera and began to set it up.

"Um, okay." This was a part of the plan that we didn't discuss. We had already made a tape, but maybe the tape I made with Brody wasn't for the Agency. Maybe it was some kind of personal insurance plan for the boys. I kept my mouth shut as Smith aimed the camera at me.

"When you're ready." He waved his hand, cuing me that it was time to shift. I closed my eyes to try to block out the room and concentrated on all the details of Cynthia. Her dark hair, her round cheeks, kind eyes, and her calloused hands. The burning began as it always did. The shifting of my skin always burned. It was painful. But I learned it was easy to block out the sensation because I knew it would be over in a few moments. I felt my mind trying to sync with my body. Trying to understand how Cynthia would think. Usually I had researched my subject, but this time there was no need for me to act like Cynthia, so I felt strange inside her skin, like a glove that was a little too loose and might fall off at any moment. When it was done, I was Cynthia, yet I was still wearing the clothing Brody selected for me to look like my stepmother.

Then, my eye caught something on the wall. It was a grainy picture of a neighborhood that I recognized. "Smith," I interrupted as he turned off his recording device. I motioned towards the picture. "What happened to Mr. Gray?" It was his neighborhood that stood out in the picture.

"Why, Mr. Gray is fine." Smith looked at the picture. "The police were called to his neighborhood that night because of the shots fired. He and others around him found the shooting suspicious, especially when they found your abandoned vehicle with the survey. They connected everything. Sadly for Mr. Gray, he resigned from the position they had offered him with the President. He knew the President's security had been compromised, and he seemed to be interested in doing what was best for the President rather worrying about his own self gain. Then again, he may have realized that night that someone could have put a bullet in his head to compromise security." Smith crossed his arms. "Why do you ask, Meda?"

I didn't know why I asked. I had never asked before. I didn't even know Mr. Gray, but it occurred to me that the people I shifted into, Cynthia and Mr. Gray, among others, had deeper lives than I imagined. "So, is there any intel on the Agency's new plan?"

"That, my dear, is what we'll get into when you return. Right now, you focus on getting your family back." I stared at Smith, with his suit and his generic, yet serious, face. I briefly wondered if he had a family. He looked to be in good health and was somewhat attractive for an older gentleman. I wondered what his story was and what was keeping him here. I nodded at him as he ushered us out of the room.

We took the elevator back down to the service area and exited through the service exit out the back of the hotel. Again, we didn't see any other employees. I had to say goodbye to Brody at the back door because we couldn't possibly enter the zoo together. If the Agency had surveillance set up, which they would, then they would recognize the boys.

A town car with tinted windows pulled up by the service area. It wasn't exactly a private exit, but considering we were in the city, it was as private as things would be. The car was very nondescript, and it was nice and clean. I rode silently in the back, buckled in behind the passenger seat so I could see the driver.

I didn't know the driver, which made me nervous. If the driver was a mole for the Agency, he could easily whisk me away and take me back to them, but he seemed unaware who I even was. He didn't look at me awkwardly; in fact, he didn't make eye contact at all. He could be a regular driver.

When we arrived at the zoo, the driver didn't park in the lot, but pulled up to the entrance and let me out. He was not going to be waiting for me.

I walked into the Lincoln Park Zoo and let my hair down around my face, which was silly because there was no way anyone knew I wasn't who I seemed to be. Still, I felt like everyone was looking at me and that they knew I was masquerading as this woman. I felt like she didn't fit. I didn't know how to act in her body or even how to walk.

I looked around, trying to remember the map of the zoo. I only had to walk a short way to get to the Primate House. From there, I went to the Park Place Café and entered through the main doors. It was still pretty empty in the building, and the lines for the eateries were short. I looked for the restroom sign, and when I spotted the ladies', I was relieved to see the "Sorry, Closed for Cleaning" sign out front.

I walked slowly, looking around to see if anyone was watching me. If someone had to go to the bathroom badly enough, they might follow me in if they saw me go. When no one seemed to be paying attention to me, I slipped inside the door, not even opening it all the way. Inside, Aaron stood near the door. He was wearing a long sleeve green shirt and khaki pants, and tufts of blond hair peered out from beneath his green hat. He saluted me.

"Ready?" he asked. He looked as nervous as I did. "Here goes, Meda." He reached out his fist. I stared at it for a moment and then reached out and tapped my own fist to his. Aaron gave me a tight smile and slipped out the door.

Outside, Aaron would be finding my dad and signaling him. My dad would then tell my stepmother we would be leaving soon and that it would be best to go the bathroom. If everything was going as planned, he had already taken the girls to the bathroom while he had Beth get a soda for him, which he shared with her. I already knew Beth did most things he told her to, so she would probably go to the bathroom. My dad had to make sure of it.

Aaron would remove the sign once he signaled my dad. Shortly after, my stepmother should enter. In the meantime, I had to wait patiently. The bathroom was a hospital scrub green, and it was damp and cold. It smelled like pee with undertones of bleach.

I jumped when Brody slipped silently through the door, which immediately alarmed me. This wasn't part of the plan.

"What's wrong?" I whispered.

"Nothing, nothing." Brody stepped quickly in front of me and reached out and gripped my hand, which was sweaty with nervousness.

"What are you doing?" I asked. I was touched he came to check on me but also afraid he would ruin the entire plan. "Brody, you shouldn't be here." My hands were shaking. I looked down at our hands, grasped together. "God, I'm nervous."

"Hey." Brody waited for my eyes to reach his face. "Soon you will be with your family. No worries. I got this end." He squeezed. I tried to smile, but it was forced. I was anxious. There was nothing he could do that would help that. Then, Brody left me alone to wait for my stepmother.

Chapter 18

I stood at the mirror, ready to pretend to be washing my hands, and though Aaron was going to remove the sign, I thought about what would happen if someone came in when I was cuffing my stepmother. I reached into my pocket and checked to make sure the shiny shackles were still there. I also checked my face again to make sure I looked nothing like myself. As I was staring at my green eyes and trying to remember if this woman had green eyes, the door opened.

I quickly hit the water and stuck my hands in. I glanced up, like anyone would, and there she was. She was a small woman, and I don't know how I hadn't noticed what a bitchy face she had before. Maybe she only looked that horrible when she let her guard down. Or maybe it was because I knew what she had done to my family. Her eyebrows sat on her forehead at an angry slant.

She glanced at me but didn't register any familiarity. Of course she wouldn't. Then she went into the stall. I went to the door, opened it, and then let it close so she would think I left. Once it was closed, I quietly locked it.

I stood by the door, trying not to breathe. And though it wasn't in the plan, I began to shift. I wanted her to see my face. I wanted her to see me before I took on her form. My skin began to itch and burn with the familiar pain.

When the stall door opened, she stepped out without looking up and walked up to the sink. I took one step, and with that tentative movement, she spotted me. She froze. She stared at me for a moment, like she was trying to place who I was, like she didn't ruin my life. Then her eyebrows went up.

"Meda?" she questioned. I didn't let her say anything else. I rushed at her and brought my elbow up, hitting her hard in the nose. She tried to back away, but she was forced up against the wall. She let out a grunt as she crumpled and held her face. I used that moment to attach the handcuff to her right wrist and then pulled her to the handicapped stall where I looped the cuff around and locked it on her other wrist, securing her to the wheelchair rail.

"What the hell are you doing?" she asked, regaining her voice. She hadn't expected me to attack. I pulled out the duct tape that had been tucked under my loose-fitting shirt and held up a strip for her to see.

"Meda, what are you doing? Where have you been this whole time? I've missed you so much." I paused to look at her.

"Oh, stop it, Beth." Then, without thinking, I grabbed her face, hard. "I know who you are. I know what you did to me. To my family."

She tried shaking my hand off her face. "I don't know what you're talking about. We've missed you. We thought you ran away." I felt a rage like never before. I wanted to hit her. I wanted to smash her stupid face in. I still had the strip of duct tape in one hand, and all I had to do was put it over her mouth. I knew I was taking too long, but her words left me unsure, frazzled.

"Why, Beth?" I took my hand off her face. "Why did you do it?" Beth looked confused.

"I don't know what you're...Meda. What's wrong with you?" I punched the stall wall next to her head, then firmly put the tape across her mouth. I would never know. I would never know if she did it because it was her job or if she did it because the Agency had something on her, like they did with me.

"You know what, Beth? I don't care. I'm taking my family back," I said. She struggled, but the cuffs didn't give her much room to work with, and I roughly continued to wrap the roll of tape around her head, covering her mouth multiple times. The tape was tangled in her hair and so tight her cheeks puffed out on either side of where the tape stuck to her skin.

I shifted again. This time into her. She looked shocked, and she tried to talk through the tape, but obviously could not. "What, nothing to say this time?" I was being childish, I knew it, and I should have been in a rush to be reunited with my family, but there was so much I wanted to say and do to her. I took a deep breath and grabbed the purse she dropped when I hit her. I walked to the door, unlocked it, and took a deep breath. I didn't look back when I left.

When I exited the bathroom, the cleaning sign was back in front of the door. They had replaced it when Beth entered. I slid out, but it didn't matter as much this time because Beth had entered and now it was Beth who was exiting the bathroom.

I took a few steps out the door and saw Aaron. I gave him a thumbs-up sign, and he saluted me with the bill of his cap and quickly walked out the side door. He would be letting the driver know we were ready, and Aaron and Brody would be departing in a separate vehicle that we would meet up with back at the suite.

I exited Park Place and scanned the faces walking around the zoo. I saw families and field trips and sometimes adults just walking, blissfully unaware I wasn't even what I seemed to be. And then I spotted him. My dad.

When I saw him, I almost ran to him. I almost called him Daddy and let tears fall down my face. I almost grabbed both of my sisters and planted hard kisses on their cheeks. Almost. But instead, I kept my composure. I walked slower than normal, making my way towards them. When he spotted me, I saw his eyes dart to my ears to be sure I was not Beth. When he saw them, his eyes rested on me, and I could tell he was fighting the same urge to run to me.

As I approached them, I got close to my father. He reached out and gripped my hand, and the moment our hands touched, I saw tears in his eyes. I looked away because I didn't want to cry along with him. As I scanned the crowd, I noticed a young girl standing by a bench. She was all alone and looked like she was waiting for someone, but she kept looking our way. It appeared as though she was watching us, but she had sunglasses on, so I couldn't be sure where she was looking. It was unsettling, and my hair stood up on my arms.

I knew I was staring, and I tried to look away, but I couldn't. Then, the girl pulled down her shades and winked.

It was Isi, the other mimic. I knew it. She stood empty-handed, arms dangling at her sides, but a smile crept up her face. If she had disguised herself, I would never have recognized her, unless she wanted me to. I scanned the crowd and didn't see anyone coming at us or anyone else who looked suspicious. When I glanced back, Isi had taken a few steps toward us.

"Dad," I whispered out of the corner of my mouth. "We have to go now." My dad looked at me with concern, but he nodded anyway, even though he didn't know the full story.

Dad patted the girls on the shoulders. They had paid no attention to me when I rejoined them because to them, I was boring old Beth. "Come on, girls," my dad called to my sisters. I wanted to pick them up and hug them or even run with them to get them out of there, but they had to remain calm. They couldn't know yet that this was a reunion. They couldn't alert anyone to the fact I was with them, even though there was one person who was already onto us.

As we made our way through the crowd, I continued to glance back. Isi didn't shift, but she continued to trail us. Why didn't she attack? She must have been under orders because she walked casually about fifteen feet behind us. "We're being followed," I whispered. Dad was smart enough not to turn around. Instead, he crouched and whispered something to one of the girls.

"Race you to the car!" Ginger, the youngest of the twins, yelled. Both girls took off.

Dad looked at me and smiled. He began to jog after the girls. "Girls!" he called out, getting in on the pretense. "Wait up!" I followed and jogged behind.

We weaved through the crowd, my sisters giggling and looking back. I tried to keep the stern face of my stepmother in place, but I knew worry crept through. We kept a slow jog so as not to draw too much attention. To anyone else, my father and I would look like two parents who were chasing after their children.

When we got to the road, the town car I arrived in hadn't reappeared. I scanned the area for the getaway car, but there was no car for us. Dad pulled the girls to him, and they looked up at him.

"Dad?" Ginger asked. "What are you looking for?" The Opposition's driver was supposed to be there, but there was no one. I started to breathe heavily as my dad looked at me. He didn't look as worried as I felt, but I also wasn't sure if he understood the true seriousness of the situation and how far-reaching the Agency was.

I looked back and saw Isi approaching from fifteen feet away with one hand in the pocket of her oversized jacket. She could easily be hiding a gun there. Then, I heard the acceleration of a vehicle, and as I turned, a black, nondescript sedan skidded to a halt in front of us.

The passenger-side window was down, and Dan was behind the

wheel. I looked at him questioningly. Dan was supposed to be the back-up. He shouldn't even be here. "Get in. Something's wrong." I didn't have time to question.

"Get in the front, Dad!" I called out as I opened the back door and shoved first Ginger and then Georgia into the back of the car. They both yelled out in surprise and were about to complain, as any kid nearing tweenhood would, but then a gunshot went off.

I tried to make myself smaller as I shoved the girls across the seat and climbed in behind them. My dad clumsily clambered into the front seat. The girls screamed, sensing the change in atmosphere. More shots went off. "Go!" I yelled helplessly from the back seat as Dan smashed his foot down on the gas pedal.

As the car jolted, I looked back out the window. Isi stood next to someone else, a young man who was in a shooter stance and firing shots off at the vehicle. Isi had her hand on his arm, and it looked as if she was trying to get him to lower the gun. People nearby were all lying facedown on the ground or huddled away. I was surprised it wasn't Isi who had taken the shot. As I squinted, I felt there was something familiar about the young man who was shooting.

The man looked like he was going to shoot again, but before I was able to duck, I saw something change, and it was so brief, I couldn't even be sure it was real. Maybe my overstressed mind was playing tricks on me, but from what I had seen, the man's face shifted to resemble the face of my mother. My real mother.

Suddenly, Dan jerked the wheel violently to the right and made his way down a side street, out of the line of fire. The girls were hugging each other, and I wrapped my arms around them, forgetting that they didn't see me, they only saw our stepmother.

I looked up and saw my dad reach over and put his hand on Dan's side. He brought his hand away and held it up, the slick, red blood bright in the dull interior of the car. "You're hit." He put his hand back, applying pressure to Dan's bleeding torso.

I gripped the girls tightly but tried to get a look at Dan's injury. "Dan," I called. "Dan, are you okay?" But he was quiet and continued to drive.

As Dan made his way to an intersection, the yellow light turned red just as we approached it. "Dan!" I yelled, unsure if he saw it. I looked up to see a white van quickly approaching from the right. I closed my eyes and waited for impact, gripping the girls tightly.

The white van slammed us hard, but I couldn't help but think it didn't feel like it looked in the movies. As the back end of the vehicle fishtailed and spun, I jostled around in the back seat, still holding my sisters in my arms. Dan didn't miss a beat as he hit the gas and we rocketed away from the van, which now had a dented hood.

"Hey," Dad called out, moving over to grip the wheel. I pulled myself closer to the front seat so I could see the side of Dan's face. His eyes looked unfocused and far away.

"Dan, are you okay?" I let go of Ginger and reached forward to grab Dan's shoulder. "Dan?"

He turned to look at me as my dad steered for him. He looked confused at first, then said, "Take that off." He sounded drunk. I removed my hand from his shoulder. "No, Meda." Dan shook his head. "Take that face off. I don't like it." He turned and tried to focus on the road with the help of my dad.

'I…" I tried to speak, but I didn't know what to say. My sisters looked up at me.

"Beth? Why did that man call you Meda?" Ginger asked between sobs. "What's going on?" She put her head down and cried. I wanted to change right then and there, for Dan and for them, but I didn't want my sisters to see and to know things they shouldn't, so I held them and let them keep thinking I was their stepmother, who was probably currently wondering where her family had gone.

Dan didn't look back again. My dad kept up a steady stream of encouragement, letting Dan know he was doing good and he was going to be okay. He had no idea where we were going, so he continually coaxed Dan to give him directions while reminding him to apply more gas or brake.

I saw the high-rise as we approached the hotel. "We're almost there, Dan," I called. I wanted to encourage him as well. I wanted to do anything I could to help him, but there was nothing I could do.

We clumsily pulled into the limited access area we departed from earlier, and I thought we were going to smash into the team of men waiting at the service doors. In a rush, the men came forward to help usher the group upstairs. As the back doors opened, I helped Ginger and Georgia out and told them to go with the men. Ginger put up a little fight, but in the end, she went when the man grabbed her hand and led her away. I got out and stood by as they pulled Dan out of the car.

Dan couldn't stand on his own, and there was blood all over the front of his shirt, soaking through the stomach area. I also noticed blood on the side of his face as though he had casually rubbed it after trying to stop his own bleeding.

I turned when I heard a commotion at the doors. Aaron came running out and was immediately at Dan's side, pushing one of the other men away. "What happened?" he yelled, looking at me.

"They knew we were there. There's a third mimic." I wanted to try to explain my mother, but I saw Aaron looking at me like it was all my fault. I continued, "They took a few shots as we were leaving, and he must have been hit then." My dad came by my side. I had barely noticed him.

"I'm a doctor." Another man stepped forward. "Help me get him inside." Aaron held one side of Dan, who was dragging his feet and leaving a trail of blood. His pale face was slack.

"You're going to be okay, man," Aaron said as they ushered Dan through the doors. As the door closed, I could see a flash of Brody, trying to help grab Dan.

I walked numbly behind. My father wrapped his arm around my shoulder. They took Aaron and Dan one way, but we were led a different direction. "I want to go with them," I said, but I lacked conviction. If they didn't need me, it wasn't necessary I go. I didn't want to be in the way.

"Your family needs you," the man directing us said and nodded at my dad, who looked scared and confused. We were led to the elevator that took us to our suite. I shifted back to myself in the elevator. My dad noticed my shifting but did not let go of me.

We made it through security, and as the door slid open, Ginger was the first one to start crying. She was shaking. I was surprised. I wasn't sure she'd even remember me. I reached out to her, and she ran to me and threw herself at me. I crouched to catch her. Her arms gripped me tightly around the neck as she sobbed in my ear, and my breath caught. I tried to pull back so I could look at her, but she wouldn't let go. "Ginger, Gingy, it's okay," I said, choking on the words. Tears started spilling around my face, and I felt another tiny set of arms reach around me. "Georgia." I looked up and grasped my sister's arm.

I held them for a while, feeling their warmth and their tears of happiness. Then I looked up at my father, and I crumbled. My father, who was stronger than most men, was crouched down in tears, as if the sight of his daughters in such an embrace had broken him. It occurred to me that I could go away with them. That we could run, hide out somewhere. The Opposition might help us. Just then, I had the chance to feel a moment of hope before it all came crashing down.

Chapter 19

Men were stationed by the door, and with no sign of Brody or Aaron, I quickly went to change into some different clothes. I found an oversized sweater and some stretchy jeans. The temperature had dropped, or maybe it was just me.

When I re-entered the living room, my father and sisters sat comfortably on the couch. They were playing a board game that had materialized out of one of the closets. I made eye contact with my dad, and he could see I was worried, so he kept my sisters distracted.

I paced nervously, waiting to hear about Dan. He was bleeding badly, but it couldn't have been that bad because he had been talking, right? I wasn't sure if I was being honest with myself. I was on edge, and when the elevator opened, we all turned, alert. The men at the door stepped forward to cover the entrance, but it was Brody who entered the room.

I held my breath when I saw his face. His eyes were red around the edges, and he had blood on his shirt. He didn't make eye contact right away. I froze, waiting for some response, some confirmation of what I was already dreading to be true.

Then he looked at me, and I saw the pain in his eyes. I still didn't want to believe it, so I moved towards him. I wanted to hear him say it. I knew I was being cruel, but I couldn't believe it until he said it.

"What is it, Brody?" I noticed he had a drop of blood on his neck. I searched his eyes, back and forth, willing him to lie to me. "Is Dan okay?" Finally, his head made one sharp movement to the right, and tears broke loose down his face.

I couldn't breathe. The vast room suddenly felt claustrophobic. I was going to be sick. I grabbed my stomach and ran to the bathroom, wanting to get away, and as I leaned over the toilet, I let loose all I'd eaten.

"Meda?" my dad called at the door. I couldn't respond. I dropped my face in my hands and began to sob. It was all my fault. Dan was the only one who had never fit into the equation. He was too innocent. Forced into these events because of what I had indirectly done to Aaron's family. I pictured what his life would have been. He probably would have worked at a garage, married young, had two children. He would have been content with that. But now?

"Meda?" It was Brody's voice. I didn't want to face him. He would say it wasn't my fault, but how could he deny it? He should resent me. He should be mad at me. Then I thought of Aaron. Aaron had every reason in the world to hate me, and now he had one more. "Meda, open the door," Brody said firmly.

I couldn't disobey, not after all he had done for me. I pushed my hair back and smoothed my clothing down. As I slowly opened the door, Brody stood, emotionless. My dad stood further down the hallway, looking over Brody's shoulder to see if I was okay.

"Brody, I'm so sorry," I finally said, my voice shaking. I didn't step forward. I wasn't sure if he was angry with me, and then I saw it. In his eyes.

"Smith wants to see you."

I studied him. "I'm sorry about Dan." I had to make him hear me. He had to know.

"Would you quit being sorry and just do something." I barely heard what he said, and it took a moment for his words to register. He seemed cold.

"Brody, what do you…"

"Just stop, Meda. Stop talking and just…do what you're supposed to do. You aren't helpless." I didn't know what he meant. His words were sharp, jabbing. This was a side of Brody I'd never seen. My stomach was boiling, but I followed Brody anyway. I owed it to him. I owed my life to him.

Everyone was on alert, even though my sisters seemed unaware of what was going on. After seeing I was okay, my father had settled back down with them. Men were talking into radios. It occurred to me that none of us were safe now, because any one of us could have been followed back to the hotel. There were traitors everywhere, possibly on both sides. No side could be trusted, the Opposition or the Agency. Isn't that what Dan told me?

I once again returned to the office behind the oak door. Smith was not as calm as he had been at our last meeting. I took a seat across the desk from him. Brody sat down in the seat next to me but didn't look at me. I tried to pretend everything was okay between us. I wondered where Aaron was. What he was doing at the moment? He hadn't returned to the suite.

Smith spoke. "Now that your family is secured, we will get them to a safe house and provide new identities for them. They will have someone from the Opposition watching over them." I thought back to what Dan had said about the three types of people in the Opposition and wondered who would be in charge of making sure my family was safe. "What we need in return is your help." I eyed him suspiciously. I stayed quiet, so he continued. "We have a mission for you."

"So soon?" I blurted out. I couldn't help it. "But Dan..." my voice trailed off. I didn't look at Brody. I couldn't help but feel trapped. Yes, the Opposition had done a lot for me, but after what happened with Dan and how wrong this all had gone, couldn't we take a breath? Couldn't we be human for a minute?

I started to get the feeling I'd traded one cage for another. Yes, they would keep my family safe, but I still wouldn't be able to see them. I was trapped. I felt the walls closing in. I would never be free. No one would ever leave me alone. Even when all of this was over, one side would want me on their team.

I looked at Brody, sitting stiffly in his chair. He glanced at me. He seemed sad, but I felt that this time it was pity for me rather than the loss of Dan. In that moment, I knew I would do whatever Smith said, for Brody, and Aaron, and for Dan. Not because I wanted to.

"You're going to need to help us stop the mimic. They already have their plan in place, and you've seen what she's capable of."

"Which one?" I asked. Smith looked at me. I began to tell him about the young man who was with Isi. The young man who had shifted at the last minute to reveal my mother's face. Smith cut me off.

"The Agency has a plan to either take over the President, much like their previous plan, or initiate a public assassination. Either way, our President will be dead. The only person who can get as close as we need without being detected is the First Lady."

I wanted to ask again about my mother, but when Smith mentioned the First Lady, he had my full attention. The Opposition, thus far, had seemed to be a reactionary group. The fact that they were going to send me out on a mission, a mission much like one the Agency would have set up, took me by surprise. I was hesitant. "So, what do you need me to do?"

"The mimic will be in place. Either as the President or the

President's security. We need you to kill her." Smith closed his hands on the desk in front of him.

I tried to speak, but my voice cracked. "But I don't kill people. That wasn't my job." I lifted my palms up, feeling helpless.

"Well, you're going to need to. You are the only one who can surprise her, and they would not expect it from you. We wouldn't normally have the power or resources to put a plan like this in place, but with you, it's our only chance." Smith leaned forward across the desk.

I planted my palms on the desk, forcefully. "There has got to be a better way. How do you know when she'll be placed? How will I know who she is?" I had a million questions running through my head. Questions that I wasn't sure they had thought of. They weren't in the business of planting mimics in assignments the way the Agency was.

"We have watched you, Meda. Your strength is that you are observant. You see everything. She doesn't. She destroys everything. You should be able to identify her before she can identify you. The Agency won't be expecting you."

I shook my head. "But why wouldn't they deviate from the plan? They know we know it."

"Now is a critical time for our nation. I will tell you something few people know." Smith crossed his arms. "The Agency tried every possible way to compromise the President. He was unshakeable, which is good for our country, but bad for them. There was no way for the Agency to manipulate the changes they need." He leaned back again.

"But what exactly is the Agency?" I finally asked the real question I'd been wondering about. "What kind of changes do they need?"

"Meda, the Agency is funded largely by other countries." He looked at me expectantly.

I furrowed my eyebrows. "I'm not sure what you mean."

"Terrorism. The Agency wants the President to authorize certain events so that there is some kind of crisis." He said it so plainly, like it was something I should have considered. But I was stunned. I hadn't thought of how large the chain of events really was. Had I still been in place, I would have been the one signing off on the papers they needed in order to get the results they wanted.

"By why would the Agency work with other countries?" I was still trying to wrap my head around how big this was.

"Other countries and terrorists pay well, which is why we, the Opposition, have never had the resources for an effective counterattack. Luckily for us, there are some people in place now at the Agency who don't believe in their end game. Not enough though. The members of the Agency know they will be protected during whatever crisis comes about."

Again, I was shocked. I looked at Brody, who stared at Smith. He didn't outwardly look surprised, but I could tell much of this information was new to him.

The three of us jumped when a sudden, shrill beep came from Smith's phone, which was sitting on his desk. He lifted it to his ear and gave quick directions, then pulled it away. "We have a security breach. They must have followed someone back."

Chapter 20

I jumped out of my chair. This was a massive building with many floors. I wasn't sure what "security breach" even meant. Did it mean they entered the building? Was the intruder on our floor? I felt trapped. I wanted to be out by my dad and sisters. I just got them back, and I didn't want to lose them again.

Smith had the phone back at his ear. "Take the family down in the elevator to the second floor, then use the employee staircase out." I moved to walk out the door, but Smith stood in front of me. "You are not going with them. We are evacuating them to a secure location, but you need to stay with us. You'll only be a danger to them."

"At least let me say goodbye." I was firm about this, but Smith shook his head. I turned to Brody.

It was clear he had no say in this and was as confused as I was. "They'll be fine," he said, trying to calm me.

Smith cut in. "They'll be safer if they aren't around you. The Agency is after you, Meda. They're trying to recover a stolen asset." He said this with no regard for my feelings, but that was to be expected. I knew he was right, but that didn't stop me from being angry. Smith turned from me. "Brody, I need you to check the perimeter and bring back security detail." Brody looked at me, nodded, and walked out the door.

"So, what are we going to do? Sit here and hide? Wait around until the mimic busts in?" I impatiently sighed as Smith listened into his phone. Minutes passed, and he didn't say a word to me. I could hear movement outside the door but still didn't know what kind of security breach we were talking about and how much danger we were in.

Finally, Smith spoke. "Okay, we're clear." As he said those words, two men in suits came in. They both had guns. When they opened the door, I glimpsed some of the chaos outside the room. Three men moved quickly down the hallway and another was stationed right outside the door. These were men I hadn't seen before, though it made sense that if this was Opposition Headquarters, there would be Opposition agents on other floors.

"Security has been breached on the upper levels," one of the men said to Smith who, in turn, saw the look on my face. He said to me, "Your family made it to the safe car." I sighed with relief.

Suddenly, there were gunshots.

Smith gripped my arm, and the two men in suits placed themselves in front of me. "We have you covered," one of the men said, and he plunged out the door. Smith pushed me from behind, and we moved the short way down the hallway, paused to search the living area, and then moved forward.

I looked over to the window where, not long ago, Brody, Aaron, Dan, and I put our heads against the glass and looked down. The room was still as bright and cheery as it had been then. I scanned the room for Brody, but I couldn't see anything right away. I couldn't see any danger either, but then I noticed a group of men surrounding the door by the elevator.

One of the men who stood in front of me spoke to Smith. "The intruder has not gained access." It had to be the mimic or mimics.

Even though there were secondary security procedures to guard against mimics, I was positive the Agency could easily find their way around those guards.

Shots went off again. They were muffled but were still deafening when they hit the door. The men that came out of the office with me placed themselves in front of me. Smith stepped around me, talking in low tones with the men. The intruder must be pinned down. Not able to enter and not able to go back down. It seemed like a stupid plan, breaking in here. Obviously, they didn't intend to get caught, but what was the back-up? There always was a back-up plan. What did they expect to accomplish? Maybe they hadn't realized how heavily armed the Opposition was.

Brody came up from behind me. The men in suits were too busy to notice. I looked around, wondering where he had come from. "Quick, we have to go. No questions." I was confused. There was nowhere else to go. Smith had it covered.

He pulled me backwards, down the long hallway, and towards the rooms. The men didn't see us leave. More shots fired in quicker succession, and the men pressed forward and knelt, ready to shoot if anyone broke through the entryway door.

I bumped into the wall and knocked a piece of artwork loose, then turned to watch where Brody was leading me. Then I remembered. The roof.

"Brody, is this a good idea?" I asked, but he didn't answer. He kept moving towards the back stairwell. It seemed unsafe. Did the Opposition have the back stairwell covered? They had to. They'd be stupid not to.

Brody pulled me through the exit door and into the stairwell, then stopped a moment. There were no lights in the stairwell. I remembered the last time we were here, there were security lights.

They weren't on now, but I could hear people a couple of flights down that sounded like agents, barking orders. They were probably making sure no one made it up the staircase the back way.

Brody didn't go any further. He pushed me up against the wall and shined a flashlight in my eyes. I didn't even see that he was carrying a flashlight. The brightness took me by surprise.

"What the...?" I held up my hand, trying to shield myself. He pulled the flashlight away so I could open my eyes again, then shined the light on his own face. I had a hard time seeing because there were still spots in my eyes, but I noticed his pupils didn't change with the light. "What are you doing, Brody?"

"I needed you to see, Meda. I'm not Brody." I immediately struggled to get free, but he had me pinned. I was about to yell out when he put his finger to my mouth to silence me. It took me by surprise, but not as much as his next words.

"Meda. I'm your mother."

I didn't react. I didn't know how. She shifted, faster than I could. When I saw her face, my mouth fell open.

"I need to talk to you," she said.

"I...I..." I struggled for words. "How do I know it's you?" I knew I shouldn't trust anyone, but I wanted to believe.

"Your favorite movie growing up was *Beauty and the Beast*. You made us watch it a million times." I stared at her. Anyone could know that. My dad could have told anyone that. "And the last thing I said to you the last time I saw you was that you would always be my girl." She studied me, trying to gauge my reaction. "Do you remember that? You will always be my girl."

"But how? What are you doing here?"

"I'm Plan B. Your assignment. I've always been Plan B."

"Wait, what are you talking about?" She let go of me and took a step back. She still gripped the flashlight in her hand but covered it with her other hand to give the illusion that we were alone in the dim stairwell. I could still hear people talking below and the crackle of their radios.

"I know you know about Plan B. That's me." She gestured to herself.

I shook my head in disbelief. "You're the assassin? But what about Isi?" My mother's eyes grew wider, as though she knew no one at the Agency would ever have mentioned her to me. As though I wasn't supposed to know her name.

"We don't have much time. I told them you'd do the original mission. I convinced them you could offer them subtlety."

"Them? What do you mean, them?" I asked.

"The Agency. I work for the Agency. They took me just as they took you. I convinced them they needed you for this mission so no one had to die, and they bought it." Shadows in the dark emphasized my mother's sharp cheekbones, and her eyes seemed to glow as she talked. "But now you're out, you can't go back. They don't trust you. We need to get you out of here. Hide you. I'll take care of the job. You can't try to stop the mission. This is your one chance to get out. I'm warning you." Her voice was piercing and urgent. She wasn't happy to see me. I hadn't seen her since I was ten, and now here she was, threatening me. It was like I wasn't her daughter at all.

"Mom, you can't do it. You can't kill the President," I said incredulously.

"Honey, it's going to happen." She said it without a shadow of a doubt. "If I do it, your father and sisters remain safe."

"They're safe." I was surprised she didn't know. "We got them. They're going somewhere safe as we speak."

She studied me. "So, they're not here?" I shook my head.

"Whatever. They let you believe what you want to believe. Do you trust the Opposition?" I thought about what Dan had said. When I didn't answer, she continued. "I taught you to be smarter than that. What I'm going to do is for you and them. If I do this last job, I stay in the Agency, prove my loyalty, but they let you live a normal life." She flicked off the flashlight and put it in the back pocket of her jeans, now baggy from shrinking down from Brody's frame.

I stepped forward. "Do you really believe that? I'm starting to think they'll never let us go."

"Meda, it is the only hope I hold onto. Anyway, what I'm doing right now is for you. Once I leave here, you will find they have Isi. When they transfer you to a new location, make sure you are in the same vehicle as her. And try to make sure there is no one else." She took a step towards the edge of the stairs. It sounded like someone was walking up.

I looked at my mother, confused. "But why?"

She continued, this time in a hurried whisper. "I can't guarantee that anyone besides you and Isi will make it out of the vehicle alive. This is our one chance to get you out of the Agency, the Opposition, everything. If you trust me, you'll do what I say." I wanted to speak, but my mom leaned in and kissed my forehead. "I have to go. Don't try to stop it, Meda. Remember, I can't help what happens to you if you do." I watched her shift back into Brody's form.

She walked to the end of the landing, turned and gave me a look, and then started down the stairs. She was smart. She was going to get through the men by pretending to be Brody. Just as she disappeared down the steps, the door to the suite flew open and banged against the wall of the stairwell. Brody stood in the doorway.

"Meda, what the hell are you doing out here?" He looked towards the steps and then back to me. "Smith said you were with them, and then he turned, and you were gone. We searched all the bedrooms because we thought you were hiding."

"Sorry. I panicked. The guns." Brody knew I didn't like guns, but I didn't tell him about my mother. Everything was moving quickly, and I didn't think he would understand, not after what happened to Dan.

"It's over. We got her." He studied my face. "We got Isi. The mimic who killed Dan."

It was like my mother had said. Brody grabbed me roughly by the hand and led me into the suite. He had no way of knowing Isi wanted to be caught. I didn't say anything and let Brody lead me back down the hallway.

When we walked into the living room, I was surprised by how quiet everyone was. They had Isi on the wide space of carpeting between the couch and the flat screen. She was on her stomach, hands cuffed behind her back, with a baggy suit hanging off her frame. She had been someone else when she entered, but with the cuffs, she was now forced to wear her own face. She watched me as I moved across the room. Her face gave away no hint of emotion.

The eight men who were in the room with Smith turned and watched me walk over to Isi. Smith stood near her.

I stood directly in front of Smith and asked quietly, "Can I speak with her?" He seemed uncertain. "Please. I'll do whatever you need me to do, but I need to speak with her." He gave me one stiff nod.

The men stood back, and Brody stayed back as well. I moved to kneel in front of her, and Brody gently called my name, but I motioned that I was okay.

"Hello, Isi." She didn't respond to me. She continued to stare, so I tried to reason with her. "Isi, you know your life doesn't have to be like this."

Isi spoke stiffly. "Anyone who doesn't do what is best for our country is a traitor."

I let out a forced laugh. "Wait, you think what the Agency does is what's best for our country? You think it's best for our country to kill people?"

Once again, Isi didn't show any emotion on her face. "Well, I learned from the best. Your mother." I heard Brody swallow hard.

I moved in closer and spoke quietly. "My mother is not a killer."

The mimic shook her head. "Your mother taught me everything I know. In fact, I've exceeded your mother at many skills, and I can tell you that she's proud of me." She stuck her chin out at me. It seemed an odd gesture, given the circumstances. I started to sense there was a reason for her animosity towards me.

"How old are you?" I asked.

"Shut up," she said. "I know what you're trying to do, but it won't work on me. I don't have feelings. I never have." I looked at her hands clasped behind her back, the shackles burning her skin, but she did not falter for a moment. Her face remained calm. I stepped away from her so I was standing by Brody once again.

"We need to move out," Smith said to Brody. He nodded. I thought about what my mother said as Smith talked to the agents about what was going to happen. I needed to be in the vehicle with Isi. My mother was planning an escape. She said that people could get hurt. I should tell Brody. I should tell Smith. I couldn't speak. I thought again about what Dan had said about trust, and when Brody placed his hand on my lower back, I flinched.

Chapter 21

We still needed to evacuate the hotel. The men grabbed Isi. I finally saw Aaron again as he entered the suite. We had all moved closer to the door, so Aaron took a few steps to be by Brody's side. He didn't even look at me as he leaned and said something in Brody's ear. Even though I was close by, I couldn't make out what he said. The words my mother said replayed in my head. She told me I couldn't trust the Opposition, but I knew, or at least I thought, I could trust Brody. I didn't know how he would react after losing one of his best friends, someone he knew much longer than me.

We were able to exit the way we came in. They seemed to think there was no more danger after the mimic was captured, but I wasn't so sure. We entered the elevator: Smith, two men carrying Isi, Aaron, Brody, and me. It was a quiet ride down, with only the empty static on the agents' radios.

We exited the elevator as a group and moved to the service door. When they opened the door, I could see other agents outside loading up two vans. Smith motioned to the first van for the agents holding Isi, and Aaron motioned for Brody to walk with him towards the second van. I took a couple of steps behind Brody and then stopped.

I looked at the first van and then back to Brody and Aaron talking by the back doors of the second van. I watched as Brody put his hand on Aaron's shoulder and grasped it. I watched as Aaron brought his hand up to his eyes and shielded them. Then I stopped watching. This was their moment. Not mine. Dan was their friend. Not mine.

I turned and walked back to the first van. Isi was in the back, and Smith was still talking to one of the men. I approached Smith. I was nervous, and I tried to hide it, hoping that he would mistake my sudden inability to look him in the eyes as anxiety left over from the gun fight. "I want to ride with Isi." I looked at her, shackled in the back of the van. She had a hood over her head so she wouldn't be able to see where they were taking her. I was glad. I didn't want to see her judgmental eyes.

Smith cleared his throat, so I looked up at him. "That's not possible, Meda. You're going to a different location."

I maintained eye contact. "After," I said. "I need to talk to her now." Smith stared at me. "I have to find out the plan. Something isn't right about this. I think I can get information out of her." I needed to talk to her. I wanted to know the plan. But I also knew I was lying and that I was putting people in danger.

Smith motioned Brody and Aaron over. They looked confused. Brody looked at me and then back at Smith. "Change of plans," Smith said. "Meda will ride with Van 1 until Checkpoint A, then switch vehicles to continue to Checkpoint F."

Brody stepped forward, looking at me. "Why?"

Smith answered for me. "She's going to try to get intel." Brody gave him a look of concern. "It can't hurt," Smith reassured Brody. My face flushed with shame.

Brody spoke while moving towards the van. "I'll go with you."

"No," I cut him off quickly. Brody froze in surprise. He looked at me, first confused, and then a little hurt, but I remembered my mother's words, and I couldn't let him get hurt.

I stepped towards him, willing myself not to reach up and twist my earring. "I'm going to talk to the mimic. It's better if we're alone. We're...the same," I added.

"No, you're not." Brody shook his head, but Smith put up his hand towards Brody, signaling him to stop.

Smith looked at me. "Meda, are you sure that's a good idea? She is a master of manipulation."

I stood my ground. "Look, I get you have your doubts with me, but there is something I need to know. I will fill you in on everything as soon as it's done." I could tell Smith didn't like deviating from the plan and that Brody didn't want me to be alone with Isi.

Brody sucked in a deep breath as he studied me. For a moment, I thought he could see through everything and that he knew something was up, but then he let out the breath he had been holding. "Let her do it," he said. "If Meda thinks there's something up, there probably is." I couldn't look Brody in the eye. What I was doing felt like betrayal, but wasn't he the one who told me that I had to make my own decisions about what was right? I was surprised when Aaron nodded in agreement. He still didn't make eye contact with me, and I was glad for it.

Smith talked into his phone. "Okay. We'll take separate routes out of the city. We should be able to converge again once we get out of the area. If you see anything suspicious, I mean anything, signal us." He waved me on.

I climbed into the back of the van and moved past the empty middle row to sit in the back next to Isi. "Isi, it's Meda." She didn't respond to me. "What's the plan?" I whispered. "What's going to happen?" As the vehicle took off down the street, I heard Isi let out a huff of breath that sounded like a laugh, but I couldn't see her face, so I took the hood off.

"Ma'am, you can't do that," the man in the passenger seat said as he looked back at me.

"I'll put it back on when we get out of the city." The man studied me, trying to decide if he should go along with it. He nodded and then turned his back on me, facing the road. I shifted my attention back to Isi. She was smiling.

"What is going on, Isi?" I asked, my body facing hers.

"What's going on is that you are in way over your head." She didn't look at me.

"What are you talking about?" I asked.

She shook her head in disbelief. "You know, they told me that you were the most observant of all of us. That I could learn something from you in that field." She finally made eye contact with me. "But what they didn't realize is that you, Meda, can't see things that are too close to you. You can't see the things that you think you already know. Your emotion blinds you."

She was taking pleasure in knowing something I didn't. I stopped speaking, not giving her the satisfaction of asking any more questions. She leaned in, whispering quickly. "You think you know your mother? Your mother is a heartless bitch. Even I know that." Her words came out even faster. "The mother you knew was just an act. That is what she is best at. The only thing that gives her pride is seeing someone practice what she preaches, which is why she took me in. I'm almost as heartless as her, though I don't think even I am heartless enough to pretend to love a child who I didn't even want." She raised her eyebrows.

I clenched my jaw tightly. I knew what she was trying to do, but I couldn't give her the satisfaction. "Go on," I said, calmly.

"She told me about your stupid father, George. About how he tainted you with his softness. About how, when she decided to leave, she originally thought about taking you with, but she knew you were more like George..." she spit the next word at me "...weak. He made you weak."

I couldn't stop myself, and I slapped her across the face. She knew which button to push. She leaned back and straightened up, looking at me, the smile not leaving her face.

The man in the passenger seat turned and looked at us. "Is everything okay back there?" he asked.

"It's fine. We're fine." I watched as he faced the road again.

"Anyway," she chuckled, "she knew your real father, your biological father, would not accept you that way. Personally, I think he would. It's your mother who doesn't accept you." She stopped looking at me and gazed out the windshield, probably trying to track our route out of the city.

I tried to comprehend what she was saying. My biological father. What did she mean? My father was not my real father? I didn't want to betray my thoughts by showing emotion, but I couldn't figure out how these lies would help her in any way. If she was trying to get in my head, why would she use this?

I tried to remain calm and rational. "What do you mean, my biological father?" Suddenly, I heard an engine rev and looked out the back window to see a black Mustang with heavily tinted windows tailgating the van. I immediately knew who was driving the car.

We were out of the city and now hit the freeway where it was easier to navigate. There wasn't a lot of traffic on the road, which also made it easier for the Mustang to maneuver around the other van in our convoy behind us. They probably thought she was just another crazy driver on the road. And now, she was there, and something was about to happen. I saw the driver look in the rearview mirror.

Isi turned and smiled at me, leaning towards me. "You might want to brace yourself, Meda." I heard the Mustang come up alongside us and tried to peer out the window, which left me unprepared when the deafening hammer crash of metal on metal pushed against the side of the van.

I had my seat belt on, but I was still smashed against the side of the vehicle. Isi's body pushed up next to me. She tried to grab the headrest of the seat in front of her, but her grip was unsteadied because of the shackles on her wrists. The driver and the man in the passenger seat were yelling.

The car collided with us again, and once again, Isi was jostled up against me. "Damn it would be nice if you could get these things off me." She looked at me. I didn't respond, so she shrugged. "Hey, third time's the charm." She bent her head down to her knees.

I saw the Mustang veering at us again, and I knew that this was going to be the worst hit. I braced myself between the seats and held on.

The van was rocked again with another collision, but this time I could feel the tires hit the rough gravel on the shoulder of the road. The driver tried righting the turn but struggled with the wheel, forcing the van to veer back and forth. The man in the passenger seat had a gun out. He turned and looked back at us. Then, in a move that wasn't the most intelligent, he unbuckled himself to try to move to the back of the van.

I'm not sure what his plan was, maybe to get closer to the prisoner. Either way, he only made it a few steps before the final impact sent the van toppling off the shoulder and down the embankment.

There was an eerie sense of weightlessness as we tumbled sideways. I could hear the crush of the metal, but the most immediate object was the man, his head bashing on the side of the van and his arms and legs tangling during the van's roll. It felt like we were in a washing machine. His gun clattered around in the vehicle, and I squinted my eyes, imagining the gun going off.

We rolled for what seemed like minutes, but in actuality was only seconds. When the vehicle finally came to a rest at the bottom of the embankment, it felt like my ears were stuffed with cotton. Everything seemed quieter after the blaring noise of the crash. I reached to unfasten my seat belt. Surprisingly, we landed somewhat upright. In movies, people were always dangling upside down in overturned vehicles.

Isi was already unbuckled and moving. "Wait," I called out. Before I could get my seat belt unlatched, there was an earsplitting boom. I flinched and tried to cover my ears. When I looked to the front of the van, I saw the driver's head flop over to the side. My mother was standing in front of the vehicle, gun pointed, glaring through the window she had fired through to kill the driver.

Isi managed to get the keys for her cuffs from the man who was in the passenger seat but was now in a crumpled ball on the floor. I didn't know if he was breathing, and I thought it better that I not check. If he was alive, there was no telling what my mother and Isi would do to him. If he was dead, well, I would have to think about that later.

Once uncuffed, Isi grabbed me by the elbow and pulled me to the front of the van. I let myself be led as we crawled through the passenger-side door. When we got out, I was surprised to see the Mustang in the ditch as well. I assumed it would be our getaway. Instead my mother grabbed me by the arm. "Come on, Meda. We have to hurry." Once again, I went along with everything.

Beyond the embankment, we jogged through the trees, scrambling our way through the patch of wooded area until we were stopped by a fence. I looked back, the highway barely visible. We vaulted over the fence and just over the rise, I saw an old abandoned barn. My mother led the way, I followed, and Isi held up the rear.

I entered the barn, squinting in the dark. I could only make out outlines of old objects. A broken-down tractor that was in pieces. Some old abandoned furniture. Some scary rusty equipment that looked like it should be in a horror movie. I also noticed a large drop cloth that looked like it was protecting a car. Maybe it was our getaway vehicle? I couldn't be sure of anything anymore.

Finally, the weight of what happened hit me, and I was angry. I was angry at my mother, who wasn't even acting like the woman I remembered. I stopped where I was standing. "What is this?" I yelled.

My mother came around behind me and slammed the barn door closed. Isi ignored me, went to the vehicle, and pulled the drop cloth away, revealing a two-seat convertible.

"Isi," my mother barked. I looked at my mom and then at the car. It only had two seats. I realized one of us wasn't going to be getting out of here in that thing.

"I said, what is this?" I directed my words at my mother. After closing the door, my mom walked right by me, heading towards Isi. I would not let her go that easily, so I took a couple of steps towards her and grabbed her by the arm, spinning her around roughly so that she was facing me. What I didn't count on was the gun in her right hand coming down and bashing me across the temple. Everything went a fuzzy shade of red and then black. Then I was out.

Chapter 22

When I came to, I was lying in dirt and dried-out old hay. I looked up, confused. I was on the ground, right where I had dropped after my mother hit me. I reached up and touched the part of my head that burned. My hand came away sticky. Part of the gun must have cut me on the head. My stomach felt weak.

"I'm not doing it." I heard Isi say to my mother.

"God. I knew you were as weak as her."

"That is not why I'm refusing. I'm refusing because Chayton will kill me. This is your vendetta. Your mission. Not mine. But maybe you aren't as unfeeling as you think you are." Isi's voice was cold, as cold as when she was talking to me. I tried to see where they were and made out their blurry shapes a dozen feet away.

My mother laughed, and it was a disgusting laugh. A malicious laugh. She was still talking to Isi. "Don't even try to play head games with me. I taught you those games."

My mother turned from her and walked in long strides over to me. She kicked me in the ribs, and I let out an "oof" that conjured up a cloud of dust. I grabbed my ribs where she hit me, this new pain dulling the pain in my head. I pulled myself up so she wouldn't kick me again.

She leaned down and looked at my head. "Oh, honey, you're

bleeding." She pulled a handkerchief out of her pocket and reached towards me. I pulled away, but just a little. Her voice sounded like it had when I was younger, but her actions were so completely contradictory. She was unstable, unhinged.

My mother tossed the handkerchief at me and turned to the younger mimic. "Keep your gun on her and don't talk to her. I have to make a call." My mother looked down at me one more time and then pulled out her phone, putting in the number as she walked towards the door of the barn and disappeared outside. Isi's eyes never left me.

She looked down at me, her head tilted suspiciously but gun at the ready. "Who at the Agency told you my name?"

I sat in the dirt with the handkerchief to my head. I didn't think it would hurt to tell her now. I wasn't feeling clearheaded. "John told me about you."

"Who's John?" She took a few steps closer, her gun aimed at my head.

I pulled the handkerchief away and looked at the blood. There wasn't a lot of it. I looked back at Isi and stared at the gun she was holding. "One of the security guards." Now, I knew I shouldn't be telling on John, but I wanted her to know I hadn't been alone at the Agency, that I had a friend, well, maybe not a friend, but someone who was kind to me. I'm not sure why it was important. Probably because deep down, even after what my mom did to me, I was jealous.

She looked at me curiously. "You didn't have a security guard named John. I know all your security. There was definitely not a John." I stared at her, wondering why she was lying to me.

She spoke again. "You don't even know who your real father is, do you?" This had to be a trick. "I've met him, you know. Your father," Isi said, smiling. "He wouldn't like what we're doing right now. He wants you alive. It's your mother who wants you dead." She motioned towards the door with her head.

I looked out and saw light coming through the crack in the door. I couldn't see my mother on the other side. "That's a lie." I gave Isi my attention. I had no idea what kind of game she was playing. I couldn't make sense of it. My mind was all jumbled. Memories of times past with my mother rushed through me. Her reading me a book at night, me feeling her belly when she was pregnant with the twins, her, dad, and I going for ice cream.

My mother leaned back in the room for a moment and looked at both of us, probably to make sure Isi still had everything under control. She pulled the phone away from her ear and stared for a couple of seconds, then put the phone back up to her ear. "Yeah?" she asked as she walked back out.

"You're stalling," Isi called after my mother, but she was out of earshot.

I held the handkerchief to my head. "So, this is the plan? To get rid of me? I heard you talking about Chayton earlier. He doesn't want me dead? Who is he?" Isi shrugged. "But it sounded like you're afraid of him, like you're going to be in trouble when he finds out, right?"

"No." She shook her head, grinning. "Because I'm not going to be the one who kills you."

I looked at the crack in the door. "What is to say she won't turn on you? I am her daughter. Her flesh and blood." I looked back to Isi. "Who are you? Some girl that she thought she could use to do her dirty work." I could tell my words stung. Isi put her gun down.

She stammered. "I am more of a daughter to her than you ever were," she said, and for a moment, I felt bad for her. That moment passed when she pointed the gun back at me.

My mother had materialized inside the barn again and was

watching us with a smirk on her face. I was sickened. "Ladies, enough," she called in a sing-song voice. She enjoyed the thought of us fighting over her, only that wasn't all I was doing. I was trying to get Isi on my side. There was something in her that needed my mother, and I was trying to speak to that part of her, to realize it was one-sided. Something that I was still trying to figure out myself.

I slowly rose to my feet and brushed the dirt off my backside. Isi kept her gun on me while my mother watched me. I broke the silence. "Who is my father?" I asked my mother.

"Oh, Isi, you little pot stirrer." She shook her head at Isi, who didn't take her eyes off me. "Well." My mom shrugged. "I guess it won't hurt for you to know now. I'm surprised George never told you this. He was soooo into honesty." She said it like it was a bad thing. "But really, that was what I liked about him. My entire life I had been lied to, and George was the only one who was completely honest. That was how I knew I would be safe. He swore to me that he would take care of you like you were his own. How many men would offer that to a pregnant woman they found on the streets? I knew I would never have to worry about Chayton and that I could disappear in the suburbs. Turns out Chayton was more interested in you than I would have expected." She raised one eyebrow.

"Who is Chayton?" I asked.

"Your real father." She paused.

"No." I shook my head. "You're playing games with me. That's all you do."

"No, Meda. This is no game. This is real, and it's big. Chayton, your father, is one of the original mimics in the Agency and one of the original founders of the Agency. He has powerful friends in high places." She spoke about him like he was a god. "He was the man who first took me in when I was a young homeless girl, having been kicked out of my own house for being different and scary. I was all alone, and he taught me everything I knew about putting on a persona and pretending to be something I wasn't."

"Oh, so he used you like you're using Isi."

"Nice try, honey. That's not going to work on my Isi. She knows better than to fall for mind games." My mother smiled with confidence, but I saw Isi looking at her out of the corner of her eye. "Anyway, how do you think I survived those years pretending to be a mother?" She laughed.

I held my breath, my jaw tightening in anger, then let it out, trying to calm myself. "You couldn't possibly have been pretending. I don't believe it. Dad told me you came back when the Agency found you. You gave him the earrings to give to me." I reached up and twisted the replacement earrings.

"I didn't leave you just those earrings," my mother said sweetly. "I left everything. Not as a gift, but because I didn't want a single trace of that life. Your father, ever the romantic, had this story in his mind about how I valiantly gave myself up for the Agency so they wouldn't come after you."

"But how would he even know about the Agency? You had to tell him something." My mother looked at Isi. Then her eyes shifted back to me.

"Stop trying to find something that isn't there, Meda. That mother you're looking for, that happy little family we had, it was all a lie. But you should know that. You're in the family business of lying. So, you, above everyone, save Isi, should be able to understand that. Your poor father never would. Anyway, you have caused me a lot of trouble, dear. The Agency still wants you, but I will never be free until you are gone. Every time you betray them, I have to make it up to them. They lose their trust in me."

"You are a psycho," I whispered. My mother stepped toward me like she was going to hit me again. Then she turned her head, and I could hear what she heard. The faintest hint of people calling out in the distance. Calling out my name.

"Damn it!" my mother yelled suddenly as the alarm on her phone went off. "She's transmitting."

I wasn't sure what she was talking about, but when my hand went up to twist my earring and I felt the diamond between my fingers, I knew why Brody gave me the earrings. I felt betrayed. Why didn't he tell me? I straightened my face and spoke directly to my mother. "They won't let you out of here if you kill me. You know that, don't you?" My mother looked frustrated. Isi looked relieved.

"Ava," Isi said quietly, trying to coax my mother. "Let's get in the car and go. This was a stupid idea. It was selfish of you. You know what happened the last time you were selfish." My mother shot her a look and then looked at me. "Well, you know. That is why she's here." Isi became firmer. "Come on." She jumped in the driver's seat and turned the key, the engine purring quietly in the vast space of the barn. She waited for my mother.

My mom stared at me, her eyebrows set in a straight line. "I'm serious, Meda. I could have done it. And if you keep messing things up for me, I will. Don't try to stop us. Even knowing that your father wants you will not stop me next time, especially if you get in my way."

Isi stared at me as my mom smoothly slid into the vehicle. Over the hum of the engine, I could hear someone calling my name. My mother aimed her gun at me. I put my hands up. "If I don't make it out of here alive, neither do you," I called out, more to Isi than to my mother. My mother was not rational. Isi at least seemed somewhat loyal to the Agency, or she was motivated by the possible repercussions of what would happen if they did get rid of me.

Isi reached across the car and put her hand on my mother's arm to lower the gun. I turned and ran as soon as the gun was off me, getting low just in case they changed their minds. When I got to the door, I barely slowed as I shoved the door open and it banged against the outside of the barn. I exited out the back, and when my eyes adjusted to the light outside, I could see a figure moving towards me across the back field. Then I saw the gun.

I threw my hands up. "I'm not armed! I'm not armed!" I called. Then I could make out the shapes. It was Smith and a few other agents. Behind them, I saw Brody and Aaron. Brody immediately pushed his way by the men, even though they tried to hold him back, but in that moment, an explosion of wood splinters and dust detonated as my mother and Isi rocketed out of the barn in their car.

The men in the suits crouched immediately into shooter stances, and Brody froze. I looked back in wonder at the blown-out side of the barn and watched as they made their way to the dirt road that led away from us. I expected helicopters and teams of vans to follow them. The Opposition had manpower, but not all-encompassing manpower, like that of the Agency. There were no helicopters. There was no fanfare. No shoot-out. No one to stop the two from driving off. The agents didn't even bother to take the shots. The car was gone in seconds around the bend of the dirt driveway.

Some of the men jogged after the car, and some went to search the barn. Aaron stood watching me from a distance, and Smith took out his phone and started talking to someone on the other end. He then pulled the phone away and watched the screen. Aaron stepped forward and peered over his shoulder. Brody came to me. He hesitated, searching my body for injuries. Looking for signs someone had hurt me.

"I'm fine, Brody," I said. He looked at me, a million questions on the tip of his tongue, but he didn't get the chance to speak.

Smith stepped forward, his phone still in his hand, and Aaron remained at his side. The look on Aaron's face was cold.

Smith's face held no emotion. He wasn't looking at me to see if I was okay. He was looking at me with suspicion. "What happened?" he demanded. Brody turned and looked at Smith, confused by the tone of his voice. When I didn't speak right away, Smith moved towards me aggressively. "What happened?" he asked again.

Brody stepped between us and held his hand up towards Smith. "What's going on, Smith?" he asked while looking at the older man.

Smith turned the screen of his phone so Brody could see. Aaron stayed where he was and watched me. I had no idea what he was looking at, but it didn't look good. I moved in closer so I could see what it was. On the screen was the stairwell of the hotel and Brody and I, but that wasn't Brody. Shit.

The video was brief, but it was clear what had happened. It looked like I went along with the whole thing. They had no way of knowing my mother and Isi wanted to kill me. That I wasn't a traitor to them.

When it was done, Brody stared at me. I could tell he wanted to ask a question, but nothing came out. Then, Smith turned to me. "So, you planned this?" he asked. "You planned a rendezvous with your mother and this mimic? You planned the mimic's escape?"

I shook my head. "No. No. That's not how it happened." I directed my words at Brody. "You have to believe me."

Brody's face clouded over. He opened his mouth but didn't say anything. Smith continued to speak. "You knew your mom was planning something. You knew enough that you needed to be in that vehicle with the mimic. You knew our men might be hurt. And you didn't alert us." He paused, giving me a chance to explain myself.

"Honestly, I didn't know what she wanted." I turned to Brody. "I thought...I thought she was someone different. I can't explain." What I needed was for Brody to believe me, for one person to be on my side, but in that moment, he took a step back.

Smith moved closer now that Brody wasn't between us anymore. "Well, there's no need to explain. It's pretty clear. If you had alerted us to an escape attempt, we would have them both right now. And two of my men wouldn't be dead." I looked to Brody. He wouldn't make eye contact. Neither would Aaron.

"But, I had no idea." I tried to convince them, my eyes prickling, but the look on Aaron's face told me it was useless. I was on my own. Even though I knew it was untrue, I said softly, "There was nothing I could do."

When Aaron heard my words, he finally looked at me. He slowly growled at me, "So, you're going to go with that old line again. Poor, helpless Meda." He spit the words at me. Brody looked down at his feet, and I saw a tear drop off the end of his nose. I started crying. I put my hands over my face, but Aaron's words continued to cut me. "Look at how many people have died because you are so stupid, Meda. What about Dan? He trusted you. People have put their lives on the line for you."

I couldn't say anything. I couldn't defend myself. I waited for Aaron to hit me, but it didn't come. I looked up to see him walking away from me, back towards the vehicle that was parked in the field. Everything in my life had fallen apart, and it only made sense that I had lost the trust of the few people I had left.

I didn't even want to look at Brody. I put my arms out to Smith, trying to fight the tears. "Put the cuffs on me," I said as Smith stared down at my wrists.

"That's not necessary," he said.

"I said put the cuffs on!" I cried out. I still couldn't look at Brody's face, even though I could sense him watching. Smith took the cuffs out of his pocket and put them on my wrists, not too tight. I only looked up once when Brody began walking away. He didn't look back, and I was glad for it. I put my head down and waited for Smith to lead me to wherever I needed to go next. I didn't need to know. I couldn't be trusted. It would be best this way. When I was responsible for making my own decisions, I screwed everything up.

Chapter 23

I stared out the window of the van. I didn't know where we were going, and I didn't care. Maybe I lost the ability to care about anything anymore. Maybe I was dead inside, like my mother. Maybe I had never cared about anyone for real, and I had only convinced myself, like I had taken on a role. Even thoughts of my father and sisters, the ones who had been my motivators throughout the entire ordeal, didn't lift me out of my despair. My entire life was a lie. My parents didn't have this fairytale relationship that I had always thought. My dad took a pregnant, homeless woman in, and she used him. My dad wasn't even my dad. My mom never cared about any of it. My whole life was a lie. I was empty.

After a while, the van stopped, and Smith crawled into the back. "Meda, do you want to say goodbye to your father and sisters? Now is your chance." I shook my head. It was all pointless. There was no one to trust. I was alone. Everything I had known about my family, about everything, was wrong. My entire life I had been lied to. Even my dad lied to me about my mother. I wanted to cry, but I didn't even have that. I couldn't summon any feelings at all.

Smith stared at me a moment like he was going to say something, but then he left me alone, and we continued our journey to who knows where. When we arrived at the location they were transporting me to, Smith crawled into the back of the van again. This time, he said nothing, but he helped me out of the vehicle. Before we exited, he covered my head, though I did glimpse an apologetic look before everything went dark.

We walked for a while, him leading me. I could tell when we entered the building, but I didn't know what kind of building it was. Then we stopped. He took the hood off my head. We were in a small room that was all metallic surfaces except for the bed. There were no windows and only one door with no handle on the inside.

Smith removed the cuffs from my wrists and let my hands fall to my sides. "If you need anything, let us know," he said. "I'm sorry it turned out this way, Meda."

I turned my back on him, and when he left the room, I heard the door lock behind me. I had officially come full circle. The Opposition needed me, so I would be a prisoner like at the Agency, except this time I had no hope.

I knew that outside this room, somewhere in this building, was Brody. And Aaron. And I had failed them both. They trusted me enough to listen to me, and here we were, back at the beginning, only this time I had also wronged Brody. I didn't want to see either of them. Ever again.

I curled up on the bed and thought about what they were going to ask me to do and how, no matter what I did, it would never make things right. They would want me to kill my mother or Isi if I had the chance, and even though I knew they probably wouldn't hesitate, I couldn't do it. I was no murderer, and killing someone could never make things right. I had already tried doing the wrong thing for the right reasons before. That didn't work out so well for me.

Maybe I wouldn't cooperate. Maybe I was done following orders. To be honest, I was done with it all. They could torture me and threaten my family, but the only thing I had left was my own willpower, and I refused to give that up.

Chapter 24

Days went by slowly in my new prison. I refused to eat. I slept most of the time or stared at the wall. When I wasn't sleeping, I alternated between feeling angry and hating everyone and feeling sad and sorry for myself. I didn't want to see or talk to anyone. Smith came in a couple of times, and every time he tried to talk to me, I turned my back on him and faced the wall. He would leave after that. I was glad they didn't send Brody in to try to talk to me, or maybe they did but he refused. I couldn't be sure. Smith never mentioned him or anyone else. They were prepared to give me some time, but I knew eventually they would force me to do what they needed me to do.

Then, one day, the door opened as I sat on my cot with my back against the wall and my knees tucked into my chest. I looked up, expecting Smith, but this time, it was Aaron.

He slowly opened the door and slid in, carrying food and a blank expression. He put the tray on the floor and shoved it towards my bed. "They said you aren't eating anything." I watched him. He didn't show any emotion. I folded my arms tighter around my legs. My clothes were a bit loose. I had lost a few pounds since my arrival, but I didn't respond to him.

"So, this is it." Aaron waved his arms around the tiny room.

"This is what you're going to do now?" He shook his head in disappointment. "You're just going to sit in here and waste away to nothing. Like nothing we did ever mattered?" I bit my lip. I knew what he was trying to do. "Like nothing Dan did ever mattered." He took a few steps toward me. "I always knew you were a coward." His voice was so angry. I looked down and hoped he wouldn't bring up his family too. I hardened myself.

"What about Brody?" he asked, his voice suddenly soft. I still didn't look at him. "Meda, Brody did everything he could to help you. He put all his trust in you, and you failed him. He doesn't deserve this." He turned, looking back at the door, and spoke in barely a whisper. "He never deserved any of this." Aaron was talking about more than what I had done to Brody. He knew, like I did, that Brody was special. He was kind. He was meant to be a leader. He was meant for great things. Not this.

I couldn't take Aaron standing there, trying to make me feel bad. "So what did they send you here to do? Beat me up again?" My cheeks burned red after I said it.

Aaron turned and stared at me, a look of guilt on his face. "I..." he started, as though he was going to try to explain himself, but he stuttered for a moment. "Look. This isn't about me and you. It's about Brody and what you owe him."

I stood up, my anger growing. I didn't want to hear about stupid Brody. I didn't want to look at Aaron's stupid face. I pointed my finger at him. "You know what, Aaron? Brody manipulated me. Just like everyone else in my life. Don't try to make him sound noble. Because he's not."

My hand dropped when Aaron stepped forward so we were nearly nose-to-nose. There would be no one to stop Aaron if he decided to beat the shit out of me. His words were sharp. "Why are you doing this? Why are you lying to yourself?" He laughed bitterly. "You think it will be easier to stomach your betrayal by convincing yourself that everyone has betrayed you. Well, that's a goddamn lie, and you know it. Brody was the only one to ever be completely on your side. To believe in you. I still have no idea why, but he did. So now you're going to turn your back on him? Maybe you are like your mother." Aaron spit on the floor in front of me. "You disgust me." He turned and walked out of the room. The door locked behind him.

I stared at the door for minutes or maybe even an hour. Then I curled back up in my bed. Maybe I was like my mother. I didn't know the next man who came in. He injected me with something and explained that it was some kind of nutrient, but it made me feel woozy. Someone else came in with a stack of books. Someone came in with a newspaper that had a terrible headline on it, probably supposed to elicit some kind of urge to protect my country. I managed to ignore it all.

Then, one day, three men came in. They lifted me from my bed, and I let myself be carried. I was probably hovering at 100 pounds. My hair was limp and greasy. My skin pasty and unhealthy. They carried me down the hallway and passed people who averted their eyes from me.

They brought me to a room and placed me in a chair seated across a sleek black desk from Smith. He even had a nameplate that said Smith. I wondered if maybe that was his real name, and then I wondered what his first name was. Probably something super boring like Jim or Steve. I almost laughed at how my mind went to such trivial things after all that had happened.

In contrast to my shabby appearance and questionable aroma, Smith was impeccably dressed, and he looked like he had gotten a fresh haircut. He didn't seem to have a care in the world. I had no respect for the man. He cleared his throat and folded his hands on the desk.

"Meda, I know this has all been tough on you. I can't imagine how you're feeling right now. And on top of all that, seeing your mother that way?" He paused to see if I would react. "We had our suspicions. Heck, I think your father had his suspicions, but he didn't want to taint the way you remembered your mother. But now that bit of ugliness is over, you need to start prepping for your job. We don't have much time. I'm positive your mother and Isi are doing the same thing at this very moment."

I tried to ignore him. I tried to look at the wall and the generic abstract art that covered it. I tried to look at the floor and its drab gray carpeting, but I knew he was sitting there with his clean hands, waiting for me to agree to do the dirty work for him. When I finally looked at him, I saw him pop a piece of gum in his mouth. I snapped.

I exploded off my chair, leaning forward and knocking his laptop off his desk. When it clattered to the floor, I roared. I stepped quickly to it and stomped down on it. I crushed it beneath my feet. Then, it was like I had forgotten Smith was even there. I tried to get out of the room, but the door was locked. I pulled my arm back and punched the wall as hard as I could, and it felt so good, so I punched it over and over and again, bloodying my knuckles. I was emotionally exhausted, but the rush was exhilarating. I wanted to break and destroy everything. My hands and arms were on fire.

Then, I heard a voice call from behind me. "Meda," Smith said. I turned in his direction. There was an end table near the door with a decorative vase on it. I picked the vase up and cocked my arm back to hurl it at him. He didn't put his arms up to protect himself. He crossed his arms and glowered at me. "I know you probably hate us right now, but this is important."

I moved towards him, lowering the vase. "Why is it so important?"

I heaved my words at him. "I feel like everyone is telling me what I have to do, but no one is telling me why I have to do it." My voice cracked with my last words.

Smith sighed and stood, his arms still crossed. "We don't have to tell you anything. I want you to remember that. But I think it would pay for you to know why because you are an honest and good person."

My face flushed, and for a moment I wanted to hurl the vase at his face. He knew I wasn't honest and good. I knew I wasn't honest and good, and Brody certainly knew I wasn't honest and good. I didn't know why Smith was pushing my buttons. Why did he continue to mess with me?

"What could possibly be that important? You need me to sign some papers? Protect the President? Well, to me, one President is as good as any. The President doesn't really have any power anyway. It's all about resources, and what I've learned is that if you have a mimic on your side, you are unstoppable." I let out a humorless laugh. "So why the hell am I so powerless? Huh?" I moved closer to him. "Why am I so powerless?"

Smith relaxed his arms and held his hands together. He spoke calmly. "Meda, there is something we didn't tell you." He waited to see if I was interested.

"Well, that's shocking." I was still standing by the door, like I wanted to bolt. I felt crazy, like I was going off the deep end, but I didn't care. I took a step back, the vase still dangling from my hand.

"It isn't about signing papers. It's more than that. The President and VP are not popular at this moment because of their response to the war. Their term is up, and they need a big event to respond to help them get re-elected. The Vice President has ties to the Agency, who also makes a habit of conferring with terrorist organizations, but only a certain group knows that; Aaron's family was one of them. Aaron's dad was the Vice President's aide and collected information on him. He suspected him before the first time he was elected and had been watching him."

Smith walked in front of his desk and leaned against it, half-standing and half-sitting. "Anyway, that was how he was turned onto the Agency. He began an investigation to see how the Vice President was getting the support of certain political leaders that wouldn't normally support him. It was through the VP's lobbying and the Agency's help. If someone doesn't want to support you, you make them. The end plan, a nuclear meltdown at one of our own power plants. The Pilgrim Nuclear Power Plant in Plymouth, Massachusetts. They pushed through Pilgrim's extended operating license and made some cuts in some of the regulatory and safety protocols, preparing a setup for failure. From what we hear, they already had a few of their own workers in place, men who don't know that when they follow the directions they're given, they will trigger a nuclear meltdown at the plant."

I was surprised at how horrible people could be for the sake of power, but that didn't make me feel anything. It reminded me how terrible the world was. "So what does this have to do with me?"

Smith continued. "Meda, you have already signed papers and pushed for these steps, lessening regulations at nuclear power plants and overworking and underpaying employees. You have done press releases, made statements, and signed off on various papers."

I pointed my finger at him. "No, you will not pin this on me. You will not make me feel the guilt for what the Agency made me do."

Smith pushed off the desk and stood up. "No. I'm not trying to make you feel guilt. I want you to know the truth. This will happen."

"Why would they risk the health and welfare of our own people just to get re-elected? It's bullshit. It doesn't make any sense." I was starting to lose my grip on the vase.

Smith took a step closer to me. "It's power. That is what it's all about. Power and money."

I shook my head. "No. There has to be an easier way."

Smith put his hand in his pocket. "Of course there is, but easy doesn't guarantee re-election. And right now, the VP is attracting suspicion from the one person who works closely with him, the President. If the Agency puts someone in place of the President, they can make decisions, and then they can easily assassinate him, leaving the VP in power, which would not deter them from any of their plans. Plus, this shows the Agency's benefactors how powerful the Agency has really become. It's a gamble, but if they pull this off, they run the United States."

I didn't know if I could believe him. I knew I couldn't trust anyone. "Why didn't you tell me about any of this before?"

"You didn't need to know," he simply added. I could tell what he meant was he didn't trust me, and with good reason. I had proven that. "But, there is a chance you will run into the other mimic." Isi was not my biggest problem. "There is also a chance you will run into your mother."

"No shit," I responded and dropped the vase with a satisfying crash. I stared down at the broken pieces. I knew I had no choice. They would make me do it, or at least try. I could go along with it and decide not to do it. There might be an opportunity for me to escape.

Chapter 25

After our little talk, Smith led me back down the hallway. I hadn't agreed, but it was now clear I was going to go along with things, which meant I was required to do my homework. The Agency had taught me well, and though the Opposition didn't fully understand what it took for a mimic to take the place of a person, I did. That meant I had to study the First Lady of the United States.

As we made our way down the hallway, I was lost in my own head. I was thinking of all the things I would have to learn, all the ways it could go wrong, and that my mother and Isi might actually kill me. I wasn't paying attention to who was walking by, but when I looked up, Brody was moving down the hallway towards me. I looked away quickly, not wanting to make eye contact, and I could feel my heart thumping in my chest. I couldn't help it, but I glanced at him. This time, he was staring at me. We were walking towards each other. His face remained expressionless.

I wanted to say something to him, and as I approached him, I realized Isi and my mother weren't the reason I agreed to help. Yes, I was prepared to face them again, but I wanted to tell Brody he was the reason I was agreeing to help. He was the sole reason. Because I knew it was what he would have done. But I was afraid he was going to spit in my face. Truthfully, I knew Brody wouldn't do that to me, or I hoped, but at this point, so much had happened that I didn't know how he felt. He was Clark Kent, but I was sure Clark Kent could only be pushed so far.

When we were about a foot away, he stopped. I wasn't sure why, so I stopped, and the men walking with me stopped too. It seemed like the right thing to do. I waited for him to say something, but he stared at me, studying my face like he had never seen it before.

Finally, his words came out, softly. "You know how you said that I always knew to do the right thing?" I waited, knowing deep down what was coming next. "I was wrong about you, Meda. I was wrong to put all my trust in you." Smith shot him a dirty look, but Brody turned and walked away. I stood for a moment, speechless. I think somewhere, in the small, unused corners of my brain, I thought that Brody would forgive me. It was stupid to think that though. He had done so much for me while I had done nothing in return.

Smith spoke into my ear. "Don't worry about him. He'll come around when he sees you are going through with it. He's still pretty upset about Dan." My mouth set in a hard line at the mention of Dan. Smith was the kind of guy who would say anything you wanted to hear to get what he wanted, and he needed me to do the mission. He needed me to be focused.

They brought me to a room that looked like a library with wood paneling and shelves filled with books. It also had video equipment, a soundboard, computers, and pretty much any kind of technology you might need for anything.

"We're going to start you out with some tapes of the First Lady." Smith directed me to a sofa with a flat screen set up in front of it. He loaded something on the laptop that was hooked up to the television, and I began to watch what would turn out to be hours of footage. I settled in and made myself comfortable, getting lost in the character I would soon be playing.

After a few hours, I finally took a break. I liked the change of scenery with this room. I had imagined a room like this in my home one day. My dad would love it. Well, not my real dad but…yes. My real dad. I didn't know my mimic dad, so he meant nothing to me.

Anyway, Smith thought it would be a good idea for me to eat on the patio and get some sun. When I agreed, I didn't know there'd be other people there. I walked out, holding my tray and tilting my head up as the sun warmed my cheeks. When I looked down, scanning the area for a place to sit, I saw Aaron and Brody sitting two tables away.

I didn't know where to go, so I stood on the freshly paved patio and held my tray close to my chest. I turned back toward the patio door, looking for an escape. Smith stood there, his arms crossed, blocking my path. This was intentional. He wanted me to make amends.

I closed my eyes and took a deep breath. When I opened them, I saw Aaron watching me. Brody had his head down and was shoveling food from his plate into his mouth. Aaron looked at Smith and then back at me, and I could see as his face smoothed that he knew what Smith was up to.

There was a small bistro table close to the door, and rather than stand there like an idiot, I quickly put my food down and sat, fumbling with my napkin before smoothing it on my lap. I didn't know where to look, so I kept my eyes down, or tried to, but with Brody so close, my eyes were like magnets drawn to him. I wouldn't admit it to anyone, but I missed him.

I picked up my fork to stab a piece of lettuce from my salad, and when I looked up again, Brody was turned toward me. We made eye contact, and this time, he didn't turn away, but I couldn't hold his gaze. I jabbed at another piece of lettuce and looked up again. This time, Brody turned away.

I tried to concentrate on chewing and swallowing in a calm and normal way, but everything seemed exaggerated. When I heard footsteps approaching, I looked up to see Brody walking past me. His jaw tightened as he approached Smith. Then, I heard a metal chair screech against the concrete. Aaron was sitting across from me.

He didn't speak but regarded me steadily. I put my fork down and placed my hands in my lap as I finished the food I was chewing, forcing it down. I wanted a drink from the bottle of water I brought out, but I didn't want to reach for it or drink it in front of Aaron.

Aaron folded his hands on the table. "So, here's the thing," he said. His words seemed forced, but whatever he was feeling, he had wrapped it in calm. "They're making us stay here until you're ready. They think if you have another...setback, that we can help. I tried to explain to them that things had changed, but they aren't having it. Brody will barely talk to anyone." He stopped and looked at his hands. I didn't speak. He was feeling something, and I could see it, smoldering at the edges. He opened his mouth as if to say something but paused. Finally, he continued. "Here's the thing. Though it kills me to say it, he still cares for you."

My breath caught in shock. Then, the heat of anger crept up my neck. Was this another game? I was angry he was telling me this. He had to see it. I couldn't hide it. Suddenly, I realized things would never be the way we wanted them to be. "I don't believe that. Not after...what he said."

"Meda, he has every right to be disappointed in you. He was way too trustworthy from the beginning, and you proved to be undeserving of his trust when you left him in the dark. You made him look like a fool."

"I'm sure he doesn't care how people see him." I couldn't imagine the confident Brody who I knew being embarrassed. "And you're right." I folded my hands, mirroring him. "I never did deserve anything Brody gave me, which is why I think it is best I stay away."

Aaron glanced towards the building and then back at me. "That might be what is best for you, but for once, you need to think about what is best for Brody."

"But how?" I reached down and grabbed my napkin, crumpling it and dropping it on my tray. "Brody won't even talk to me. How do you expect me to fix anything?"

Aaron got up from his chair. "I don't know. But you're pretty smart. I'm sure you'll figure it out." He pushed his chair in and walked by me and through the patio door. I pushed the tray aside. I wasn't hungry anymore. In fact, I felt sick to my stomach.

Chapter 26

After my run-in with Brody, I went back to my studies, but I lacked focus. I tried to watch hours of videotape of the interactions between the President and the First Lady, but I found myself zoning out. I read over transcripts that were uncomfortably intimate and tried to mimic her exact words, but I couldn't put myself into it. I didn't know what it was like to be in a relationship. I had no clue how to talk to someone that way. With every loving and alien word that tumbled out of my mouth came a flood of doubt.

I was a couple of days into my cram session, reading a book on the President, when I looked up and noticed that I was alone. There was always some man in a suit lurking in the background, but at this moment, the room was eerily quiet and empty.

I stood up and walked over to the shelves of equipment that lined the walls. I ran my fingers across some of the items. Tapes, discs, video equipment, books, and file folders containing photos and transcripts. There was so much information that there was no way I'd be able to get to it all. My pulse kicked up, and I felt like I was going to have some kind of panic attack. I would never be ready. I would never make it through this.

I took a deep breath and tried to concentrate on the items in front of me rather than the job that I was doomed to fail at. There was an old video camera on the shelf in front of me, so I picked it up, pressing the side to open it. It had one of those mini tapes in it. I powered it on, surprised that the batteries worked, and looked at the screen as I scanned the room. It was calming, looking at the world through the screen, as though I wasn't there. Still looking through the screen, I walked over to the sofa.

An idea was forming in my head, an idea born out of fear but developing quickly because of the camera in my hand. I couldn't hide from the world behind a camera lens, but I could use it to get a message out. A message I was too afraid to say in person.

I moved over to the television stand that held the flat screen and placed the camera down on the space in front of the TV. I did not stop recording. Instead, I crouched down so my face was in the camera shot. I took a deep breath and stared into the lens. I didn't know where to start. I thought about all I had been through and all I had done, the people I hurt along the way, and the task in front of me. And then, I spilled my guts.

I started talking about my dad and my sisters, then continued with everything I thought I knew about my mother, about what happened with my mother, and about how I felt about her, including the anger, hurt, and confusion. I talked about all I had done wrong, and I apologized over and over again. As I talked, I knew exactly who I was talking to, and I told him how much I cared for him and appreciated him. I told him I wasn't worthy of having someone care about me like he had. And then I apologized again and again.

When I ran out of things to say, I stared into the camera. I leaned forward and pressed the stop button, then took the camera in my hands and ejected the tape. With the camera in one hand and the tape in the other, I went to the door of the study and knocked on it with my elbow.

A suited man opened the door and looked me up and down. I handed the tape to him. "Make sure this gets to Brody," I said. The man looked confused at first as he stared down at the object in my hand. Then, he took it from me and nodded curtly. He looked at me, waiting to see if I had anything else to say, but I turned and walked away.

I went back to the sofa and plopped down. As the man in the suit shut the door, I had a sudden overwhelming urge to run back and snatch the tape from him. I tried to think back on everything I said. Then I tried to imagine Brody's response to my words, to my feelings. I never let anyone see the real me. I felt so vulnerable. What if he laughed? What if he showed the video to everyone and they all laughed at what an idiot I was? What if he never cared, and he was only mad at me because I had made a fool of him? My pulse quickened again, and my vision blurred around the edges. I took a few deep breaths, trying to calm myself. I reminded myself that I couldn't change anything and I didn't care what Brody thought. I didn't believe myself, but I knew I deserved whatever happened to me.

Chapter 27

A while later, there was a short rap on the door. I must have dozed off because I found myself slumped over on the arm of the sofa. I quickly sat up and wiped my hand down my face as Smith walked in.

When I saw him enter, I stood. He wasn't stopping in for a friendly visit. There was something important he was going to tell me, and I could see it on his face.

"What is it?" I asked, trying to hide the concern in my voice.

He waited until he was standing directly in front of me. "We are putting you in place tomorrow." I started to shake my head, but Smith continued talking. "We have a security breach. The First Lady is available for a swap. We need to go now."

"But I…" I ran my hand through my hair, "but I'm not ready."

"Sure, you are. But the last thing we need you to do is some gun training." I knew he could see the look of horror on my face. I was frightened of guns, but he continued before I could protest. "It will mostly be handling a gun at close range." I took a deep breath. "Meda, you have to be prepared. If the other… mimics are there," I noticed he didn't mention my mother, "you have to eliminate them. We're going to have quite a mess to clean up when it's all over, but it will be better than a nuclear mess."

I sealed my lips and closed my eyes. I couldn't imagine myself pulling the trigger on anyone, much less my mother. But if I couldn't do it, I'd be dead, and so would a lot of other people. Brody intruded my thoughts. There was no telling if he would see the video before I left. I might not ever get the chance to hear what he thought about what I had to say.

Smith continued one more time. "Before we go to the range, I've arranged a video chat for you and your father." He turned from me and walked over to the computer on the desk in the room.

"Wait, why?" I blurted out. I knew why, but I wanted to hear Smith say it. He didn't answer as he bent down by the computer to cue up the chat. I wasn't prepared. There were so many questions I had and things I wanted to say to my dad, and they weren't all good things. They weren't the kind of things you would say to someone who you might never see again.

The monitor showed the call going through, and before I could even think, my dad's face filled the screen. First, he had Ginger and Georgia speak to me. They excitedly popped into view and had so much to say but had obviously been coached by my father not to ask any questions. We had a generic discussion, and before Dad sent them away, we all said our "I love yous," and I could see Ginger start to cry. When they disappeared, I looked back and saw that Smith had left the room. He had given me privacy so I could have the conversation I needed to have. It was just my father and me.

I tried to cautiously choose the words I wanted to say, but then it all came out. "Dad, how did we get in this position?" I stared at the man looking back at me. The man who I thought had been my real father all of my life. "Who was Mom? She wasn't the mother I knew. How could you fall for her act?"

My dad took a deep breath. He knew he didn't have much time, so he didn't hold back. "Meda, I knew your mother was not who she said she was, but I loved her anyway. When she told me there were people looking for her, I knew that it wasn't some ex-lover. When she showed me what she could do, I began researching mimics. I mean, come on, I'm a librarian. I came across some stuff, and I knew I had to stop. I didn't want to know that much, for her sake and for yours." He wiped his eyes.

I stared at the screen. He started to look less and less like my father and more like just a regular guy. A tired, regular guy. "So, you went on living with a complete stranger?"

"She wasn't a stranger. The Ava I know was a wonderful mother and a caring wife. When you love someone, you don't care what came before for them."

"What about what came after? Did you know she chose to return to the Agency?" I watched my father shrug, and it irritated me. "Dad, how can you be so nonchalant about all of this? After all that has happened? After all the lies?"

"Meda, you have to understand. The best things in my life are things that your mother gave me. Ginger. Georgia. You. How could I regret the time I spent with her?"

"But she hates you, Dad. She looks at you with pity. She regrets ever meeting you." My dad's smile disappeared. I felt bad for what I had said, but I couldn't take it back. I knew I had gone too far.

"The Ava you met is not my Ava. My Ava is right here." He pointed at his head. "And right here." He pointed at his heart. I understood what he meant. We believe what we want to believe. But it also reminded me what I had suspected all along. No one truly knows anyone, at least on the inside. So what was the point of it all? Like Dan said, don't trust anyone. That was easier when you didn't put yourself in a situation where you had to rely on someone.

"Dad, I know you're not my real dad."

"Yes, I am," he said firmly.

"You know what I mean."

"And you know what I mean, and that is all we are going to say about that. Now, I'm guessing you're going to be doing something dangerous, which is why they are giving you this time with me. Be strong, Meda. Be confident. You are not like your mother. You are like me. You will do the right thing. I have faith in you."

As I looked at my dad, I began to cry. He stayed on for a couple of minutes, trying to give me words of encouragement, but he didn't even know what I was going up against. He didn't know how bad it could be.

He said, "I love you," about a billion times before the video ended. When it was over, a suited man came in to take me for my gun training. Luckily, my mind was still on my dad and my sisters, so I didn't have time to be afraid.

Chapter 28

After talking to my father and shooting at the range for two hours, I was exhausted when Smith brought me back to my room. My shoulders were sore. I had a headache. I felt like crying, but I couldn't because I was too tired, too worn out. I knew this wasn't a good way to go into this thing, but I couldn't control myself. I collapsed in my bed, thinking I was going to fall right to sleep. It didn't happen.

I lay in the bedroom/cell. It was dark, and I stared at the wall, trying to see it. I was scared. If I failed, I didn't know what that meant for me or for the world. I was lost in the middle of the ocean with no life raft. I wasn't sure why I cared about what happened with the world at that moment. From my perspective, there wasn't a lot of good in it, but there was my family and there was Brody. Not that Brody was speaking to me or ever would again. He seemed to have a set of morals and standards above anyone, so I knew there was no way he could forgive me again, like he had instantly forgiven me for what I had done to Aaron's family. I knew that and accepted it, but it didn't mean it didn't hurt.

I continued staring at the wall and trying to see in the dark when the door opened. I didn't turn. From my experience, whenever the door opened, it wasn't good. The only time people talked to me anymore was to give me bad news or to give me orders.

The door clicked closed. That was different. Usually, visitors announced themselves when they entered, but this visitor remained quiet. A few padded footsteps moved towards me.

"Meda?" Brody's voice whispered in the dark. My heart began to pound. That was the last voice I expected to hear. I was frozen. My mouth felt dry, and my palms were sweating. I couldn't answer. There were a few more padded footsteps, and I felt the bed shift under his weight. I still couldn't move. I didn't know how to respond. He wasn't touching me in any way, but I could feel his body heat as he perched on the edge of my bed, close to my thigh.

"Are you awake?" Brody whispered again.

My breath hitched, and I hoped he couldn't hear it. I finally was able to speak. "Yes," I answered. He didn't say anything. I could hear my own breathing, and I tried to stop, or at least be quiet about it. I closed my eyes, even though I knew he couldn't see me. Part of me wished he would go away because I didn't know how to react to this. Another part of me prayed for him to stay and never leave me, to curl up around me, ask me to run away with him, tell me he loved me. So instead, I waited.

The pillow crumpled behind my head. He was now lying down behind me. I held my breath. We weren't touching in any way, but we were so close that I felt like we were.

"I can't let you leave like this." The cot vibrated as he motioned with his free arm. "I can't let you go without saying what I need to say." I stayed where I was, facing the wall. Motionless.

Brody took a deep breath. "Meda, would you face me?"

I let out the breath I was holding and shifted my weight, rolling over but inching back so I wasn't on top of him. We lay face-to-face on the bed. Even though it was dark, I could see the shadow that his jaw cast. My brain jumped to the video, and I squeezed my eyes shut in embarrassment.

"Are you…ready for this?" he asked.

I tried to be brave. I tried not to show what I was feeling. Trust no one. But this was Brody, and it was only seconds before I blurted out, "No." I tried to fight back tears. "But I don't have a choice." The tears spilled sideways down my face. Brody reached out and tried to wipe them off my cheek, but there were too many. Instead he pulled me to him and wrapped his arms around me. It was as though I was underwater, holding my breath for so long, and had just emerged to the surface. I let out ugly sobs, the ones easier to do in the dark when someone is holding you. He didn't say anything, and he didn't need to. The smell of him, the soap in his hair, his deodorant, it comforted me.

"I'm so sorry, Brody. I'm so sorry," I sobbed, my voice cracking.

He whispered in my ear. "You have nothing to be sorry about." He pulled back and brushed the tear-drenched hair from my face.

"I should have told you that I talked to my mother. I should have told you their plan to get me out of there. I put people in danger." I squeezed my eyes shut in the darkness, trying to unsee the memories of all I had done.

Brody let out a big sigh. "I wasn't as angry about that as I was angry about the idea of you putting yourself in danger." He held my head in both his hands, and without warning, he pulled me toward him and began planting gentle kisses all over my face.

Then he stopped and whispered in my ear, "And after, I was angry that you were giving up. That's not you. That's not what you do." He kissed me on one of my eyelids.

This time, I grabbed his face. I pulled him back where I could see him. "Brody, I worry that you have this romantic notion of who I am because of what I can do. You see more in me than what's there." I held him away from me.

"No, Meda…" he began, but I cut him off.

"No. I do give up, and that's why I do whatever I'm told. I'm not worried about what is right or wrong." Brody went to speak, but I squeezed his face. "No, listen. That is who I am, or who I was. But because of you, I realize that there is more to it than my own existence. I mean, I still don't know if I could kill someone, let alone my own mother, but I know I'll do what needs to be done, not because Smith told me to, but because I know what will happen if I don't stop them."

Brody pulled me toward him once more, and I surrendered. His gentle kisses soothed me, and soon, I was lost in his lips and his hands. We were entangled in the small bed, and it wasn't like when I was shifting into someone else. We were two, and we remained two but became connected in a way that I could never imagine. And I knew that I could never betray Brody or let him down again. Dan said not to trust anyone, but Dan had trusted Brody and so would I.

I jolted awake and was surprised to find that Brody was still in the bed with me. I thought maybe he would sneak out so Smith wouldn't find us together. But even though I woke up early, it was only seconds before Smith walked in. I was tucked under Brody's arm, staring at the wall, when the door opened.

I jumped up, which awoke Brody and made Smith chuckle in a dry laugh. "Well, I'm glad to see you two are getting along once again."

Brody placed his hand protectively on my head. "We'll be out for breakfast in a minute." Smith didn't say another word, and left us alone.

"Well, I guess this is it," I sighed. I didn't move to get up. In fact, I didn't want to move at all. Brody began stroking my hair.

"I love you, Meda," he said. It came out so naturally, I didn't realize what he said at first. And this was the moment. I never let anyone know how I felt because I was taught to be secretive. I was taught to feel guilt for revealing anything. I couldn't show feeling, I couldn't reach out and touch someone when I cared about them because that would be one step closer to revealing my big secret, but with Brody, I had nothing left to hide. He knew everything.

"I love you too, Brody."

Chapter 29

We ate breakfast quietly. I tried not to think about what we had said to each other. It was so natural, but it also seemed reckless, especially with the shadow of the mission looming over us. When Aaron joined us, he could tell something was different. He ate quietly but glanced back and forth between me and Brody, trying to gauge what had changed. Even if Aaron couldn't guess, I knew that just because Brody and I were together, that didn't mean Aaron would forgive me. That was not how he operated. He would need time, and once I was gone, he would have all the time he needed. Even if he didn't forgive me, I hoped that in the future he would find some peace.

After breakfast, I made my way back to the small room to get ready. I looked at the bed, thinking of Brody and last night. I wished we could stay here in this little room, or better yet, run away, but that wasn't in the cards.

On the bed was a dress suit in the style that the First Lady would wear. I walked over and touched the thick, expensive fabric. I rubbed it between my fingers, still in thought. Once I got dressed, that would be it. I reached up to twist at my ear, but I stopped myself. It would be a dead giveaway in the field.

I carefully and slowly got dressed. When I was finished, I looked down, smoothing the fabric, when there was a knock on the door. I turned, half-expecting Smith, but it was Brody. This was it. I bit the corner of my lip to prevent it from shaking. I needed to be strong if I was going to make it out alive.

Brody walked over slowly and stood in front of me, staring at me. I wasn't sure if he was waiting for something.

"Wha—" I began to ask.

"Shh," he said, smiling. "I want to memorize your face, before you change."

"You say it like you won't see me again." I said it jokingly, but when it came out, it instantly soured the mood. His smile disappeared.

"I didn't mean it like that." Brody reached for me, and I intercepted his hand, taking it in both of mine.

"I know," I said. "Let's not do this. Let's not say goodbye. We'll see each other soon."

He looked at me for another second and then pulled me into him. "Yes, we will," he said, wrapping his arms around me. We stayed like that for a little while, but we both knew it was time to go. This time, it was my turn to be strong. I pulled Brody over to the door when it opened. Smith had been standing on the other side, in wait.

"Come on, folks, we're on a schedule," he said. I felt Brody looking at me, but I couldn't make eye contact otherwise I might break down, so I looked straight ahead and followed Smith down the hallway and into the depths of a dark basement parking structure.

They walked me to the vehicle they had waiting. Smith had informed me earlier, when briefing me on the mission, that the Opposition had pooled all of its resources for this. The First Lady was doing an appearance at a fitness center for her women's health campaign. There was security, but it was the easiest place to make the switch. The plan was risky because while the Opposition didn't hire hits like the Agency did, they still had to hold on to the First Lady, which meant they would have to keep her safe and comfortable, but also hide what was going on. They weren't in the business of kidnapping, but in this case, it was the only way.

Smith explained they were not taking the First Lady to the compound for fear people would find it. They had an undisclosed location outside of D.C. where they planned to house her. It would be scary for her at first, but their plan was to dress like security and explain that there had been an attempt on her husband's life.

"So, where will the President be?" I asked.

"He is at a different engagement."

"But what will happen to him? You know the Agency is making an attempt to put a mimic in his place."

"Don't worry about that. We have it covered," Smith reassured me.

"How again do you have it covered?"

"We're working with someone at the Agency." Smith looked down when he said those words, as though he was lying to me or trying to keep something from me.

"And, is this someone I know?" I thought there was no way they could be working with my mother, but there was some hope in me that maybe that other business with the kidnapping had been a show, put on for Isi's sake.

"I can't tell you now, Meda. We can't blow their identity. It's best you don't know." I was frustrated. Of course, it would be better if I knew what was going on, but I knew that there was no way Smith would reveal it to me.

So now I stood, ready to enter the vehicle and leave behind the one person in the world that I ever trusted. I knew now it wasn't silly to put trust in people, because sometimes that was all a person had to hold onto.

An agent opened the door for me, but before I got in, I turned to Brody, leaned in, and kissed him one last time. It wasn't big or dramatic. I didn't want it to seem like a goodbye. There would be no goodbyes.

Just then, Aaron entered the parking structure followed by two more agents. He stayed by the entryway and didn't smile or wave or make any kind of indication that he was there to wish me good luck. I was certain he was there for Brody, but I was glad to see him.

Without wasting any more time, I ducked into the back of the car. Brody stepped forward like he wanted to say something, but the door quickly shut behind me. I slid across the leather seats and clicked my seat belt in place. Then, I looked out the deeply tinted windows, and even though I knew Brody couldn't see me as we pulled away, I gave him one final wave.

Chapter 30

I was alone in the back of the vehicle. In the front were two men in suits, generic men that I hadn't seen before, or if I had, they blended in with the rest of them. I stared out the window as we exited the parking structure and made our way to the point of the swap. I couldn't think of Brody or Aaron anymore. I had to focus on my job. What I was doing now was going to be bigger than anything I had done, and I could either be responsible for saving many people, or, well, I didn't want to think about the consequences of my failure. So the rest of the way, I remained lost in thoughts of what was expected of me as the First Lady.

When we slowed down, I noticed we were in a well-manicured area around D.C. I wasn't sure the town, but it didn't matter. In the last few weeks, I had been all over the place, but it didn't seem that way because whether I was in D.C., Chicago, or some suburb, I was always confined to the small place that someone had put me in. A walking prison.

In no time at all, we pulled into the packed parking lot of the fitness center. There were news vans and parking attendants directing traffic, and people were scattered all over the place. This wasn't the quiet swap I was used to.

The parking attendants stopped us, and the driver showed them something, and we were directed to the back of the building. They even moved one of the road barricades that they had in place. We pulled around back to a service entrance with a garage door.

We pulled to a stop, and only moments after, the large metal door opened where a man was waiting for us. I ducked down, covering my face. I knew it was important that no one see me, especially if my mom or Isi were anywhere nearby.

I concentrated on shifting into Cynthia, the hotel staff member I had used when we did the swap at the zoo. It seemed like bad luck, but it was best I didn't shift into any of the politicians I had been using in the last year. For all I knew, they had probably met the First Lady.

My skin prickled with heat, and then it was over in a moment. I exited the back of the vehicle, led by one of the men in suits, and we walked to the large door. The man waiting for us ushered us inside and then shut the door, but not before he studied me closely. He probably had never seen a mimic up close.

The man who stood in front of me had a deep tan and a shiny bald head. He didn't speak to me, but he spoke in a firm, hushed tone to the man in the suit. "The First Lady is just finishing up her appearance. She is going to exit this way, but they have asked that she freshen up in the bathroom. We were required to clear the locker room." Great, I thought. Another bathroom swap. It made sense though. It was the only place people truly had privacy.

Even though he wasn't talking to me, I cleared my throat. "How will you remove her security detail?" I was sweating underneath the bright lights in the access way. We stood in what seemed like a receiving room, and I felt too exposed.

He paused a moment before answering me. "We have one of our own with her. He will be the one to do the sweep and will stand just inside the door. He knows what you need to do. He will also administer a sedative to the First Lady which will knock her out long enough to get her to the next location."

"It won't hurt her at all, will it?" I grabbed for my ear but then corrected myself.

"No, ma'am. We wouldn't think of it. Now, let's get you in place." He grabbed my arm to lead me, but I stopped him.

"You know, she's going to be terribly frightened, watching me change. You'll have to expect that. I've seen it a million times."

"Yes, ma'am. We'll do our best to make sure she is as comfortable as can be given the situation."

"Thank you," I said and let myself be led to the locker room. The locker room wasn't far from the service entrance, and the bathrooms were located directly next to the showers in the far back corner. It was completely empty, so I quietly walked through, slipped into the back stall, and waited.

The minutes dragged. I was sweating in the ridiculous skirt suit, peering through the crack in the stall door. I kept thinking I heard something, but then minutes would pass, and no one would appear. I began to think maybe they changed their plans. Security teams did that all the time so no one could guess where the person they were guarding was going to be. How dangerous was life for the First Lady? She wouldn't need as much security as the President, but there were still threats on her life. As I was thinking about that, I heard someone speak.

"If you need anything, I will be right out here, ma'am." The man spoke in an overly loud voice so that I was aware that she was on her way. I held my breath and waited.

As it turned out, the switch was uneventful compared to the last one, probably because this woman had done me no wrong and she wasn't expecting what was going on. When I exited the stall, she looked at me, surprised.

"Oh, sorry, I didn't think anyone was in here," she said. I stepped forward and grabbed her hand, shaking it. "Oh," she said again, surprised.

"It's nice to meet you, ma'am," I said. Her mouth twitched, but even nerves didn't erase her impeccable manners. I continued to shake her hand when I felt the pins and needles and the burn. I must have grimaced and probably gripped her hand a little too hard.

"Are you okay?" she asked. "Paul?" She called out to her security guard, and when she turned back to look at me, he snuck up behind her and injected her with the sedative. I let go of her hand, and she put it up to the spot where he had injected her, confused. Then she turned back to me. Her eyes opened wide at the horror of seeing herself standing in front of her. Before she could call out for help, her eyes rolled back in her head, and Paul caught her.

"You're up," he said, still holding the First Lady. "Be careful, and may God be with you."

"Thanks," I said as I stepped around them and exited out the door. I was not an expert in walking in heels, and though I had walked in with the heels on, I knew as I walked out that I would have to be just a little bit better, just a little more graceful.

The rest of the security detail met me at the door, and we walked out into the back service entrance. The vehicle I arrived in had been moved, and a different one was in its place. This one would take me to The White House.

No matter how much I studied for this, nothing prepared me for our drive to the White House, the symbol of America, our government, and most importantly, our President. The massive columns tucked away by trees revealed themselves as we approached and eventually came to a stop. This would be the backdrop for what I hoped would be my final mission.

Chapter 31

The car door opened, and a security guard reached in to help me out. I tried to be ladylike as I slid across the seat and took his hand, nodding and smiling. I stood and demurely straightened my suit, not wanting to look anything but my best. I thanked the man and began walking behind the security officer. A few men were posted around, and I wondered if this was a normal security detail or if they had gotten wind of what the Agency was up to.

As we walked up to the sprawling, pristine building, I smiled and nodded at the men and women who were stationed at the entrance. I was going to try to talk as little as possible because speaking was a way to get caught. A person can usually tell when someone they know is off by what they say, and though I studied the tapes, I knew it was best if I played it safe.

As I was led inside, I tried not to look too awestruck, but it was difficult not to be. It was my first time visiting the White House. My security team informed me that my husband would be arriving home at 8:00 pm. I mentally checked. That gave me about eight hours to wander around this place without getting recognized as someone other than the First Lady.

I knew the presidential bedroom along with the private sitting rooms and private office, the one the President used when he wasn't in the Oval Office, were located on the second floor in the residential area. With all of the people wandering around, I couldn't imagine the President and First Lady ever having any private time. I felt a brief moment of sadness. That had to be difficult. Much more difficult than being a celebrity. No privacy and massive, world-changing decisions? I knew I couldn't imagine the half of it. I stopped imagining and focused on my surroundings as we made our way up to the second floor.

I was surprised that once we got upstairs, they basically left me alone. I hadn't known what to expect, but I wasn't banking on having a lot of privacy. I was so wired that I decided to do a little wandering to get the lay of the land. Everything was so beautiful and picture-ready. There were fresh flowers, the rooms smelled clean, and each room had a color scheme. My thoughts rushed back to my own home growing up. We lived in a nice family home on Kenilworth Avenue, an old home my father updated as we grew into it. My father's parents left it to him after they passed. They died one after the other because that was what two people in love did. Two people who couldn't live without one another. I shook my head, feeling ridiculous for being so cheesy.

My thoughts turned to my mother. She had a garden in the back of that house, and I remember standing to the side, watching her tend to it. She'd wipe her hair back from her face, leaving dirty marks, and I would step forward and wipe them away. She would look up and smile at me, like she hadn't known I was even there, and then she would go back to work, concentrating solely on the garden.

Then I remembered one other thing. Something I hadn't thought of until that moment. My mother, when my father was gone at work, used to sit up at her vanity where she had a cushioned chair, a sprawling table of makeup, and a large mirror. She would sit up there for hours, staring at herself. I remembered thinking that my mother was the most beautiful woman in the world. Then, she would slowly apply makeup. Bright red lips, multiple sweeps of mascara, powder. The strange thing was she wasn't going anywhere. After we did our homeschool lessons, she would go back upstairs and wipe most of it off before my father arrived home.

I was young at the time, and my mother was still in her early twenties. Now that I knew something about her, this ritual took on a new meaning. Rather than changing faces in the mimic sense, she changed her face using makeup. I remembered asking her to put makeup on me, and she said that I wasn't ready yet. And then, at the age of ten, about a month before she left, she told me I would never need it. I was too beautiful for it. I didn't understand. I looked exactly like my mother, except my skin tone was a little bit darker and my eyes were a bright shade of green. I didn't understand why I wouldn't need makeup because she used it and she was the most beautiful woman I knew. Now I understood. It wasn't the makeup she was talking about. It was putting on a different face.

Thinking it would be safer if I kept to myself, I entered the master bedroom, curled up on the bed, and stared at the ceiling, waiting for something to happen.

A phone rang in the bedroom and startled me awake. I jumped up, embarrassed that I had fallen asleep. I knew I should be ready for anything, but I wasn't. I picked up the phone. It was one of the staff letting me know that my husband wanted to see me in his office. I hung up, wondering if someone had walked in and seen me sleeping there and thought it odd and un-First Lady-like. Then I wondered if the President was really the President at all.

I straightened out my clothing, realizing I probably should have changed into something more appropriate for wearing around the house. I walked out of the room, slowly making my way down the hallway, and wondered if my mother was lurking out there somewhere, ready to put a bullet in the President's head as well as my own. Maybe Isi was out there. Maybe the President was already dead. There was no way of knowing.

The hallway was dark, and I padded quietly, my feet making a light noise as they hit the floor. Although there was security, there was none here in the inner sanctum, only service staff, and for the first time since everything started, I felt completely alone and scared. I knew it wouldn't end until I finished this job and stopped the nuclear meltdown, or died trying. The Agency's job was clear, and the Opposition's one and only mission was to stop them. Brody, Aaron, Dan, and I had all been pawns in this game, and though we liked to believe that we, or more accurately they, had some kind of power or say in what happened, any side would use us to get what they wanted.

When I arrived at the end of the hallway, I felt a bit turned around. I had studied the maps, but everything seemed different, bigger, in real life.

At the door stood a member of the residential staff whom I recognized from a photograph. I was sure his name was Steven Karr, but he looked a lot like another staff member, Joe Belino. Luckily, he spoke first.

"Hello, ma'am." He nodded curtly, then approached me. "Do you need anything?"

"Oh, no, sorry." I wanted to call him by name, but I knew if I made a mistake, it would be trouble. "Have you seen my husband?"

"Sure, he's in his office. Let me walk with you." I tried to look at the man's eyes, check his pupils, see if it was really a man in there or someone else, but it was too dark, and then suddenly I was following him.

"Oh, you don't need to," I began.

"I insist, ma'am." We went a little bit further to a beautiful solid wooden door. The man opened the door for me and stepped out of the way so that I could walk in. The President was sitting at his desk, papers sprawled out in front of him.

I couldn't move for a minute. No matter who you are, when you see the President for the first time, it is a surreal moment. After years of seeing him on television, it was crazy to see him in real life. He didn't look up. I turned and glanced back, and Steve/Joe/whatever his name was watched me. I stepped in. Steve/Joe stepped into the room, shut the door behind us, and faced the President.

"Yes?" The President regarded the man. Then he saw me standing there and broke into a big, warm smile.

"I found her wandering the house." I gave Steve a once-over; I was sure it was Steve now. I was surprised he was in here and that he spoke to the President first. It seemed like a very disrespectful thing to say about the First Lady.

Before I could reach for my gun, which was tucked into the inner pocket of the suit jacket, a shot went off. I looked down at myself, checking for blood. I thought the shot had come from the security guard, but when I turned towards him, I saw the red blooms blossoming on his shirt. I knew who the shot had come from.

The President remained seated at his desk, but he held a gun that was now pointed at me. "Meda, why don't you have a seat? No one will be coming. This room is soundproof." I stared in disbelief, trying to catch my breath. I couldn't help but think that I never stood a chance on either side. I thought about Brody, who would be out there somewhere waiting for me to return. It wasn't fair to him.

I stared, trying to see through the false skin. "Isi?" I asked. I had no way of knowing if this was the mimic my mother had trained or if it was my mother. There was no giveaway. But if this was the stone-cold killer, I didn't understand why I was still alive. Or, maybe it was my mother, turned on Isi so that she could save me and make things right. My head spun.

A knock sounded on the door. I jumped. "Mr. President. Is everything all right in there?"

I turned and watched the President. He answered, voice raised and sounding presidential. "Everything is fine, Watkins. I'll be finishing up momentarily, and I'll check in with you before I turn in. And, Watkins, please don't disturb us again."

With that, we were alone. I looked at the security guard lying on the floor and wondered who he was. Was that another mimic? Where was the real President? Were we too late?

The President rose from his seat and walked over to me. I felt the gun, strapped beneath my clothing, pressed tightly against my body. Even now, I didn't think I could use it. "So, tell me, how does it feel to be in the big leagues? Do you at least feel some kind of pride?" I looked at the mimic in front of me. It was a strange question. It was even odder to hear it in the President's formal tone.

"I don't know what you're talking about, sir." I added the "sir" for effect.

"Come now, Meda. You're in the big leagues. The Opposition has finally made it, though they will never be as powerful as the Agency. They don't have the resources. So, are you proud?"

"I don't know what you're talking about."

"Come on." The President gestured with his hands. "The big leagues!" he called out excitedly. "They couldn't have done it without you. You must be proud."

I knew there was no point in pretending anymore. "No, I'm not proud," I answered calmly. "In fact, I don't even think I can do what they want me to do." I was surprised I said it, but I figured it wouldn't hurt to be honest. Isi prided herself on being number one, and I was perfectly fine with her taking the title, and my crazy mother, well, I wasn't sure it mattered what I said to her.

"And that, my dear, is why your mother was always disappointed in you. In fact, the first time I ever saw a little bit of pride in her was when she found out you escaped. At least that took some spine." It had to be Isi. I heard the jealousy in her voice.

Steve moaned from the floor, which jolted me because I thought he was dead. The President stood from behind his desk and turned his gun on Steve, and we both watched as Steve struggled to get to his feet. He was holding his side where he had been shot.

"Oh dear," the President chuckled as he watched the guard struggle. "I mean, Steve," he said exaggeratedly.

Steve grimaced as he propped himself on the corner of the side table that stood by the door. "How could you?" he asked the President. There was a pained, betrayed look on his face. "I mean, I knew you were deceitful, but I thought…after everything…I didn't think you could actually do it." He chuckled but there was no humor in his laughter.

"Mom?" I asked, hoping I was right. Steve glared at me and shook his head slowly. Then he looked back at the President and began to shift. I was surprised when his face began to form. It was the face of Isi. I was confused. Isi hadn't even gone for her gun. She had done nothing to provoke an attack. I was trying to figure out what was going on when a voice spoke from behind me.

"I guess it's my turn," the President said. His face began to melt, and he started to shrink down. I recognized the features instantly. Mom.

Chapter 32

I couldn't speak, and I couldn't make sense of what was going on. The mission was completely forgotten.

"Meda, honey." My mom turned her head, looking exactly like my mother always had, but still wearing the President's now baggy suit. There was a trace of condescension in her voice. The horrible things she said to me flashed over my brain.

"It's true," Isi spoke up. "You thought I was bad, but I only learned from the best. What I can't figure out is why she shot me." Isi gripped her side but managed to straighten herself.

My mom sighed, lowering the gun a few inches. "Well, it can't hurt now." She took a deep breath. "I'm authorized to do a clean sweep if I feel it is necessary. Sorry, Isi, but this has all been too much trouble. I hate to see you go, but you have been careless, and you haven't gotten the job done. I saw you falter when you had the chance to stop Meda at the zoo."

"What about you?" Isi spit angrily. "You tried to kill her. You didn't stop her either."

My mother's jaw was set and her smile a grim line. "That wasn't my job. That was your job. And what you need to realize is that the most important thing with these guys is doing your job. If you show momentary weakness, you're done. I've told you that before.

It's too bad you didn't listen to me."

"That is a load of crap," Isi hissed at her. "You're the one who went rogue to try to off your own daughter and then didn't have the guts to follow through. Our job wasn't to kill her. It was to stop her. To get her back."

I stared between them. I heard what my dad had said about my mother and hoped there was a trace of that woman left. She didn't kill me at the barn. She could have. I looked at my mom. "Who are you?" I asked.

"Meda, honey. Catch up. And wipe that face off. There isn't time to go into all this. Let's just say that sometimes, once you've been so many people, you forget who you are. It's easier for you because you never knew who you were in the first place. Same with Isi. It turns out I am not who I thought I was, or who your father thought I was, or the mother you thought I was."

It finally hit me. Before, in the barn, when she was saying all of those awful things, I didn't believe it. I thought someone was forcing her to say it. But now, stuck in this room with no contact from the outside world, I knew it was all true. I knew my mother was now what she had always been, and she had only taken a detour as a mother. And now she was wiping all traces of that detour and making a devastating decision that would put many people in harm's way. I let myself shift back into my own form.

"All I have to do is get rid of the two of you, help them waste the nuke plant, and then shazam, I'm on the top of the world again."

"What, you didn't think you could compete with me?" Isi laughed, then clutched at her side, feeling the pain of the gunshot.

My mother smiled, tilting her head. "Dear, the beauty of it has always been," she took a breath, "that I don't have to compete." She leveled the gun on Isi and pulled the trigger. I was aware enough to pull my own gun out and point it at my mother as Isi tumbled down, grimacing and making low growling noises.

My mother turned her gun on me, knowing that I wouldn't be able to fire, maybe ever. We stood and faced each other, completely forgetting Isi.

"I know you don't want to do this. You aren't cut out for this life." Her tone was comforting, motherly. "Just think how much easier it would be for your father and your sisters if you were gone. No one would watch them anymore. I mean, they aren't watching them for me." She shook her head. "Meda, I know you wanted the dream. The family. But it isn't in the cards for us. Look at Isi. She was abandoned. Unless we are with people of our own kind, we will never be accepted. I had the same problem. My dad was a mimic, but my bitch of a mom didn't get it. She kicked me out of the house after I pretended to be her, but what did I know? I was a teenager. Of course, I was going to try things. That was how I ended up at the Agency. That was how I ended up with you." She took a step closer to me. I didn't lower the gun an inch.

"Your real father was the only one who ever accepted me and was proud with what I was able to do. Now, it didn't help that we were both being controlled by the Agency, and I don't like being controlled. I was afraid that once I got pregnant, they would discard me or use me in a way that I didn't want to be used, which is why I ran. It was only by chance that I ended up in that library in Oak Park. I was going to find some fancy ritzy place in Chicago and get a man to take care of me. But there he was, your father, who had money, a job, and wanted someone to care for. He didn't even care that I was pregnant with another man's baby. It was perfect."

"Stop it!" I yelled at her, shaking my head. I didn't want to hear what she was saying. "You cannot possibly be that heartless. You are my mother. You raised me for ten years. You taught me how to read. You taught me how to multiply."

"I know," my mother replied. "I was surprised that I was so good at that. I guess us mimics can adapt to pretty much anything." She laughed. I gritted my teeth, trying to contain myself.

"There is no way it was all an act." The gun in my hand was an exclamation point following each word. I was so angry, yet I still would never be able to pull the trigger on her. I knew the only reason that she was holding off on pulling the trigger on me was because she had to be concerned with Isi as well. It was a good thing she told us her plan.

She tilted her head quizzically for a moment. "No, you know, you're right. At first it wasn't an act. It was who I thought I was outside of all this. I thought I finally discovered myself. You were a well-behaved child, Meda. It wasn't that. It wasn't even you. It just got so…tedious, mundane. You had to know what my life was like before that. It was exciting and dangerous. And I think that I convinced myself I was happy with you and George, but he wanted children of his own. So, I decided to want that too. And then I was pregnant with twins. And while you came out this dark-haired, bright-eyed little thing, wild by nature, they came out little redheads, destined to be pale, freckled bores like their father."

I tried to contain my anger, but I was breathing heavily through my nostrils. She continued. "Then I got to watching you. You had picked up so many of George's mannerisms even though he wasn't your real father. I resented him for forcing me to have the twins and taking you away from me. I began to resent all of it. Then I took a closer look at my situation and realized I didn't have to stay." She smiled, gesturing openly with one hand. "So, I went back to the Agency, and they welcomed me with open arms."

"What about my biological father?" I asked.

"We're not like that anymore." My mother smiled. "Chayton was a great deal older than me when I got pregnant."

"So, what does he think of me?" I didn't want to sound needy, but I knew it came out that way. Of course I wanted to know what my father thought, and even if I hadn't known he existed, once I came to the Agency, he surely knew who I was.

"He doesn't think of you. Why would he? You were raised by a librarian. Barely a mimic. You don't have many skills."

"That's where you're wrong," Isi suddenly spoke up between grimaces. "You know it, Ava. You know the reason the Agency would never get rid of Meda is because she was born of two mimics, the only one of us. Which means she's more of a mimic than any of us."

I kept my eyes on my mother to gauge her reaction and to watch for any sign of movement, but she showed nothing. I was confused. "What does that mean?" I asked Isi, making sure I didn't take my eyes off my mother.

My mother faked a yawn. "I'm bored with this conversation," she said. She raised the gun again, but she had no way out. It was two against one.

Isi continued. "It means that there are things you can do that even we can't do. And you will learn them, eventually. First, they had to convert you. They couldn't have you switching sides."

My mother suddenly turned, pointing her gun at Isi again. "Shut up!" she demanded.

"Stop!" I yelled at her. She turned and looked at me.

"What?" she snarled. "You wouldn't. You couldn't. I am your mother, and she is nothing." She walked towards Isi and pointed her gun at Isi's forehead. Isi stared down the barrel of the gun.

"Oh, do it already," Isi said. "I'm sick of your threats. Just do it."

My mother smiled. "Oh, honey, I will. There is nothing stopping me. Certainly Meda won't stop me." She looked at me out of the corner of her eye. Isi looked at me as well. "The funny thing is," my mother continued, "you two both needed a mother so badly that it was sad."

Now it was Isi's turn to look angry. She always seemed to be in control, but my mother had hit a sore spot. "Shut up. You are not my mother. You never were." She leveled with my mom. "Did it ever occur to you that I treated you that way because I knew you were such a narcissistic, egotistical bitch? That the only way I was going to be able to work with you was to suck up to you?"

My mother laughed. "You can stop, Isi. I know your true feelings. I saw the videos of you crying at night in your room. They were worried about your mental state. Worried you would crack. I vouched for you because I knew you were weak. That I could bend you to my will." I watched as Isi's tough façade crumbled. Her chin quivered. My mother grinned wickedly. "You know, at this point, it's probably better that I end your misery." I watched as my mother's grip tightened on the gun. I watched as Isi steeled herself for the final blow. Then, I closed my eyes.

Chapter 33

My eyes were still closed when I gently squeezed the trigger, like I was taught. The kickback was minimal. The silencer muffled the gunfire, but it still was loud in the room. I clenched my jaw and jumped.

For not being an assassin, I had deadly aim. My mother dropped instantly and landed with her face towards the ceiling. She didn't even have time to wipe the smug look off her face or be surprised that her weak daughter was the one who took her life.

Isi stared at me, still clutching her side wound, as though she wasn't sure if I was going to fire on her next. When she saw I still had my gun trained on my mother, she lifted herself up, grunting as she moved. Doubled over, she moved towards my mother and reached down, still glancing my way. She checked her pulse, then looked at me again.

I had killed my mother with one shot. I had killed my own mother to save this trained assassin orphan who I didn't even know.

I watched Isi struggle to stand back up, so I went to her side to help her. She looked at me quizzically. "I didn't think you'd actually do it."

I didn't respond. I didn't think I would either, but maybe I was more like my mother than I cared to admit. "Bring me to the desk,"

Isi groaned, and I did as she asked. I had only been in control for a moment, but now I felt like I was losing my mind. I had gone off script, and I didn't like it. I wanted someone there telling me what to do. I knew it was a stupid thought. I knew I was better and smarter than that. I knew I had learned a lot over the events in my life and that I should be in control, but I didn't feel it. Maybe control was only an illusion, and even people who looked in control felt the same way I did.

I placed Isi in the cushiony chair behind the desk. She grimaced, then spoke through her teeth. "The President is safe," she said. I looked at her, surprised by her words. "We were able to switch, and during the switch, he was taken to the same location as his wife. That was the plan all along. I wasn't sure the Opposition could pull it off, considering they barely had enough resources to handle your switch. I guess your boys are helpful." She eyed me, waiting for a response.

I looked at her, confused. "So what side are you on?"

"I'm on no side, Meda." Isi lifted her bloodied hand for a moment to look at her wound. "I just don't like being double-crossed."

I stared at the blood on her hand. "But you don't mind being the double-crosser?"

"Hell no." She looked back up at me and laughed then winced.

"Now what?" I asked, unsure of what to do. "Are we staying in place? What do we do with...?" I motioned towards my mother's body.

"So here it is. Right now, the Agency doesn't know Ava is dead. They know I am here with her, ready to step in and take her place if something goes wrong." I thought about Isi's words. She couldn't be sure the Agency wasn't on to us, but for some reason, I trusted her instinct.

"Do they know I'm here? Would my mother have alerted them?"

Isi studied me. "Are you kidding me?" When I didn't respond, she continued. "No. Your mother's plan was to kill me, saying that you had done it, kill you, and come out looking like the hero of the Agency, the one who saved the mission from going belly-up. So no, there is no way she alerted anyone to the fact that you were here, and she was too arrogant to suspect anything from me." I nodded in agreement.

Isi continued. "And right now, the Opposition doesn't know if you've succeeded or not. They know I helped them hide the President and that I am in place, but they know nothing else. So, there are a few ways we can play this." I was surprised she said we. She assumed I would go along with her, and though I knew that I shouldn't trust her, I decided to hear her out.

"We can both walk out of here right now and go our own ways, being on the run but never being pawns again." I stared, waiting for option two. "Or we can finish this, with one of us staying in place." I nodded, still confused. She paused, "Which means one of us needs to be caught."

I took a few steps away from her. "What do you mean, caught?"

"Well, for this entire plan to come crashing down, the Secret Service has to be alerted that something is going down. We have to show them."

"I'll do it." I said it without even thinking, but I felt like I owed that much to everyone who had sacrificed something.

Isi laughed and shook her head. "You are an idiot and a terrible liar, and you don't think things through, do you?" She took a deep breath as I scowled at her. "I will be caught. I'm already shot up." She held up her bloody hand. "I'm a better liar than you, and the Agency will send someone in to get me anyway after it's all done."

"But you can't talk. The Agency won't let you come back if you talk." My eyebrows creased.

"Don't worry about me. I always know exactly what to say. What you need to do now is shift into one of the staff and get the hell out of here. I'll tell them you got away."

"I can't leave you, Isi. Not after everything." I moved close to her again.

She put a hand up, halting me. "Stop. Meda, you are not good at this. How about you follow my lead. I was built for this." I stared at her, trying to decide if I could trust her. She was a terrific liar and a brilliant assassin, but she was also a young girl who was double-crossed by a woman she thought of as her mother. I could totally relate.

"Alright. Deal." I nodded. "What do you need me to do?"

"Help me up," Isi said.

Chapter 34

Isi moved my mother's body out of sight as I watched. I felt bad, considering Isi had just been shot, but I couldn't lay a hand on my mother's body. Isi fluidly shifted into the President, having prepared for it when she took him to the safe house. Her suit was a little ill-fitting, but she was passable. She would still have her wound; just because she shifted didn't mean that she would heal or the flesh would form fully. That was a common misbelief.

Isi picked up the phone and dialed 0, which called out to staff members. When she hung up the phone, she stared at me. "Um, First Lady?" she questioned.

"Oh," I said. I felt the familiar prickles as I shifted back into the First Lady. We waited only a few moments before a woman entered.

I remembered my research. This woman was a newer staff member. Isi, in her best presidential voice, introduced the woman to me. The woman was so excited to meet the First Lady. We shook hands.

Then, Isi told the woman that we were celebrating a special occasion and to go to the kitchen to help with some food. She listed off a bunch of food items she wanted and sent her on her way.

"That should keep her busy enough that you can sneak out as her. You'll use the entrance you came in." I nodded.

Isi went back to the phone and called for a cleaning crew from the Agency. I didn't know how they would get clearance or how they were going to remove a body from the White House, and I didn't want to know. I didn't need to know anymore. I quickly shifted into the new staffer.

I walked towards the door, steeling myself to put on a show. Isi cleared her throat. "Meda?" she called. I turned around. "There is one thing I want you to know."

I stared at Isi wearing the face of the President. I was worried about what was going to come out of her mouth. A double-cross? Maybe she'd pull out a gun and shoot me.

"There was no John at the Agency." I continued to stare, not sure what it meant. "I was confused when you told me that you talked to a John and that he told you about me. But there is no John. That means someone shifted and posed as your security."

"But that doesn't make sense. John was kind to me. He talked to me. He brought me books. Who would do that?" My eyes traveled to where my mother's body had been. I looked up at Isi, who shook her head.

"No way it was Ava, and it certainly wasn't me." But that only left one other mimic. My father. Chayton.

I tried to breathe, but questions caught in my throat. Why would he come see me? Why would he pretend to be someone else? What did he want from me? Did he want to know me? I had to stop myself. Hope was building, and I knew that was dangerous, like the dangerous hope that had bloomed when I saw my mother again. I opened my mouth to speak, but before I could say anything, Isi cut me off.

"We don't have time. You can leave out the servants' exit. If anyone sees you, don't talk to them. Just keep your head down. There should be someone waiting for you there. Someone you recognize."

And there was. As I exited, I squinted at the black sedan that was parked down the driveway. Brody was behind the wheel, and my heart murmured at the sight of him. Security stood next to him. "I'm sorry you aren't feeling well, Monique," the security guard said to me. "Your son is here to pick you up."

"Thank you," I said, putting my hand to my mouth to muffle my voice. I didn't know enough about the woman I had changed into to accurately pretend to be her. I hoped that any oddities the security guard noticed would be chalked up as illness.

He helped me into the vehicle, and when I was situated, closed the door for me. I kept my head down, not wanting to reveal that anything was amiss. Brody eased down the driveway, not saying a word. It was as though he felt the tenuous line might snap if we broke the silence. I held my breath as the sedan glided through the gate, then I looked back. No one was chasing us. No one was shooting at us. I turned back around. There was nothing in front of us. I raised my head, looking at Brody.

He was looking at me, his eyes awash with questions. I knew he didn't know anything that had gone on behind that gate. I didn't even know where to begin or how much I wanted to tell him. So, I kept it simple.

"We did it," I said, and he reached out and grabbed my hand. Tears ran down my face as Brody squeezed my hand. The tears weren't exactly tears of happiness. I had killed my mother, the mother who had never loved me. I had possibly met my real father, and I didn't even know how to feel about it. Also, I didn't know what was going to happen to Isi, and even though we were far from friends, I felt like because we were both stuck in something we hadn't signed up for, there was a bond. I didn't know how strong it was, and I didn't know what would happen when I saw her next, but I felt connected nonetheless.

It turned out that Isi did her job and she did it well, which was to be expected. She played President for a little while, but when one of the staff members saw her blood, they reported it to the Secret Service. I'm not sure what she had to say to the Agency, but even they couldn't expect her to maintain her cover when she was full of bullet holes. Plus, Ava's betrayal proved there was something wrong with the inner workings of the Agency, misdirecting all suspicions so that Isi was looked on as the hero.

I learned all this in a meeting I was invited to attend with Isi and Smith. As we sat in Smith's office, Isi gave all the details of what happened. Smith applauded her for being loyal to the Opposition.

Isi sat next to me, hands folded in her lap. "What you need to know about me is that I'm going to take the best deal. You have to understand that I don't have feelings like others do."

I tried to hide my smile. Isi did have feelings, which is why she turned on my mother. She felt the sting of betrayal, but to her, feelings were a sign of weakness, so I would keep her secret for her. And for a moment, I felt like she could be my younger sister. In fact, I might have felt closer to her than my own sisters, but then I remembered what Isi was, a trained assassin, and I pushed that hope away. We would see what happened.

But Isi did listen to my next plan, and then laughed in my face and walked out of the office. For her, doing things for purely redemptive purposes was ridiculous, but I would do it anyway, with or without her.

Chapter 35

I wasn't nervous, even though this was one of the most important assignments I would have. This time, the assignment was mine. It was my choice. Isi had laughed at it, Smith said that it wasn't worth it, but to me it was. It was the beginning of my new life. A life in which I could choose.

Brody stood next to me. "Are you sure about this, Meda?" A few suited men stood around us, but none of them were listening.

"I'm positive. I finally feel like I'm doing the right thing for once." I straightened out my suit, then reached up and touched my face, which wasn't really my face. I was wearing the face of a middle-aged, redheaded woman. I looked down at my hands where wrinkles were starting to develop.

Aaron stepped forward, and I looked up at him. I was happy he was here. I wanted him to see what I was about to do. He might not ever be at peace with all that happened to him and his family, but maybe this would help ease some of his pain.

"Meda," Aaron spoke quietly. "Really. This isn't necessary. I know the truth, and we know the truth, that's all that matters." He stood, cracking his knuckles and shifting uncomfortably from foot to foot. He looked awkward dressed in a suit, but I wasn't sure that was what was making him uncomfortable.

"No." I reached out, placing my hand on his shoulder. "It's not, Aaron, and you know that." His gaze hovered on my face for a moment, but then he looked down. I remembered that he wasn't seeing my face anyway.

"Ms. Collins?" A Secret Service officer asked me. "We're ready for you." He directed me towards the platform.

I didn't think I would be back at the White House so soon. And as I took my place behind the podium at the front of the Press Briefing Room, my hands started to shake and I gripped the edges of the podium to steady myself. Cameras flashed, and a room full of faces stared at me without really seeing me. They thought I was here to talk about the recent assassination attempts on the lives of the President and the First Lady. But I had my own agenda.

I cleared my throat and began to speak. "Good morning. I'm here today to talk about the recent assassination attempt on the life of our President. But before I give you a detailed brief on the event, I'd like to begin by saying our President is an honorable man. But even honorable men can be led astray by the people closest to them." I paused.

There was a subtle shift in the room. Before there was an atmosphere of business-as-usual with a tinge of apathy, but after I spoke those words, a hush came over the room. I had everyone's attention.

"We have looked into the death of one of the men who once worked closely with the Vice President. The man's name was Reginald Monroe, but many knew him as Reg. He was a family man, which is why it came as a surprise when he allegedly killed his family and committed suicide himself. After reopening the case . . ." I lied. No one was looking into the case now, but after this they would. "After reopening the case, we have found evidence of foul play, and in Reginald's own files, we have found implications of our Vice President working with groups to aid terrorism on United States' soil."

I paused as a buzz rippled through the room. The Secret Service to the sides of me looked like they wanted to tackle me. They were talking in their earpieces, trying to decide what to do.

"If you look into the regulation changes of the Pilgrim Nuclear Power Plant in Plymouth, you'll see the Vice President has been lobbying for changes to make the plant unsafe. He was planning to cause a failure at the plant." I continued sharing much of the information that the Opposition had gathered over the last year against the Agency and the VP. I left out any part about mimics; I wasn't going to divulge that information and put a target on my own back. If they figured that out on their own, well, good for them.

When I finished, people were calling out questions, and the Secret Service was crawling around the room. I stepped off to the side, but I knew they wouldn't just let me go. Two men with suits and earpieces came up on either side of me and gripped me by the arms. I let them take me, not daring to make a scene.

"You'll have to come with us," the agents said. I let them lead me out of the room and tried to fight the smile of satisfaction that threatened to break through. Behind the scenes, I was surrounded by complete chaos. I could hear the press yelling out questions from the Press Room. People were running around barking orders and whispering behind nervous hands. The agent to the left of me squeezed my arm tight enough to get my attention. I glanced at him. "That was ballsy," he whispered, and with a flash of his face, I saw Isi.

I tried to hide my smile and turned slightly so that she could hear me. "I thought you didn't agree with this."

She let out a dry laugh. "I don't agree with pretty much anything you do. But it is in the best interest of both parties involved that you don't get busted."

"So, are you here for the Agency?" I asked quietly so no one else could hear me.

"Yes, believe it or not, they still think you are an asset to them." She shook her head. We continued to walk down the hallway, people still rushing around on all sides of us. They were trying to get a look at me but didn't want me to see them looking.

"Even after I just revealed everything? They don't want me dead?" That came as a surprise. I thought I might be target number one.

"Stratagem," Isi whispered to me.

I turned to look at her to make sure I heard correctly. "Stratagem? What do you mean?"

"Stratagem. Schemes. Subterfuge. If you know yourself but not the enemy, for every victory gained you will also suffer a defeat. Sun Tzu said that in *The Art of War*. He also said, 'He will win who, prepared himself, waits to take the enemy unprepared.'"

"I never pegged you as a reader." Isi stared at me. I hoped she wasn't my enemy, but then again, there was so much I didn't know about her.

Chapter 36

After the meeting, it was just Brody and me. We got in the car to visit my father and sisters. The Opposition had set them up with a new life. They also got rid of Beth and the Agency's hold on them...for now. The Agency had bigger fish to fry in the fallout of their failures.

I didn't know how to feel about seeing my father, knowing that he had kept the truth from me all those years but not knowing why. Then again, I had also wanted to believe the best in my mother up until the end. But my father was the only one who could give me real information, and before Brody, he had been the only one I could trust, which was why his lie stung a little bit more than I expected. But I knew everyone deserved another chance. I had used a few up myself.

My father had built up this wonderfully impossible image of what my mother had been. Maybe after she left, he even romanticized. That was in his nature. He was a lover of fiction and books, and more than anything, my father deserved a happily ever after because he was a good man, too good for my mom.

When we arrived at their new house, which was in a small neighborhood near D. C., I felt a stab of jealousy. Smith told me they found a library position for my father, which was good for him, and then there was their cute little home complete with a white fence, well-manicured shrubs, and a porch swing. Smith also informed me that with blood samples from me and Isi, they could compare our DNA makeup to that of my sisters, and they were almost positive that neither of my sisters would shift. I shouldn't have been jealous that they were happy, but I was. They were going to be able to live a normal life. I was condemned to always be on the run. To always keep secrets.

When I walked into the foyer, I stopped and smelled the air. It smelled like fresh-cut flowers, and vases of all different types of wildflowers that my sisters had surely picked were set up. My sisters ran to me when they saw me, and I hugged them tightly, patting their auburn hair and rubbing their freckles. I told them to be good and that I would see them soon. The closer I was to them, the more danger they would be in.

My dad led me through French doors into a sunlit room. It was his office. He brought me to a couch that was up against the wall and held my hand and waited for me to tell him about the mission, about what was going to happen next.

I didn't mess around. There wasn't time. "Mom's gone." He looked down at his hand holding mine. When he didn't say anything, I continued. "I killed her." Only then did he look up at me with pain in his eyes. I saw tears forming. "Say something, Dad."

"I don't know what to say."

"Well, are you crying because you're upset with me? Are you ashamed I killed someone? Are you sad she's dead?" My anger built. "You know that she was there to kill me, right?" He shook his head, tears falling down.

"Meda, stop." He let go of my hand and wiped his face. "Of course I'm sad your mother is dead. I'm heartbroken." He shook his head again. "There was always a part of me that thought she would come back." My mouth formed a thin line. I couldn't believe what he was saying.

"Dad, this woman was going to kill me."

"That woman was still your mother." His tone was stern, like he was scolding me.

I jumped up and backed away from him. "Who are you?"

My dad stood and moved towards me. "I'm sorry, Meda. I'm sorry. I didn't mean that. I mean, this is difficult. I know it had to be difficult for you. I can't even imagine what you've been through in the last year." I watched emotions play out in his eyes. "Don't take this the wrong way, but I hardly recognize you as my daughter. I just…with all you've been through, I don't want you to forget that there is good. There was good in this family. Please don't forget that."

"What do you see now when you look at me if you don't see your daughter?" My dad moved forward and grabbed me in a hug. I let him hug me, but I couldn't speak. I knew that if I did say something, it would come out wrong. I knew it would be best if I had time, if he had time.

We stood like that for a while. Finally, when he let go, I cleared my throat. "I better get going." He didn't say anything, so I turned and made my way to the front door. He didn't stop me; he followed me, like a shadow.

I opened the door and half turned. I wouldn't let go of the handle because I didn't want him to hug me again, not at that moment. He lifted his hand in a wave. I did the same and then walked out, closing the door behind me. I realized I used to be like my dad, trying to push away the bad and only see the good. Only see what I wanted to see, but I was beyond that now. I guessed I had changed.

Brody was behind the wheel. I slipped in the passenger seat. He looked at me and could tell there was something wrong. He reached out his hand, and I put mine in his. "Want to talk about it?" he asked. I shook my head.

He only briefly took his hand away to put the car in gear, and then his palm returned to mine, and we drove that way for a while, each mile unraveling the tangle of emotions I felt inside.

The freeway turned into a highway, and the highway turned into winding dirt roads. We stopped at a few gas stations and rest stops, got some snacks, and continued on the road. I didn't know where we were going, and I was perfectly fine with that. I watched the trees go by. My only experiences in the country were with my father and when I was first taken by Brody, Aaron, and Dan. Needless to say, I didn't have good memories of the wilderness.

After hours of driving, we made our way down one last windy country road. I could make out a small cottage in the distance.

When Brody pulled next to the building, I asked, "What are we doing?"

"I thought it would be nice to get away," he answered and studied me, waiting for my reaction. Before I could respond, he continued. "I thought we needed to change your perspective of the country. Don't laugh at me," he said preemptively. "I was hoping one day we would be able to find a place to settle down."

Speechless, I shook my head. "What do you mean? One day? Settle down?" I couldn't make sense of those words, especially the use of "we."

"We both know the Opposition needs you, not only for their own reasons, but to help people like you and families like yours. But one day, when we decide we've done enough, we will live our lives for us, not them."

I laughed. "Do you forget we're only seventeen?" Brody flushed red. "I didn't mean that, about me and you, I mean. I meant that it seems like you have our lives planned out. Some of the missions are dangerous. How can you be sure we'll get the chance…?" I couldn't finish. I didn't want to sound hopeless, but after all I had seen, I wasn't so sure about life after missions.

"Meda, if it ever gets too dangerous, if they stop caring about you and only care about the mission, I promise you I'll take you away. In fact, if you told me right now that you were done, I would love to disappear with you." I went to speak, but Brody cut me off. "Now, I know you wouldn't do that, but I'm just saying. I'm with you to the end. And I didn't mean to make it sound like you were stuck with me. I'm not proposing marriage. But this is what seventeen-year-olds would do. You know, seventeen-year-olds with no adult supervision. They are irresponsible." He grinned and took a deep breath. "I love you."

"I love you, Brody. I would love to disappear for a little while."

"See, I always knew you were capable of doing the right thing."

SNEAK PEEK!

Resistance
STRATAGEM BOOK TWO

Chapter 1

The paint-chipped wood cooled my bare feet as I stepped out onto the porch to survey my surroundings. Happiness couldn't last forever. I should have learned that by now. Not that I thought at seventeen my life would be without troubles, but it seemed possible with Brody by my side, especially because there were no Isi or Agency members around.

One week had passed since the incident at the White House, but the pain of the events leading up to the mission wasn't really behind us. I could see the moments of grief in Brody's eyes as he stared off in the distance, and I thought of poor Dan, who had died helping me. Aaron's family. My mother. All gone because of my actions, like a pebble thrown into the water, the casualties rippled and flowed out to sea with far-reaching effects. I'd foiled the Agency's assassination attempt on the president by eliminating my mother, and I implicated the vice president in the press conference that followed. As a reward, they whisked me off to the wilderness to go into hiding with Brody.

The sun blazed in the sky, but the days grew shorter. In this cozy cabin in the woods, protected by tall trees that had stood like guardians for decades, it was easy to forget the problems in the world.

While Brody was off in town, picking up a few supplies, I sat on the deck drinking lemonade. The familiar rumble of an approaching vehicle, the gravel crunching under tires, alerted me to an incoming presence. My body tensed with anticipation, but it was just Brody, driving the nondescript sedan that had been gifted to us by the Opposition for helping them with the mission. The Opposition didn't have the funding that the Agency did, but they were strategic in how they used their money, and they would do anything to keep me, a mimic, out of the hands of the Agency.

He put the vehicle in park, and the trunk popped open as he stepped out of the car. He disappeared around the back and, after some rustling, reappeared carrying two reusable grocery bags.

"Hey, there." I smiled at him, my stomach fluttering with the sudden shyness that popped up at the oddest of times around him. I wasn't used to the freedom of living without someone giving me orders or watching over me, but I also wasn't used to sharing a space with anyone, let alone a boy. But Brody was not just any boy, as he had proven time and time again. He was intuitive and gentle, and after everything we'd been through, we both needed time to recover, so we made sure to give each other space and privacy.

He climbed the porch steps with a smile stretching across his face. As he reached the top, he bent over and placed the groceries on the deck. Then with that same smile plastered on his face, he stood and studied me.

"What?" My cheeks burned hot as I pulled at the hem of my sweater.

"Nothing, you just look…" he tilted his head, "happy."

A wind whispered a warning through the trees, but I ignored it. I waited for Brody to come over and plant a kiss on my cheek, but he held up one finger. He bent over and rifled through the grocery bag before standing and taking the two steps over to where I sat.

He held out a paperback book. It was *Little Women*. My favorite.

I shook my head in surprise. It was a minor detail from my life from before the Agency took me and forced me to be an operative, but it meant a lot to me that he remembered. Although I felt like I didn't know myself because I was never allowed to be myself, Brody knew me through and through. I counted myself lucky that the Agency assigned him to kidnap me that day. Who knows what would have happened if they'd assigned Aaron alone? He'd held me solely responsible for the death of his entire family and believed I was to blame, but all I did was impersonate his father and make him look capable of killing his loved ones. It was no wonder that Aaron had hated me when he first helped kidnap me and shoved me into the trunk of his car.

"Do you need help with supper?" The chair creaked under my shifting weight.

He put his hand up. "Let me, Meda. Read. Relax. Do what you want. I got this." He scooped up the groceries and disappeared through the door.

I flipped my legs over the arm of the chair and opened the book. Jo lamented on holidays without their father in the first few lines. It made me think of my father. Not my biological dad, but my dad who raised me. I'd need to check with Brody to see if it was okay if I called him soon. Maybe tomorrow. I hoped he and my sisters were okay. The Opposition looked after them, but we couldn't be together. Being anywhere near a mimic like me was dangerous. It seemed like a lifetime had passed since I had lived under the same roof as them.

After we ate, I took my book to bed, and as I was reading, Brody crawled in beside me. I placed my book down on my chest and looked at him.

When we had first arrived, he offered to sleep on the couch, but that night, he checked on me four times in the first hour, worried about the guilt that gnawed at me. The fifth time he tiptoed into the room, I invited him to sleep by my side. He'd propped pillows between us, acting as a barrier to comfort me. I'd removed the *Great Pillow Wall* sometime near the early morning hours and pulled his arm over me. He'd asked if I was okay, and I assured him I slept better with him near me.

Now, he was staring at me, and I wondered if he remembered that first night the same way I did. "What is it?" I reached over and folded my hand over his.

"I was thinking about us." He brought my hand to his lips. Then he pressed his other hand on my cheek and drew me in for a kiss. I leaned into it, letting the comfort of our touch wash over me like ocean waves as our lips dissolved into one another. I didn't want to worry about my family or the future. I just wanted to be in the present.

I kissed him back, and he pushed his fingers through my hair, gently pulling me closer. I parted my lips, and his tongue grazed mine.

He broke away from our kiss, whispering, "I love you." Brody looked at me with wide eyes. "I love this face. Your face. I love being with you. Here."

"I love you too," I whispered, surprised by the ease of those words.

"I also love watching you read." He touched the tip of my nose with his finger before settling back against his pillow.

I let out a laugh. "How boring."

He nodded like he agreed. "Yes, boring and normal. And real." He smiled but kept his eyes on me.

I reached over and patted his hand. There was a strange flash of light and a stabbing pain in my temple, and suddenly, I saw myself lying down on the bed. It was like I was looking at myself from his perspective.

I let go of his hand, gasping. Confusion wrinkled Brody's forehead as I rolled over so he couldn't see my face. Meanwhile, my mind raced, working to run down the list of all the things that could be wrong with me. I focused on staying still so as not to make a noise or draw his attention.

"Are you okay?" Brody asked.

I took a deep breath and rolled back to face him. "I'm fine." I felt guilty for lying, but I didn't want to worry him.

I grabbed my book and pretended to read, but the words swam in front of me. I couldn't concentrate, and my head felt funny, like it was wrapped in a fuzzy blanket.

I felt his gaze as he dozed off. The fuzzy sensation in my head spread like a warmth through my body, making everything heavy and tired. When my eyelids were too weighty to hold up, I turned the lamp off and curled into Brody. My brain flashed a faded signal that something was wrong, but I lost it in the fog of sleep that enveloped my thoughts.

CHRISTINA HAGMANN grew up in rural Wisconsin, climbing trees, swimming in creeks (pronounced "cricks"), and running amok. She began reading Stephen King in 5th grade and was hooked. That year she wrote her first short story, and she's been making up stories ever since. When not writing short stories and novels, Christina can be found spending time with her family, coaching, teaching English, and reading anything and everything.